Disney

DuckTales

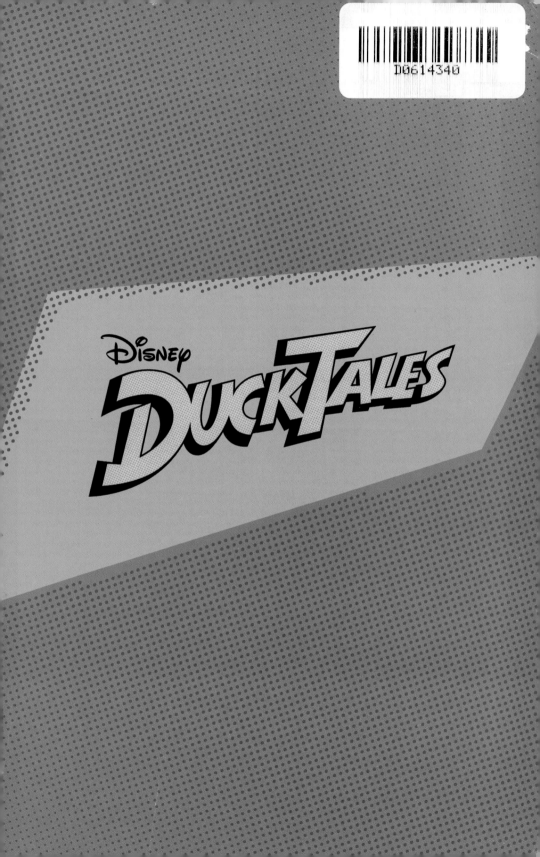

Facebook: **facebook.com/idwpublishing**
Twitter: **@idwpublishing**
YouTube: **youtube.com/idwpublishing**
Tumblr: **tumblr.idwpublishing.com**
Instagram: **instagram.com/idwpublishing**

ISBN: 978-1-68405-230-1   21 20 19 18   2 3 4 5

COVER ARTIST
MARCO GHIGLIONE

COVER COLORIST
DARIO CALABRIA

LETTERER
TOM B. LONG

SERIES EDITOR
JOE HUGHES

COLLECTION EDITORS
JUSTIN EISINGER
and ALONZO SIMON

COLLECTION DESIGNER
CLYDE GRAPA

PUBLISHER
GREG GOLDSTEIN

Originally published as DUCKTALES issues #3–5.

Greg Goldstein, President & Publisher

Robbie Robbins, EVP & Sr. Art Director

Matthew Ruzicka, CPA, Chief Financial Officer

David Hedgecock, Associate Publisher

Lorelei Bunjes, VP of Digital Services

Eric Moss, Sr. Director, Licensing & Business Development

Ted Adams, Founder & CEO of IDW Media Holdings

Special Thanks to Carlotta Quattrocolo, Julie Dorris, Eugene Paraszczuk,
Chris Troise, Daniel Saeva, Manny Mederos, Roberto Santillo, Marco Ghiglione,
Stefano Attardi, Stefano Ambrosio, and Jonathan Manning.

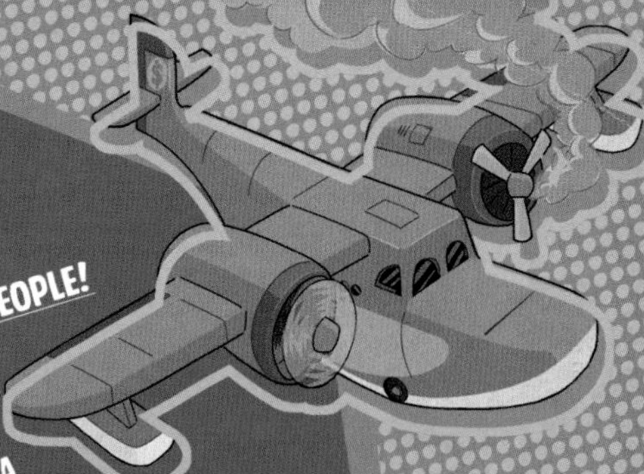

CHEATING LIKE NOSTRADOGMUS!
WRITER: JOEY CAVALIERI
ARTIST: LUCA USAI
COLORIST: GIUSEPPE FONTANA

BEWARE OF THE PHENOMENAL PUMPKIN PEOPLE!
WRITER: JOEY CAVALIERI
ARTISTS: GRAZIANO BARBARO, ANDREA GREPPI, & ROBERTA ZANOTTA
COLORISTS: GIUSEPPE FONTANA & DARIO CALABRIA

HAPPY, HAPPY VALLEY!
WRITER: JOEY CAVALIERI
ARTIST: LUCA USAI
COLORIST: DARIO CALABRIA

FIGHT!
WRITER: JOE CARAMAGNA
ARTIST: GIANFRANCO FLORIO
COLORIST: STUDIO KAWAII

GO, GO, GOLDEN YEARS!
WRITER: JOEY CAVALIERI
ARTISTS: EMILIO URBANO, ANDREA GREPPI, MICHELA FRARE, & CRISTINA STELLA
COLORISTS: LUCIO DE GIUSEPPE & GIUSEPPE FONTANA

A SERIES OF UNFORTUNATE SUBSTITUTIONS!
WRITER: JOE CARAMAGNA
ARTISTS: ANTONELLO DALENA, MANUELA RAZZI, GIANFRANCO FLORIO, & ROBERTA ZANOTTA
COLORIST: GIUSEPPE FONTANA

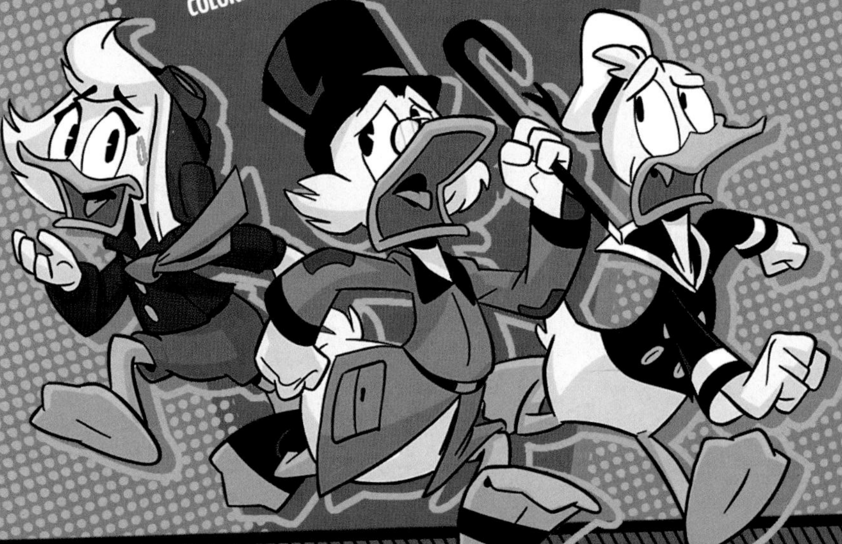

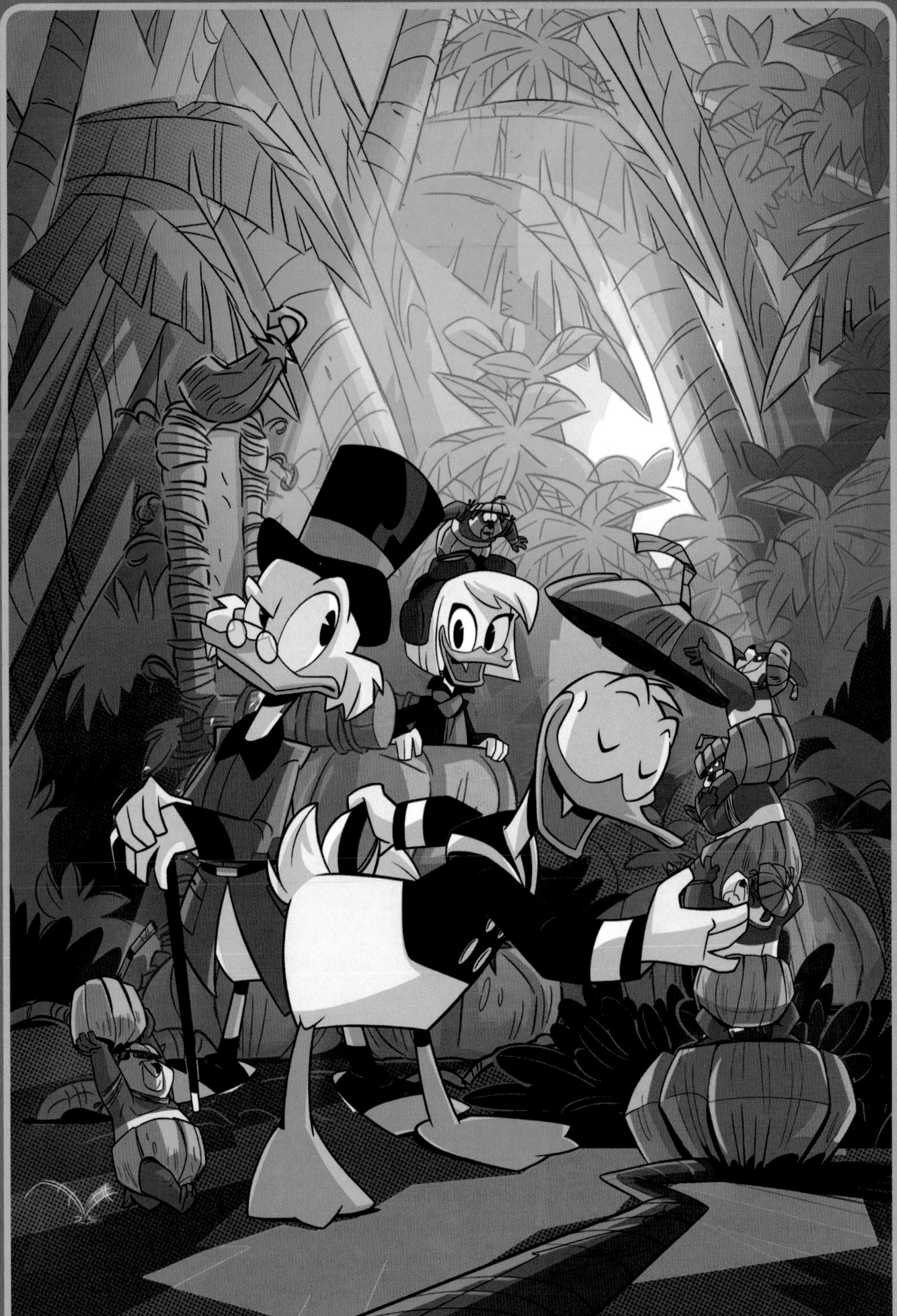

Art by Marco Ghiglione, Colors by Giuseppe Fontana

Disney DuckTales

AWESOME EXPLOITS and QUESTS for rare and wonderful artifacts culled from foreboding terrain and forbidden lands! These are our journeys, these are: The Daring Adventures of Scrooge, Donald and Della Duck!

CHEATING like NOSTRADOGMUS!

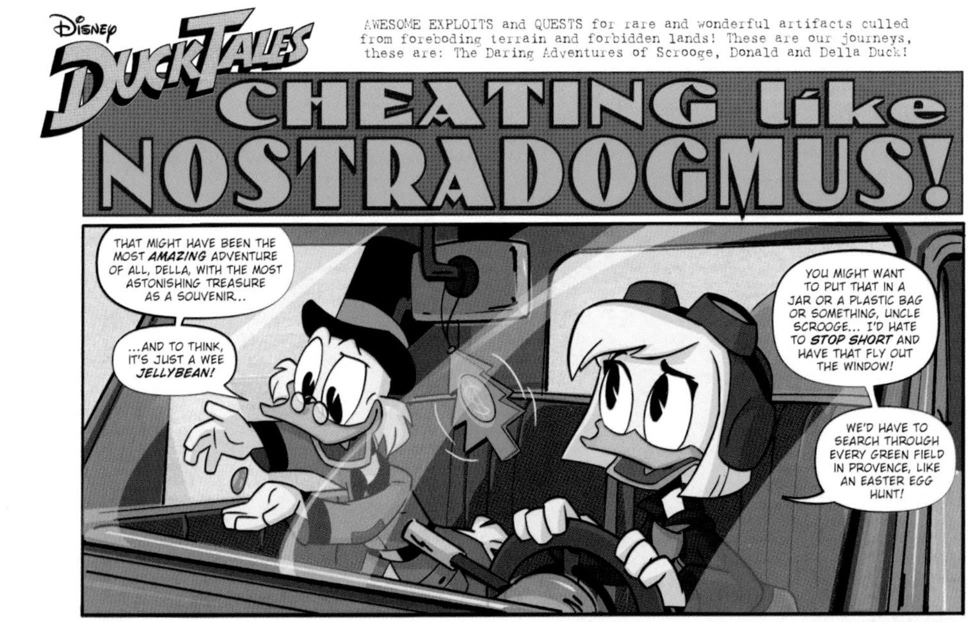
THAT MIGHT HAVE BEEN THE MOST AMAZING ADVENTURE OF ALL, DELLA, WITH THE MOST ASTONISHING TREASURE AS A SOUVENIR...
...AND TO THINK, IT'S JUST A WEE JELLYBEAN!
YOU MIGHT WANT TO PUT THAT IN A JAR OR A PLASTIC BAG OR SOMETHING, UNCLE SCROOGE... I'D HATE TO STOP SHORT AND HAVE THAT FLY OUT THE WINDOW!
WE'D HAVE TO SEARCH THROUGH EVERY GREEN FIELD IN PROVENCE, LIKE AN EASTER EGG HUNT!

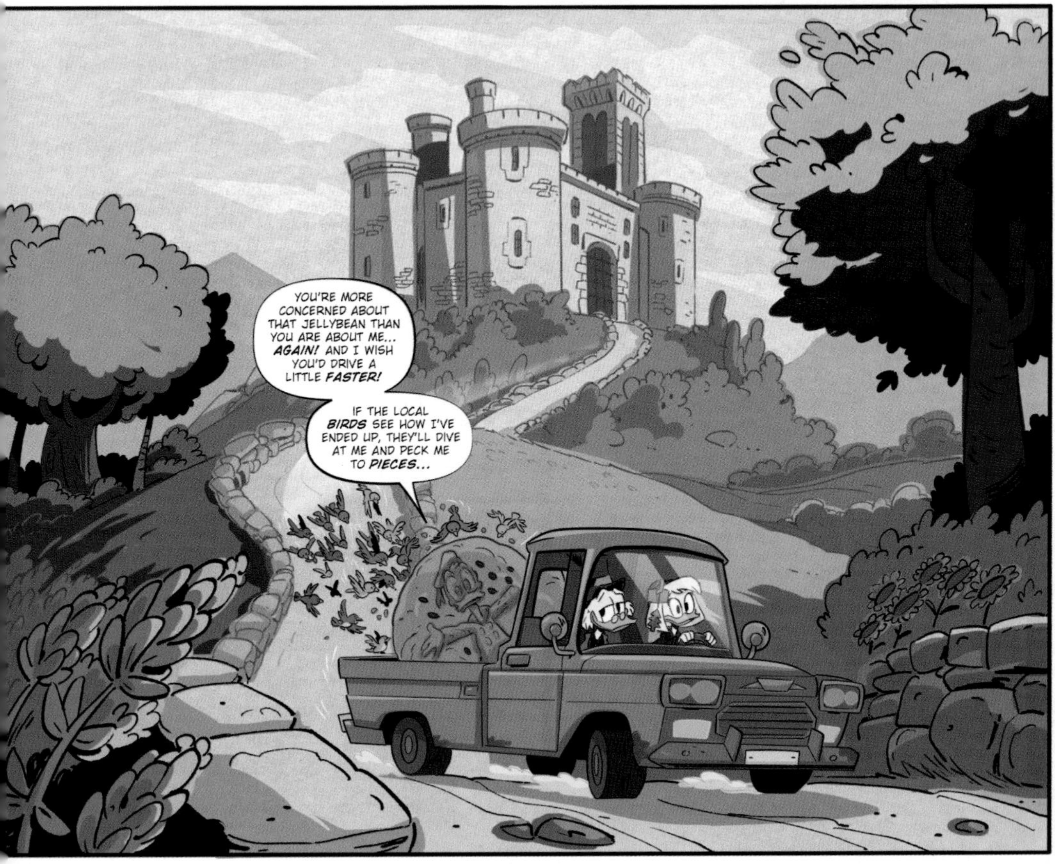
YOU'RE MORE CONCERNED ABOUT THAT JELLYBEAN THAN YOU ARE ABOUT ME... AGAIN! AND I WISH YOU'D DRIVE A LITTLE FASTER!
IF THE LOCAL BIRDS SEE HOW I'VE ENDED UP, THEY'LL DIVE AT ME AND PECK ME TO PIECES...

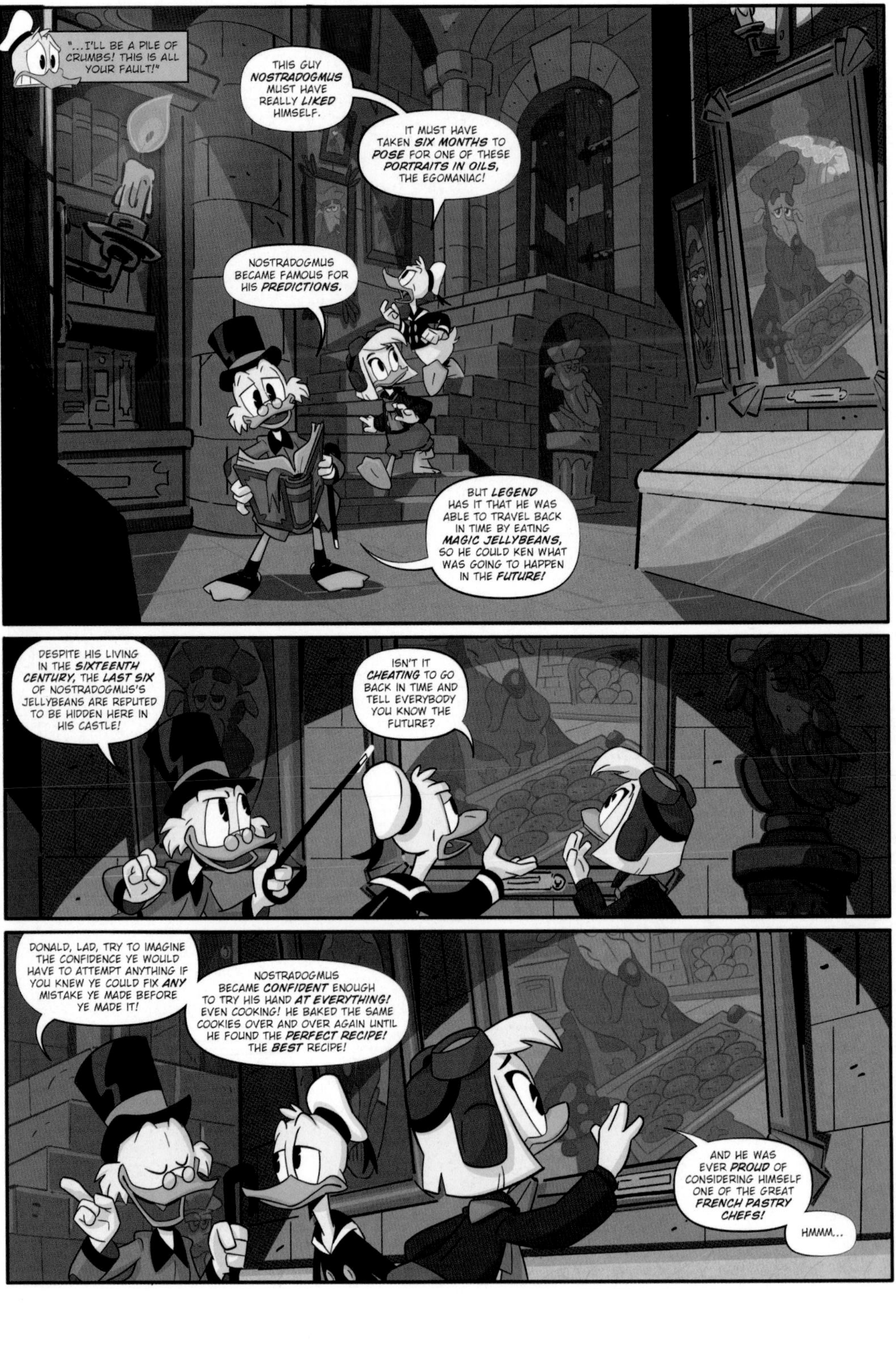
"...I'LL BE A PILE OF CRUMBS! THIS IS ALL YOUR FAULT!"
THIS GUY NOSTRADOGMUS MUST HAVE REALLY LIKED HIMSELF.
IT MUST HAVE TAKEN SIX MONTHS TO POSE FOR ONE OF THESE PORTRAITS IN OILS, THE EGOMANIAC!
NOSTRADOGMUS BECAME FAMOUS FOR HIS PREDICTIONS.
BUT LEGEND HAS IT THAT HE WAS ABLE TO TRAVEL BACK IN TIME BY EATING MAGIC JELLYBEANS, SO HE COULD KEN WHAT WAS GOING TO HAPPEN IN THE FUTURE!
DESPITE HIS LIVING IN THE SIXTEENTH CENTURY, THE LAST SIX OF NOSTRADOGMUS'S JELLYBEANS ARE REPUTED TO BE HIDDEN HERE IN HIS CASTLE!
ISN'T IT CHEATING TO GO BACK IN TIME AND TELL EVERYBODY YOU KNOW THE FUTURE?
DONALD, LAD, TRY TO IMAGINE THE CONFIDENCE YE WOULD HAVE TO ATTEMPT ANYTHING IF YOU KNEW YE COULD FIX ANY MISTAKE YE MADE BEFORE YE MADE IT!
NOSTRADOGMUS BECAME CONFIDENT ENOUGH TO TRY HIS HAND AT EVERYTHING! EVEN COOKING! HE BAKED THE SAME COOKIES OVER AND OVER AGAIN UNTIL HE FOUND THE PERFECT RECIPE! THE BEST RECIPE!
AND HE WAS EVER PROUD OF CONSIDERING HIMSELF ONE OF THE GREAT FRENCH PASTRY CHEFS!
HMMM...

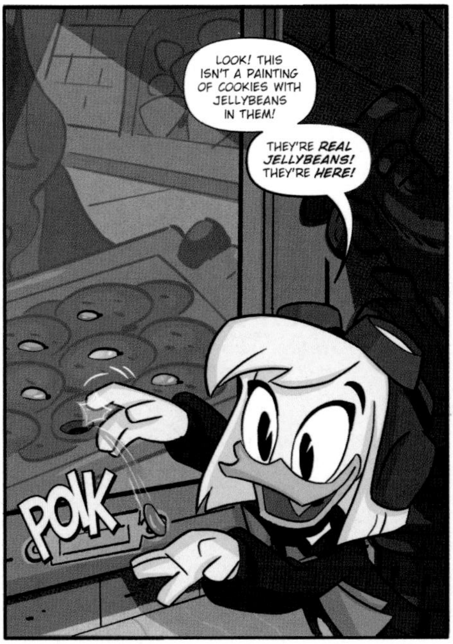
LOOK! THIS ISN'T A PAINTING OF COOKIES WITH JELLYBEANS IN THEM!
THEY'RE REAL JELLYBEANS! THEY'RE HERE!
POK

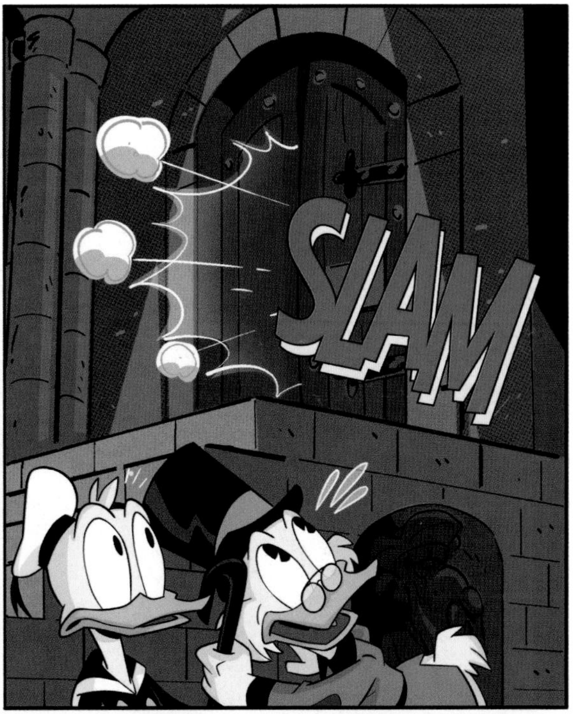
SLAM

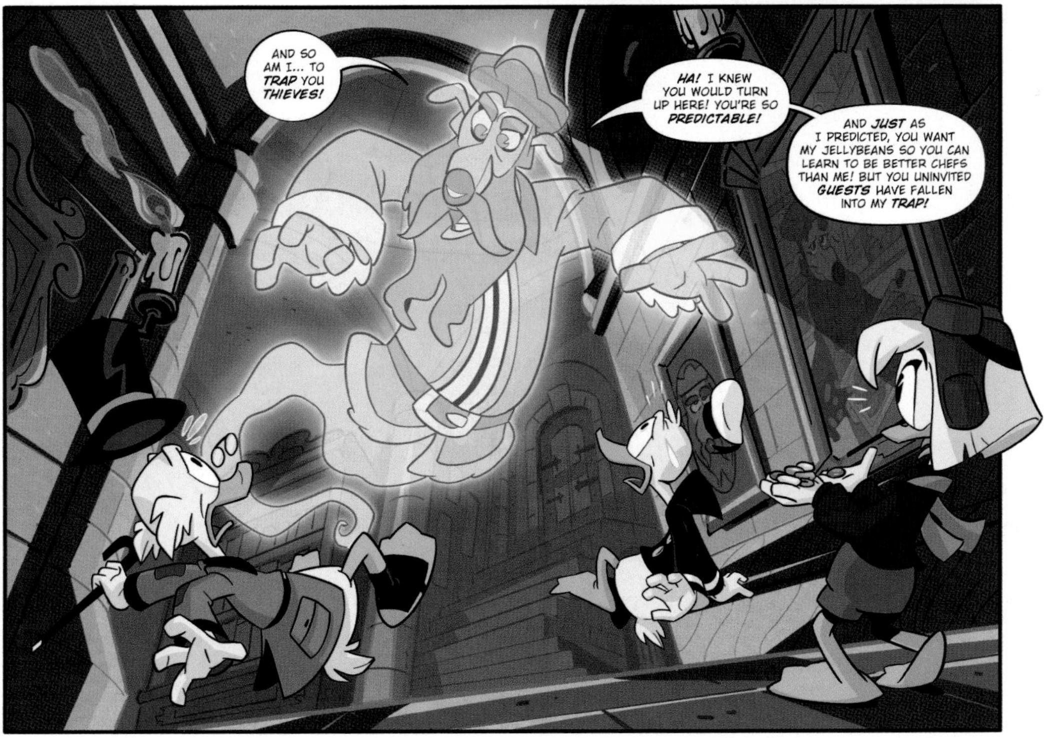
AND SO AM I... TO TRAP YOU THIEVES!
HA! I KNEW YOU WOULD TURN UP HERE! YOU'RE SO PREDICTABLE!
AND JUST AS I PREDICTED, YOU WANT MY JELLYBEANS SO YOU CAN LEARN TO BE BETTER CHEFS THAN ME! BUT YOU UNINVITED GUESTS HAVE FALLEN INTO MY TRAP!

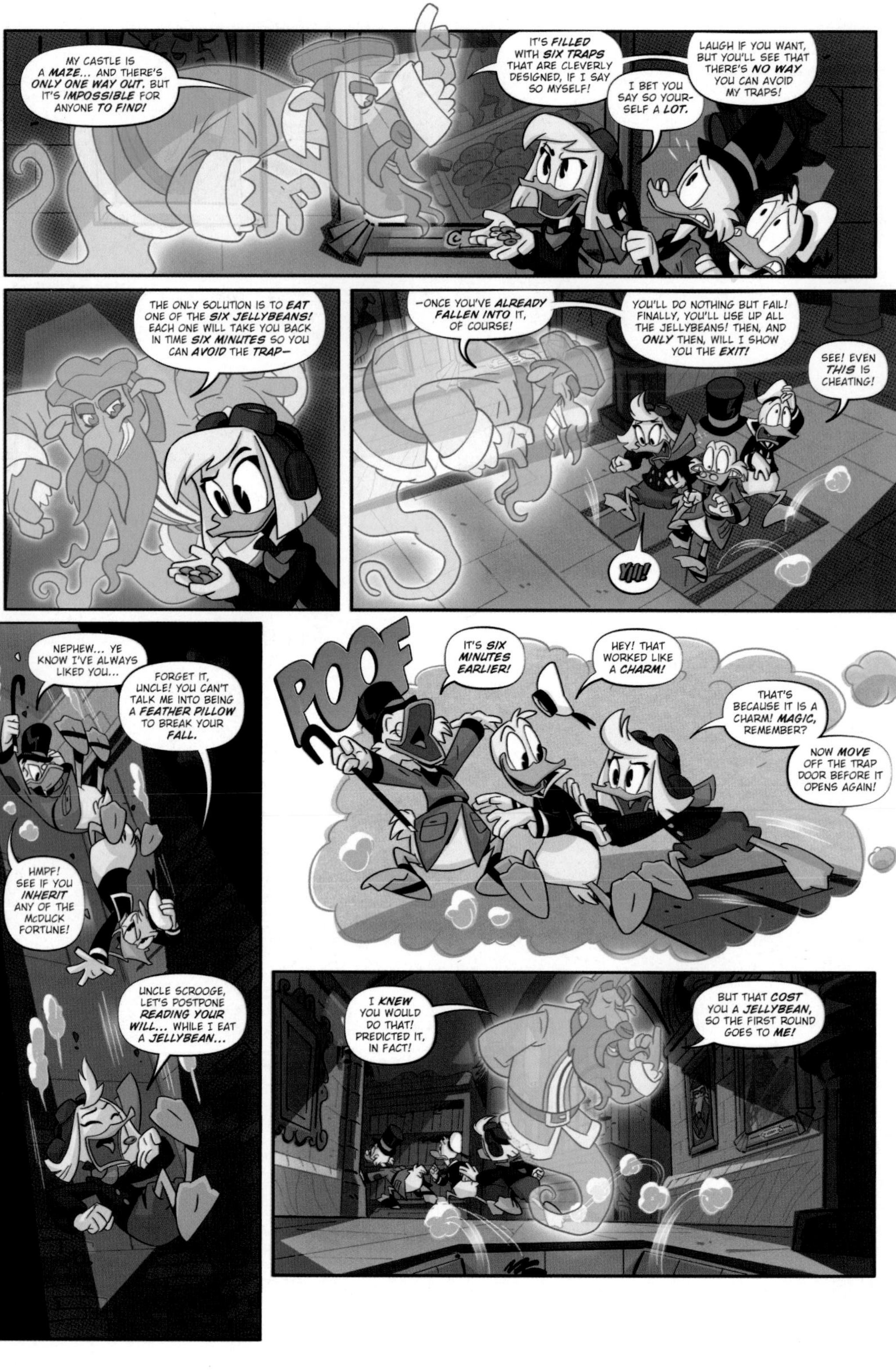
MY CASTLE IS A MAZE... AND THERE'S ONLY ONE WAY OUT. BUT IT'S IMPOSSIBLE FOR ANYONE TO FIND!
IT'S FILLED WITH SIX TRAPS THAT ARE CLEVERLY DESIGNED, IF I SAY SO MYSELF!
I BET YOU SAY SO YOURSELF A LOT.
LAUGH IF YOU WANT, BUT YOU'LL SEE THAT THERE'S NO WAY YOU CAN AVOID MY TRAPS!
THE ONLY SOLUTION IS TO EAT ONE OF THE SIX JELLYBEANS! EACH ONE WILL TAKE YOU BACK IN TIME SIX MINUTES SO YOU CAN AVOID THE TRAP—
—ONCE YOU'VE ALREADY FALLEN INTO IT, OF COURSE!
YOU'LL DO NOTHING BUT FAIL! FINALLY, YOU'LL USE UP ALL THE JELLYBEANS! THEN, AND ONLY THEN, WILL I SHOW YOU THE EXIT!
SEE! EVEN THIS IS CHEATING!
YIII!
NEPHEW... YE KNOW I'VE ALWAYS LIKED YOU...
FORGET IT, UNCLE! YOU CAN'T TALK ME INTO BEING A FEATHER PILLOW TO BREAK YOUR FALL.
HMPF! SEE IF YOU INHERIT ANY OF THE McDUCK FORTUNE!
UNCLE SCROOGE, LET'S POSTPONE READING YOUR WILL... WHILE I EAT A JELLYBEAN...
POOF
IT'S SIX MINUTES EARLIER!
HEY! THAT WORKED LIKE A CHARM!
THAT'S BECAUSE IT IS A CHARM! MAGIC, REMEMBER?
NOW MOVE OFF THE TRAP DOOR BEFORE IT OPENS AGAIN!
I KNEW YOU WOULD DO THAT! PREDICTED IT, IN FACT!
BUT THAT COST YOU A JELLYBEAN, SO THE FIRST ROUND GOES TO ME!

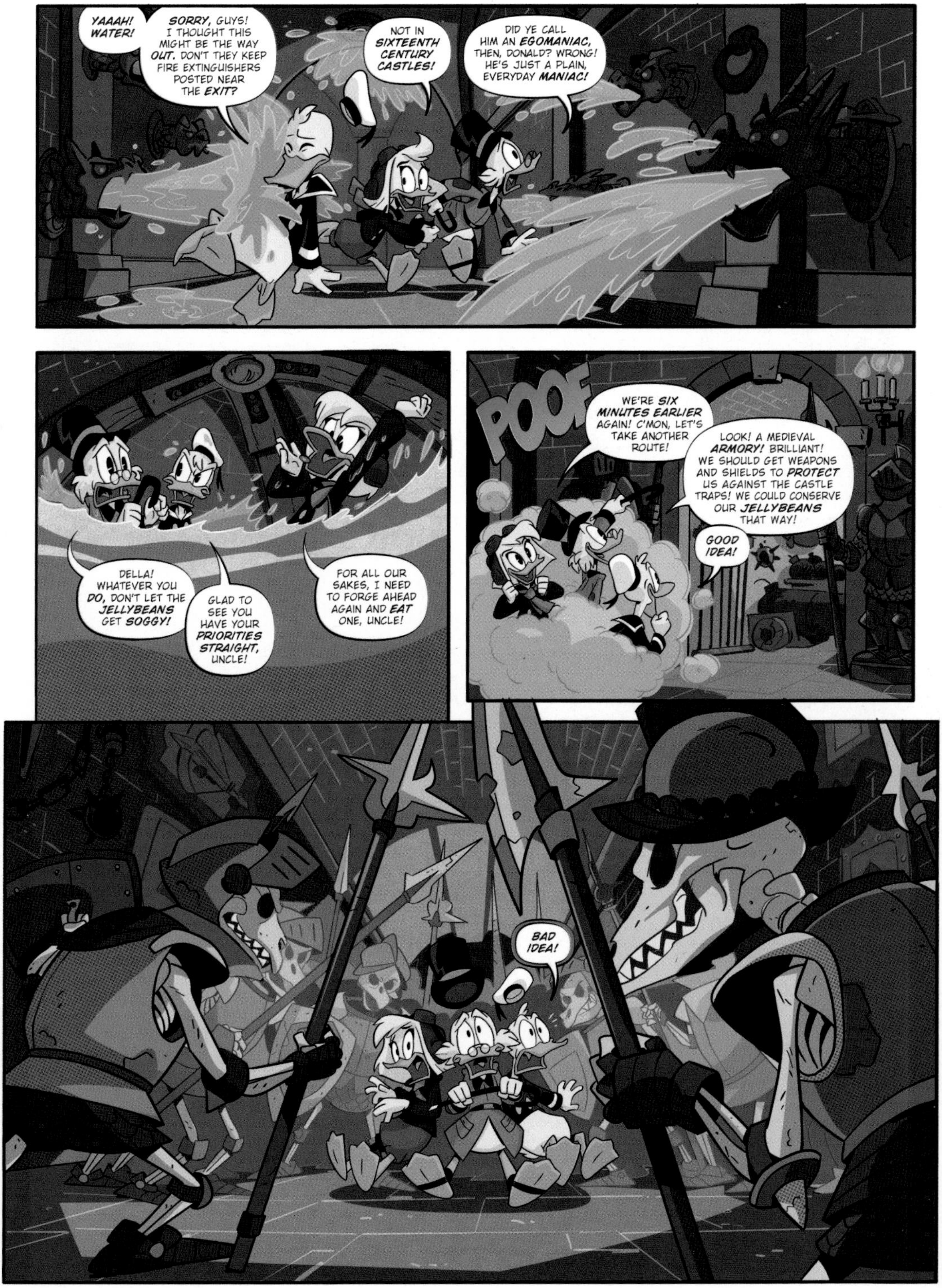
YAAAH! WATER!
SORRY, GUYS! I THOUGHT THIS MIGHT BE THE WAY OUT. DON'T THEY KEEP FIRE EXTINGUISHERS POSTED NEAR THE EXIT?
NOT IN SIXTEENTH CENTURY CASTLES!
DID YE CALL HIM AN EGOMANIAC, THEN, DONALD? WRONG! HE'S JUST A PLAIN, EVERYDAY MANIAC!
DELLA! WHATEVER YOU DO, DON'T LET THE JELLYBEANS GET SOGGY!
GLAD TO SEE YOU HAVE YOUR PRIORITIES STRAIGHT, UNCLE!
FOR ALL OUR SAKES, I NEED TO FORGE AHEAD AGAIN AND EAT ONE, UNCLE!
POOF
WE'RE SIX MINUTES EARLIER AGAIN! C'MON, LET'S TAKE ANOTHER ROUTE!
LOOK! A MEDIEVAL ARMORY! BRILLIANT! WE SHOULD GET WEAPONS AND SHIELDS TO PROTECT US AGAINST THE CASTLE TRAPS! WE COULD CONSERVE OUR JELLYBEANS THAT WAY!
GOOD IDEA!
BAD IDEA!

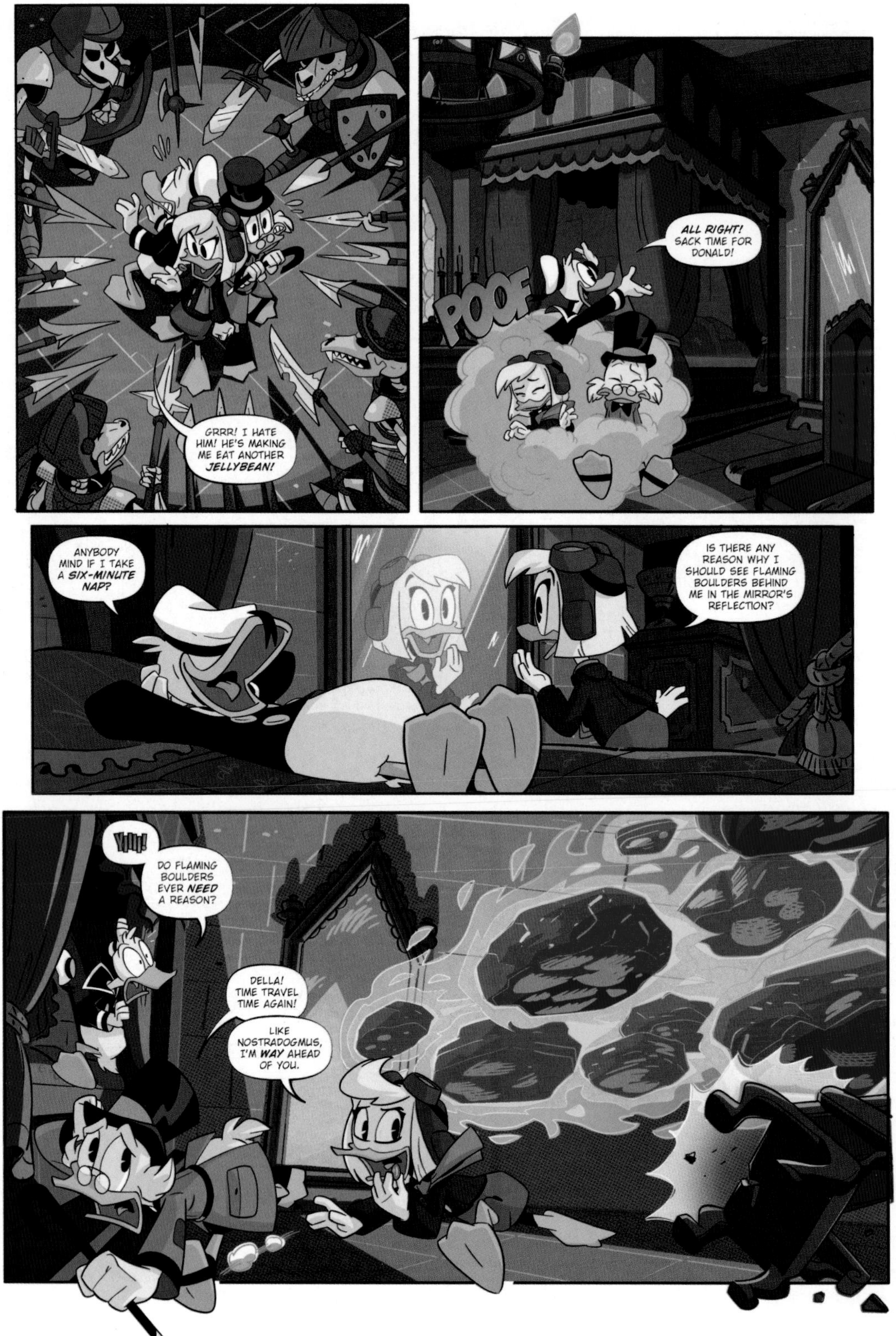
GRRR! I HATE HIM! HE'S MAKING ME EAT ANOTHER JELLYBEAN!
ALL RIGHT! SACK TIME FOR DONALD!
POOF
ANYBODY MIND IF I TAKE A SIX-MINUTE NAP?
IS THERE ANY REASON WHY I SHOULD SEE FLAMING BOULDERS BEHIND ME IN THE MIRROR'S REFLECTION?
YIII!
DO FLAMING BOULDERS EVER NEED A REASON?
DELLA! TIME TRAVEL TIME AGAIN!
LIKE NOSTRADOGMUS, I'M WAY AHEAD OF YOU.

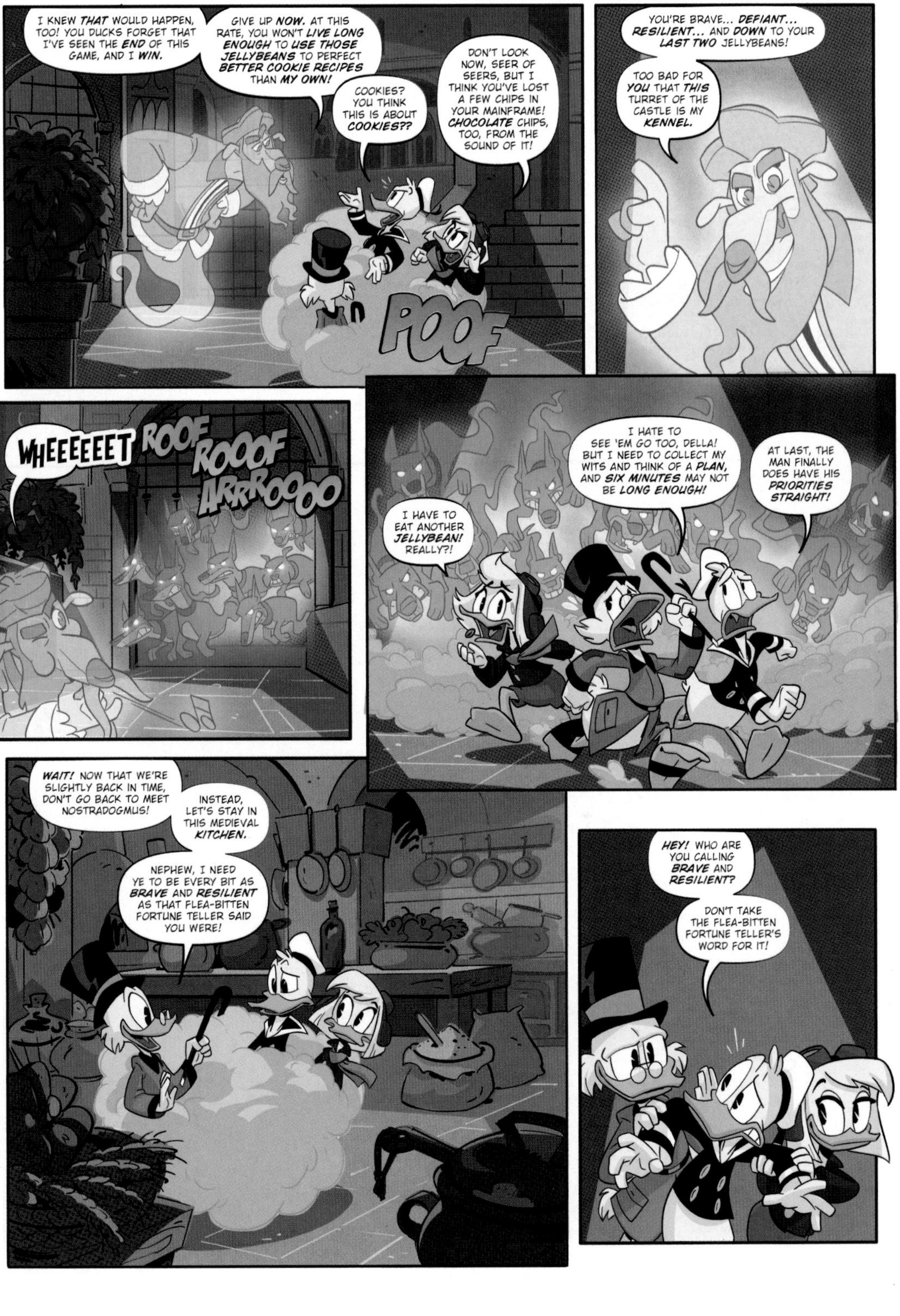
I KNEW THAT WOULD HAPPEN, TOO! YOU DUCKS FORGET THAT I'VE SEEN THE END OF THIS GAME, AND I WIN.
GIVE UP NOW. AT THIS RATE, YOU WON'T LIVE LONG ENOUGH TO USE THOSE JELLYBEANS TO PERFECT BETTER COOKIE RECIPES THAN MY OWN!
COOKIES? YOU THINK THIS IS ABOUT COOKIES??
DON'T LOOK NOW, SEER OF SEERS, BUT I THINK YOU'VE LOST A FEW CHIPS IN YOUR MAINFRAME! CHOCOLATE CHIPS, TOO, FROM THE SOUND OF IT!
POOF
YOU'RE BRAVE... DEFIANT... RESILIENT... AND DOWN TO YOUR LAST TWO JELLYBEANS!
TOO BAD FOR YOU THAT THIS TURRET OF THE CASTLE IS MY KENNEL.
WHEEEEEET
ROOF
ROOOF
ARRROOOO
I HAVE TO EAT ANOTHER JELLYBEAN! REALLY?!
I HATE TO SEE 'EM GO TOO, DELLA! BUT I NEED TO COLLECT MY WITS AND THINK OF A PLAN, AND SIX MINUTES MAY NOT BE LONG ENOUGH!
AT LAST, THE MAN FINALLY DOES HAVE HIS PRIORITIES STRAIGHT!
WAIT! NOW THAT WE'RE SLIGHTLY BACK IN TIME, DON'T GO BACK TO MEET NOSTRADOGMUS!
INSTEAD, LET'S STAY IN THIS MEDIEVAL KITCHEN.
NEPHEW, I NEED YE TO BE EVERY BIT AS BRAVE AND RESILIENT AS THAT FLEA-BITTEN FORTUNE TELLER SAID YOU WERE!
HEY! WHO ARE YOU CALLING BRAVE AND RESILIENT?
DON'T TAKE THE FLEA-BITTEN FORTUNE TELLER'S WORD FOR IT!

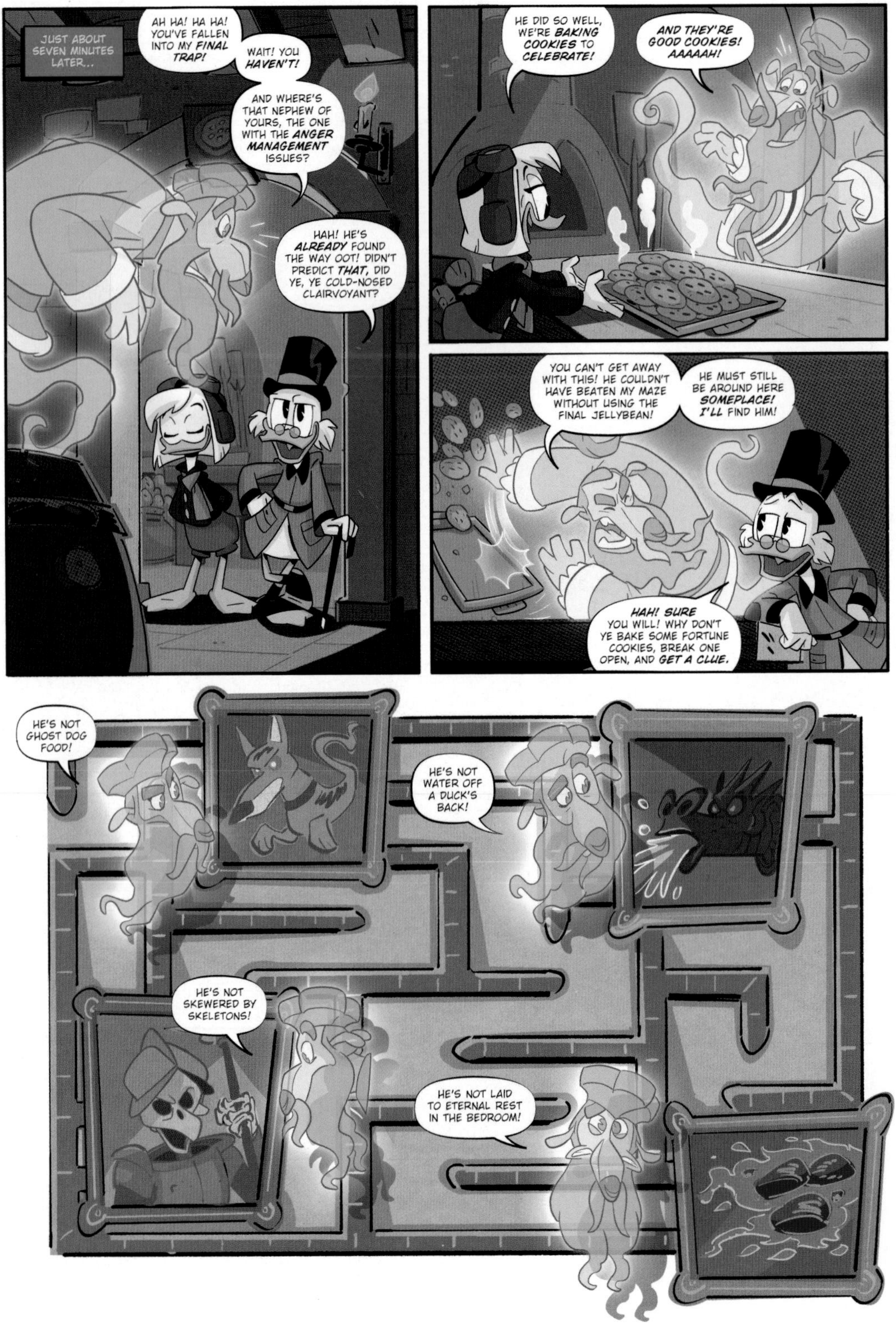
JUST ABOUT SEVEN MINUTES LATER...
AH HA! HA HA! YOU'VE FALLEN INTO MY FINAL TRAP!
WAIT! YOU HAVEN'T!
AND WHERE'S THAT NEPHEW OF YOURS, THE ONE WITH THE ANGER MANAGEMENT ISSUES?
HAH! HE'S ALREADY FOUND THE WAY OOT! DIDN'T PREDICT THAT, DID YE, YE COLD-NOSED CLAIRVOYANT?
HE DID SO WELL, WE'RE BAKING COOKIES TO CELEBRATE!
AND THEY'RE GOOD COOKIES! AAAAAH!
YOU CAN'T GET AWAY WITH THIS! HE COULDN'T HAVE BEATEN MY MAZE WITHOUT USING THE FINAL JELLYBEAN!
HE MUST STILL BE AROUND HERE SOMEPLACE! I'LL FIND HIM!
HAH! SURE YOU WILL! WHY DON'T YE BAKE SOME FORTUNE COOKIES, BREAK ONE OPEN, AND GET A CLUE.
HE'S NOT GHOST DOG FOOD!
HE'S NOT WATER OFF A DUCK'S BACK!
HE'S NOT SKEWERED BY SKELETONS!
HE'S NOT LAID TO ETERNAL REST IN THE BEDROOM!

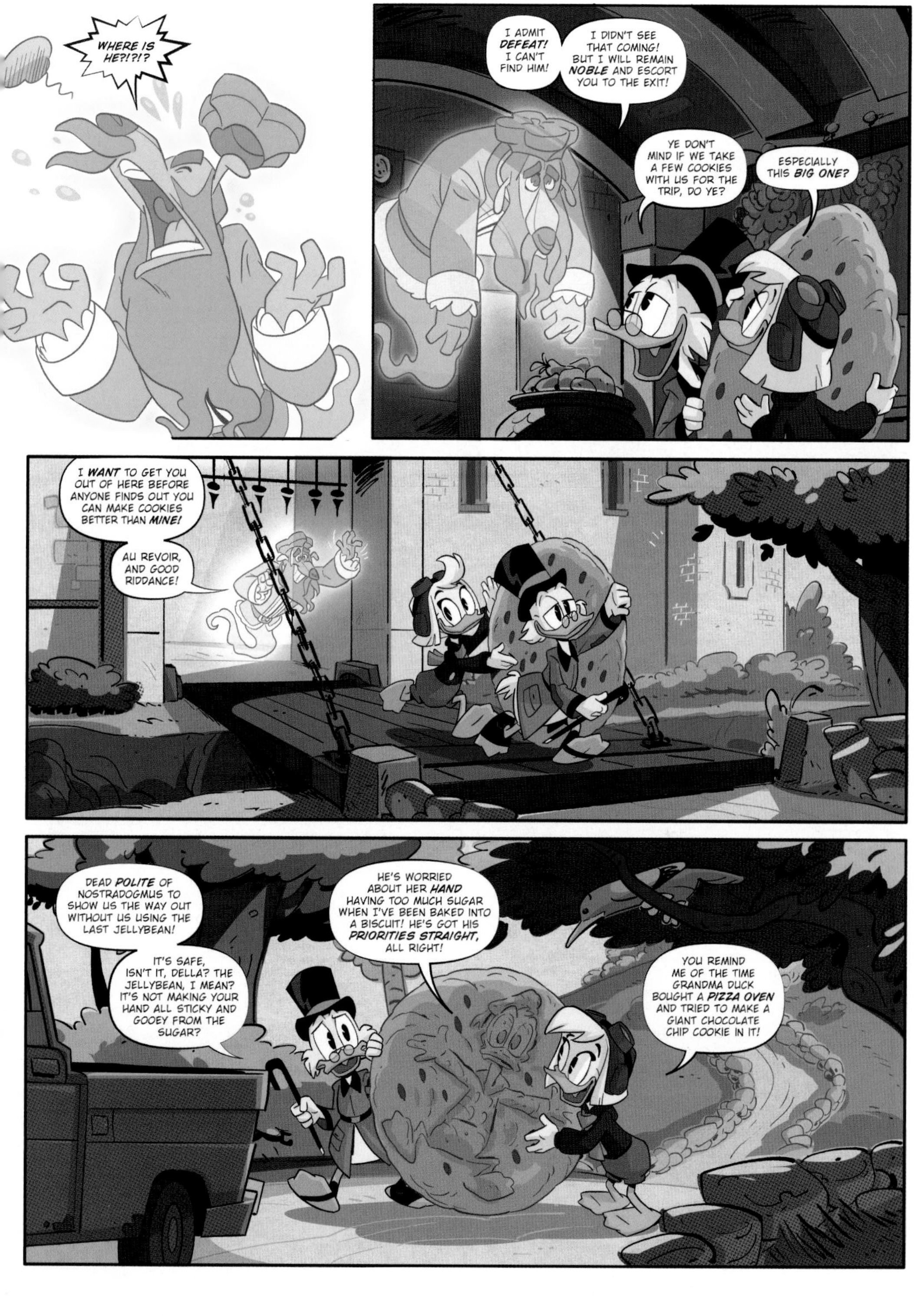
WHERE IS HE?!?!?
I ADMIT DEFEAT! I CAN'T FIND HIM!
I DIDN'T SEE THAT COMING! BUT I WILL REMAIN NOBLE AND ESCORT YOU TO THE EXIT!
YE DON'T MIND IF WE TAKE A FEW COOKIES WITH US FOR THE TRIP, DO YE?
ESPECIALLY THIS BIG ONE?
I WANT TO GET YOU OUT OF HERE BEFORE ANYONE FINDS OUT YOU CAN MAKE COOKIES BETTER THAN MINE!
AU REVOIR, AND GOOD RIDDANCE!
DEAD POLITE OF NOSTRADOGMUS TO SHOW US THE WAY OUT WITHOUT US USING THE LAST JELLYBEAN!
IT'S SAFE, ISN'T IT, DELLA? THE JELLYBEAN, I MEAN? IT'S NOT MAKING YOUR HAND ALL STICKY AND GOOEY FROM THE SUGAR?
HE'S WORRIED ABOUT HER HAND HAVING TOO MUCH SUGAR WHEN I'VE BEEN BAKED INTO A BISCUIT! HE'S GOT HIS PRIORITIES STRAIGHT, ALL RIGHT!
YOU REMIND ME OF THE TIME GRANDMA DUCK BOUGHT A PIZZA OVEN AND TRIED TO MAKE A GIANT CHOCOLATE CHIP COOKIE IN IT!

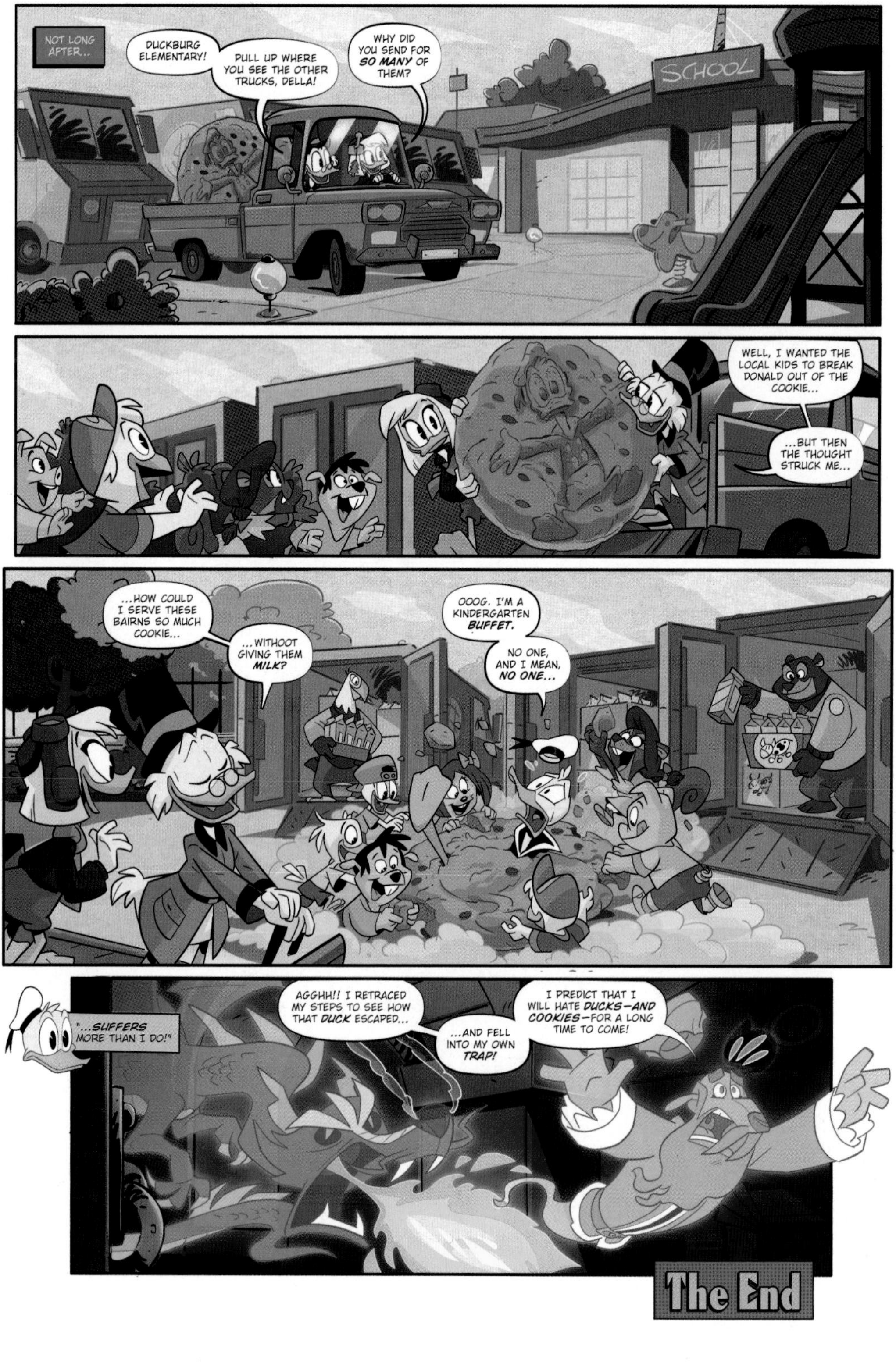
NOT LONG AFTER...
DUCKBURG ELEMENTARY!
PULL UP WHERE YOU SEE THE OTHER TRUCKS, DELLA!
WHY DID YOU SEND FOR SO MANY OF THEM?
SCHOOL
WELL, I WANTED THE LOCAL KIDS TO BREAK DONALD OUT OF THE COOKIE...
...BUT THEN THE THOUGHT STRUCK ME...
...HOW COULD I SERVE THESE BAIRNS SO MUCH COOKIE...
...WITHOOT GIVING THEM MILK?
OOOG. I'M A KINDERGARTEN BUFFET.
NO ONE, AND I MEAN, NO ONE...
"...SUFFERS MORE THAN I DO!"
AGGHH!! I RETRACED MY STEPS TO SEE HOW THAT DUCK ESCAPED...
...AND FELL INTO MY OWN TRAP!
I PREDICT THAT I WILL HATE DUCKS—AND COOKIES—FOR A LONG TIME TO COME!
The End

Disney DuckTales

AWESOME EXPLOITS and QUESTS for rare and wonderful artifacts culled from foreboding terrain and forbidden lands! These are our journeys, these are: The Daring Adventures of Scrooge, Donald and Della Duck!

BEWARE of the PHENOMENAL PUMPKIN PEOPLE!

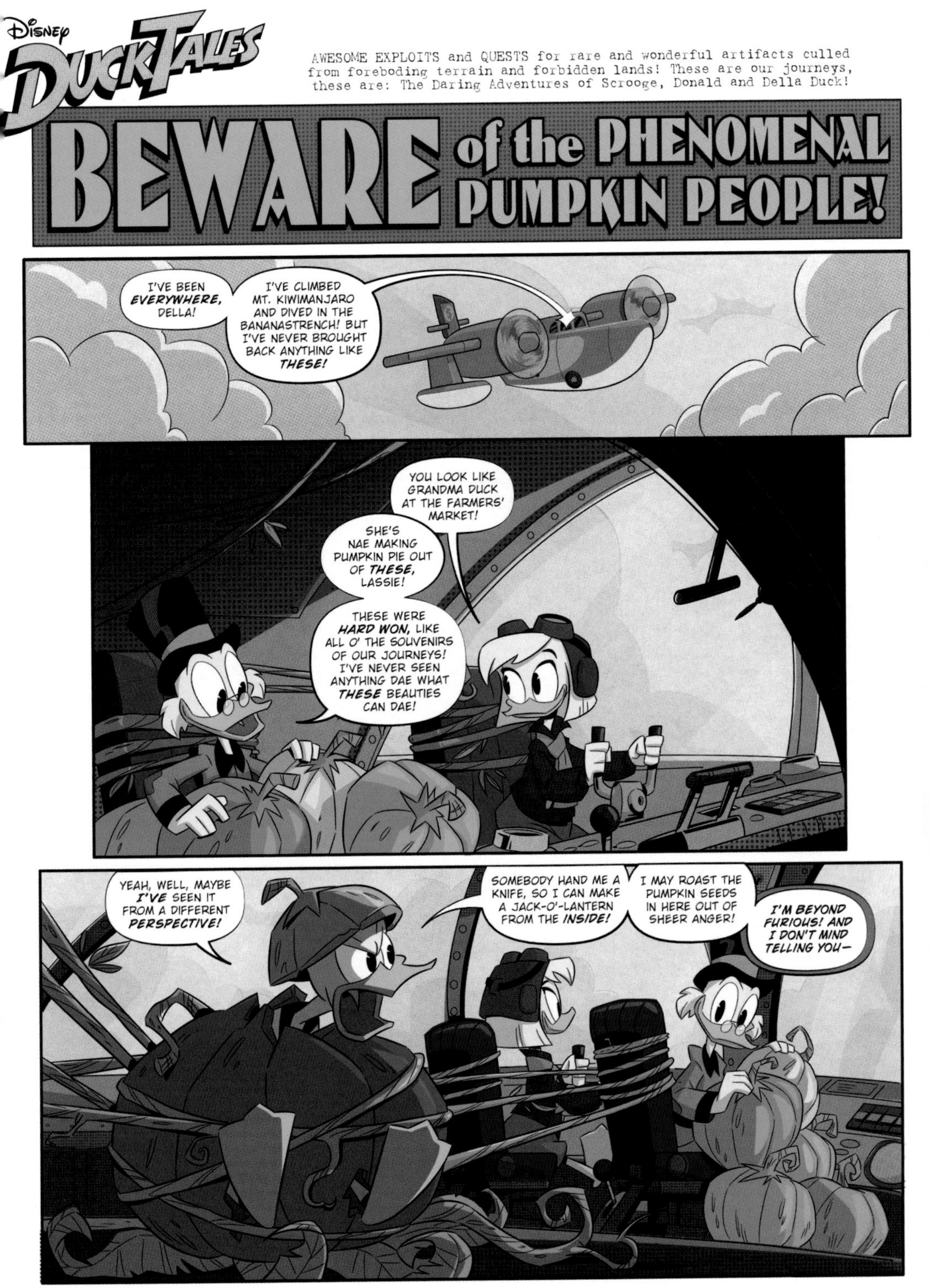

I'VE BEEN EVERYWHERE, DELLA!
I'VE CLIMBED MT. KIWIMANJARO AND DIVED IN THE BANANASTRENCH! BUT I'VE NEVER BROUGHT BACK ANYTHING LIKE THESE!
YOU LOOK LIKE GRANDMA DUCK AT THE FARMERS' MARKET!
SHE'S NAE MAKING PUMPKIN PIE OUT OF THESE, LASSIE!
THESE WERE HARD WON, LIKE ALL O' THE SOUVENIRS OF OUR JOURNEYS! I'VE NEVER SEEN ANYTHING DAE WHAT THESE BEAUTIES CAN DAE!
YEAH, WELL, MAYBE I'VE SEEN IT FROM A DIFFERENT PERSPECTIVE!
SOMEBODY HAND ME A KNIFE, SO I CAN MAKE A JACK-O'-LANTERN FROM THE INSIDE!
I MAY ROAST THE PUMPKIN SEEDS IN HERE OUT OF SHEER ANGER!
I'M BEYOND FURIOUS! AND I DON'T MIND TELLING YOU—

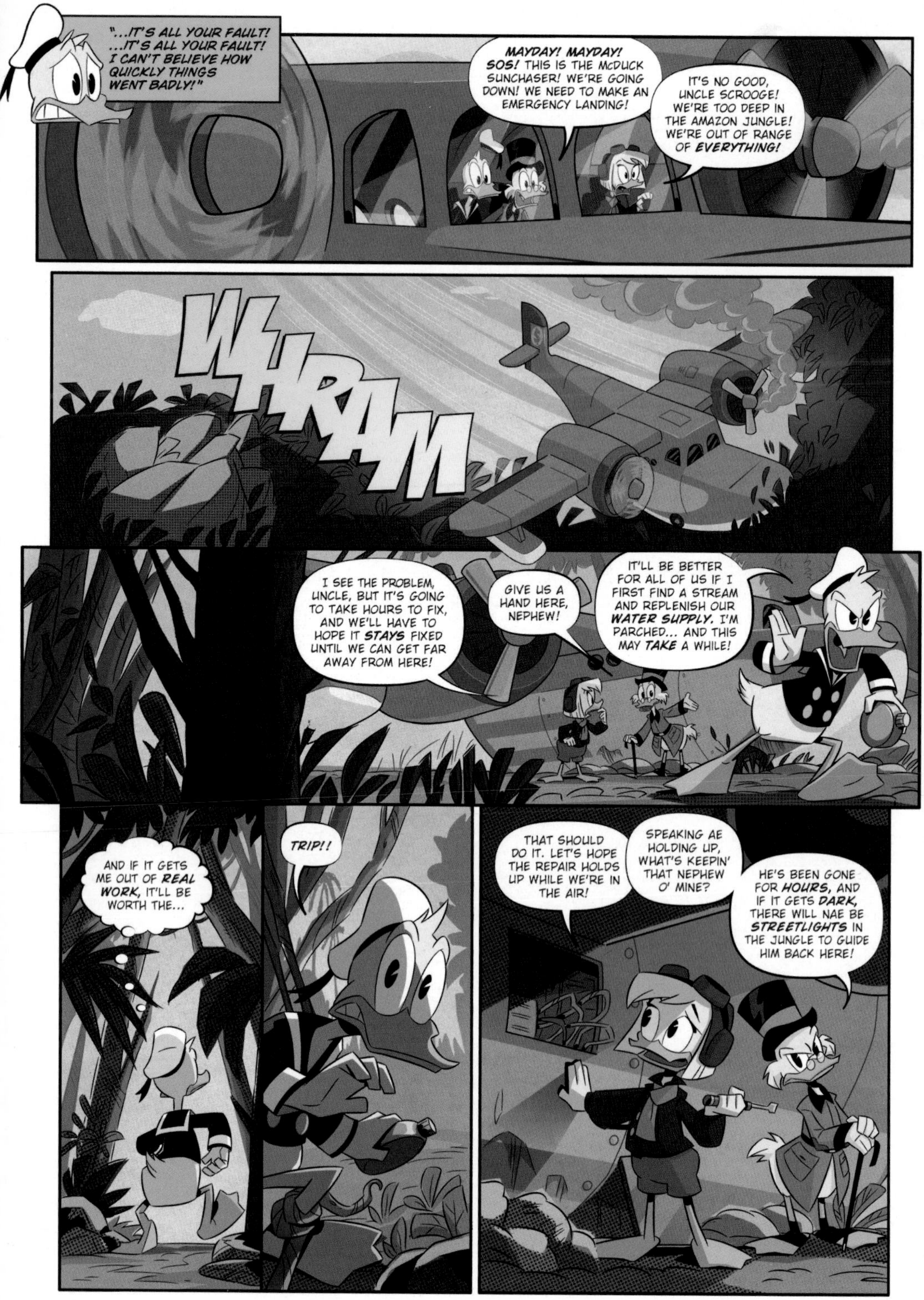
"...IT'S ALL YOUR FAULT! ...IT'S ALL YOUR FAULT! I CAN'T BELIEVE HOW QUICKLY THINGS WENT BADLY!"
MAYDAY! MAYDAY! SOS! THIS IS THE McDUCK SUNCHASER! WE'RE GOING DOWN! WE NEED TO MAKE AN EMERGENCY LANDING!
IT'S NO GOOD, UNCLE SCROOGE! WE'RE TOO DEEP IN THE AMAZON JUNGLE! WE'RE OUT OF RANGE OF EVERYTHING!
WHRAM
I SEE THE PROBLEM, UNCLE, BUT IT'S GOING TO TAKE HOURS TO FIX, AND WE'LL HAVE TO HOPE IT STAYS FIXED UNTIL WE CAN GET FAR AWAY FROM HERE!
GIVE US A HAND HERE, NEPHEW!
IT'LL BE BETTER FOR ALL OF US IF I FIRST FIND A STREAM AND REPLENISH OUR WATER SUPPLY. I'M PARCHED... AND THIS MAY TAKE A WHILE!
AND IF IT GETS ME OUT OF REAL WORK, IT'LL BE WORTH THE...
TRIP!!
THAT SHOULD DO IT. LET'S HOPE THE REPAIR HOLDS UP WHILE WE'RE IN THE AIR!
SPEAKING AE HOLDING UP, WHAT'S KEEPIN' THAT NEPHEW O' MINE?
HE'S BEEN GONE FOR HOURS, AND IF IT GETS DARK, THERE WILL NAE BE STREETLIGHTS IN THE JUNGLE TO GUIDE HIM BACK HERE!

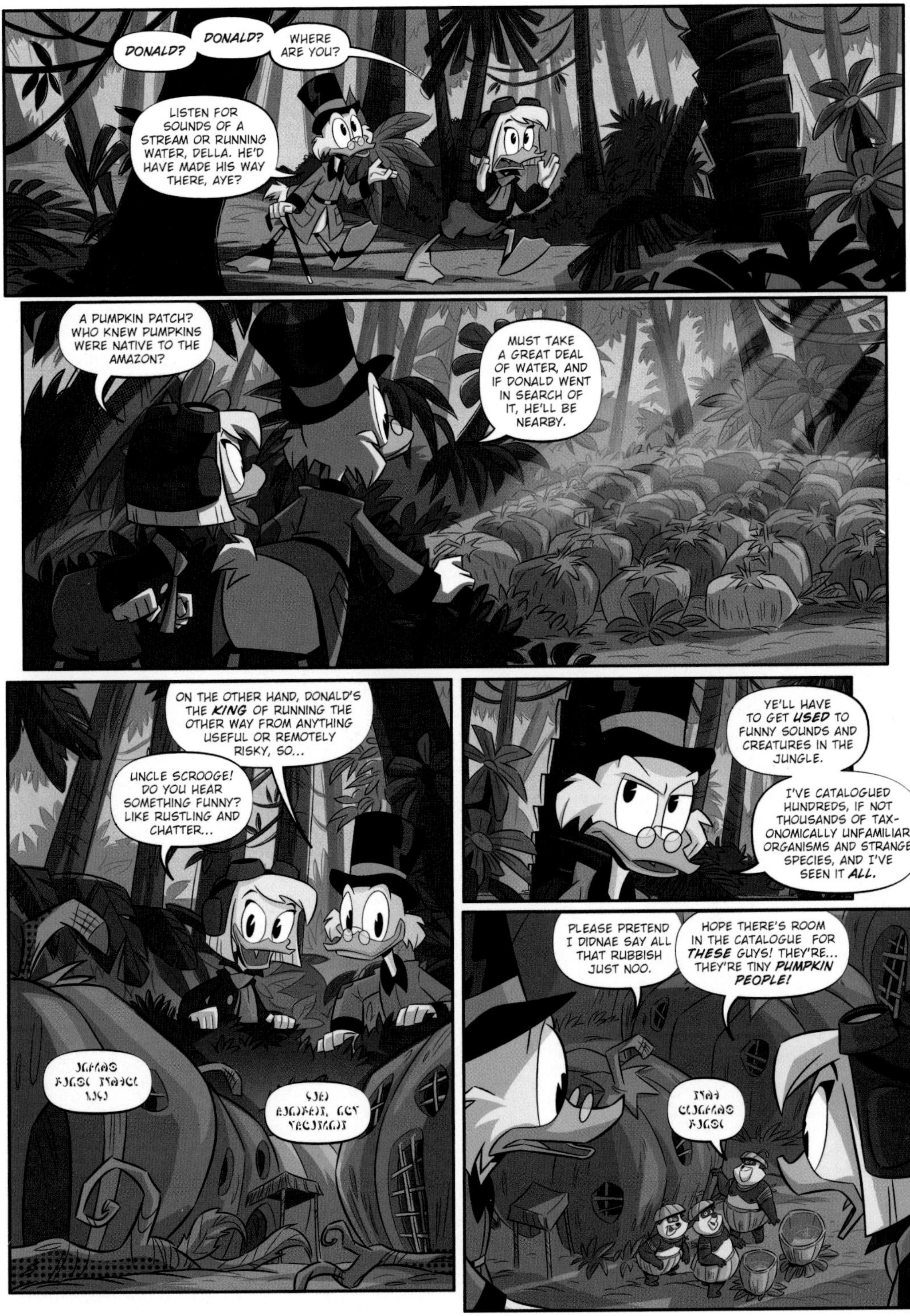
DONALD?
DONALD?
WHERE ARE YOU?
LISTEN FOR SOUNDS OF A STREAM OR RUNNING WATER, DELLA. HE'D HAVE MADE HIS WAY THERE, AYE?
A PUMPKIN PATCH? WHO KNEW PUMPKINS WERE NATIVE TO THE AMAZON?
MUST TAKE A GREAT DEAL OF WATER, AND IF DONALD WENT IN SEARCH OF IT, HE'LL BE NEARBY.
ON THE OTHER HAND, DONALD'S THE KING OF RUNNING THE OTHER WAY FROM ANYTHING USEFUL OR REMOTELY RISKY, SO...
UNCLE SCROOGE! DO YOU HEAR SOMETHING FUNNY? LIKE RUSTLING AND CHATTER...
YE'LL HAVE TO GET USED TO FUNNY SOUNDS AND CREATURES IN THE JUNGLE.
I'VE CATALOGUED HUNDREDS, IF NOT THOUSANDS OF TAX-ONOMICALLY UNFAMILIAR ORGANISMS AND STRANGE SPECIES, AND I'VE SEEN IT ALL.
PLEASE PRETEND I DIDNAE SAY ALL THAT RUBBISH JUST NOO.
HOPE THERE'S ROOM IN THE CATALOGUE FOR THESE GUYS! THEY'RE... THEY'RE TINY PUMPKIN PEOPLE!

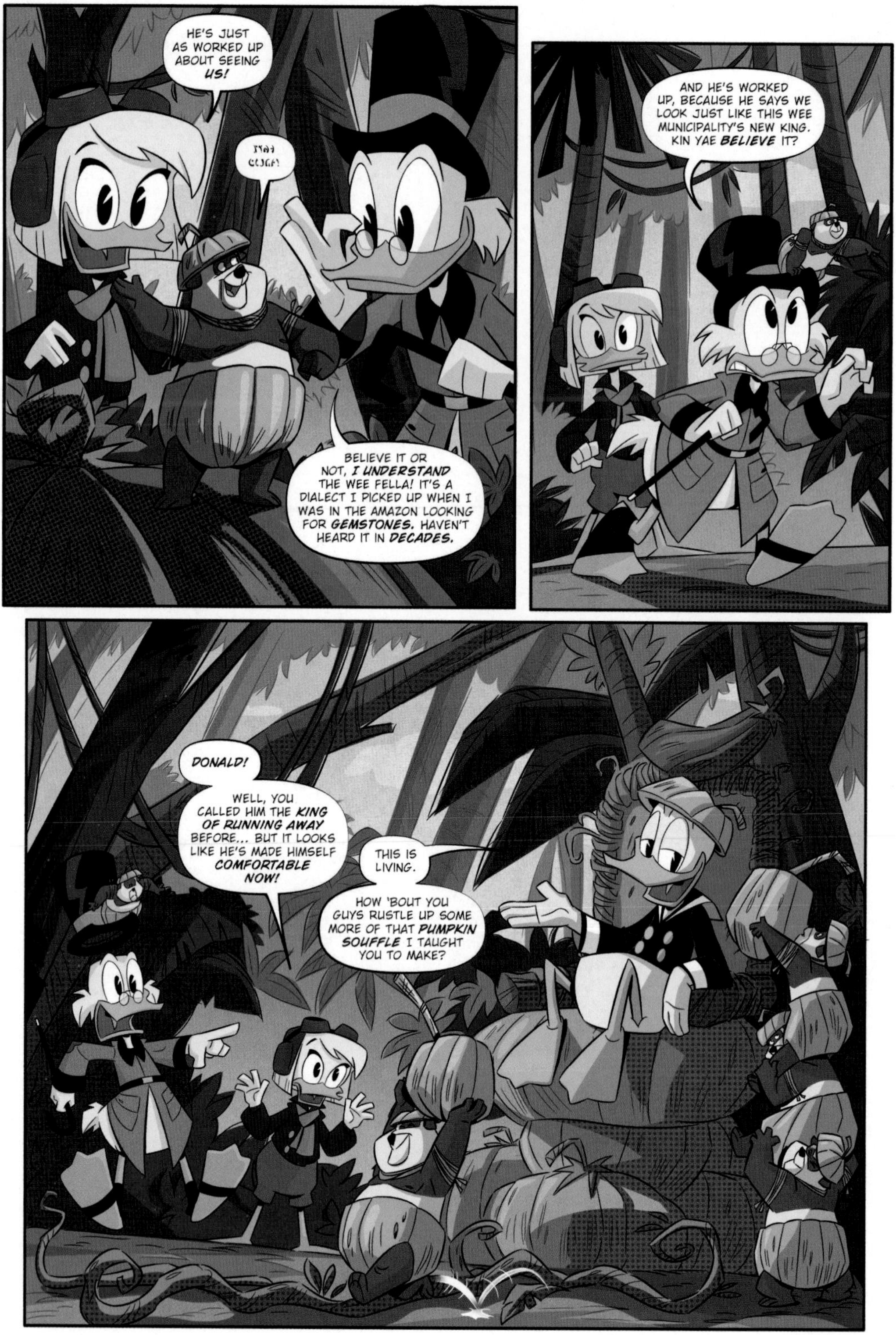
HE'S JUST AS WORKED UP ABOUT SEEING US!
BELIEVE IT OR NOT, I UNDERSTAND THE WEE FELLA! IT'S A DIALECT I PICKED UP WHEN I WAS IN THE AMAZON LOOKING FOR GEMSTONES. HAVEN'T HEARD IT IN DECADES.
AND HE'S WORKED UP, BECAUSE HE SAYS WE LOOK JUST LIKE THIS WEE MUNICIPALITY'S NEW KING. KIN YAE BELIEVE IT?
DONALD!
WELL, YOU CALLED HIM THE KING OF RUNNING AWAY BEFORE... BUT IT LOOKS LIKE HE'S MADE HIMSELF COMFORTABLE NOW!
THIS IS LIVING.
HOW 'BOUT YOU GUYS RUSTLE UP SOME MORE OF THAT PUMPKIN SOUFFLE I TAUGHT YOU TO MAKE?

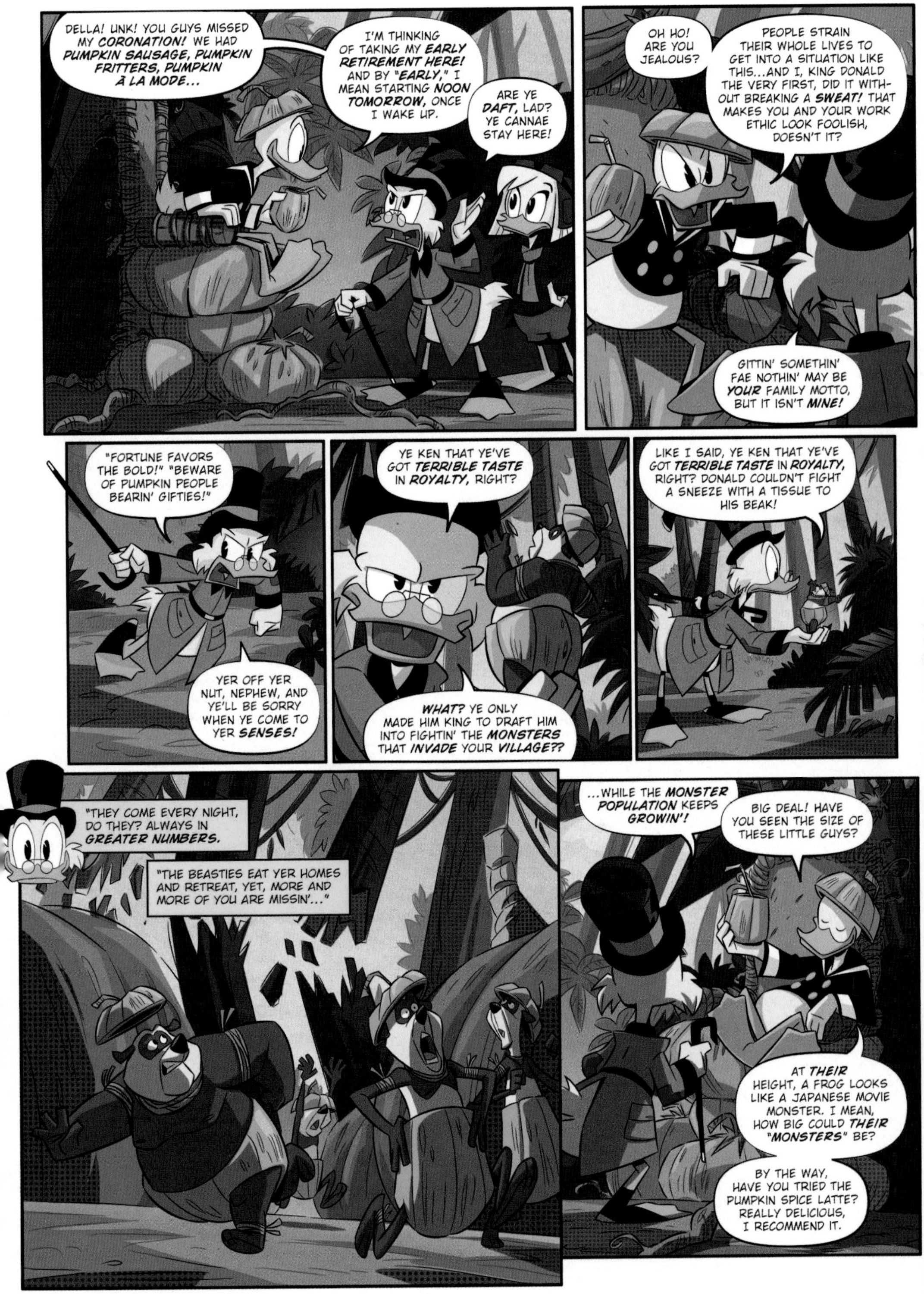
DELLA! UNK! YOU GUYS MISSED MY CORONATION! WE HAD PUMPKIN SAUSAGE, PUMPKIN FRITTERS, PUMPKIN À LA MODE...
I'M THINKING OF TAKING MY EARLY RETIREMENT HERE! AND BY "EARLY," I MEAN STARTING NOON TOMORROW, ONCE I WAKE UP.
ARE YE DAFT, LAD? YE CANNAE STAY HERE!
OH HO! ARE YOU JEALOUS?
PEOPLE STRAIN THEIR WHOLE LIVES TO GET INTO A SITUATION LIKE THIS...AND I, KING DONALD THE VERY FIRST, DID IT WITHOUT BREAKING A SWEAT! THAT MAKES YOU AND YOUR WORK ETHIC LOOK FOOLISH, DOESN'T IT?
GITTIN' SOMETHIN' FAE NOTHIN' MAY BE YOUR FAMILY MOTTO, BUT IT ISN'T MINE!
"FORTUNE FAVORS THE BOLD!" "BEWARE OF PUMPKIN PEOPLE BEARIN' GIFTIES!"
YER OFF YER NUT, NEPHEW, AND YE'LL BE SORRY WHEN YE COME TO YER SENSES!
YE KEN THAT YE'VE GOT TERRIBLE TASTE IN ROYALTY, RIGHT?
WHAT? YE ONLY MADE HIM KING TO DRAFT HIM INTO FIGHTIN' THE MONSTERS THAT INVADE YOUR VILLAGE??
LIKE I SAID, YE KEN THAT YE'VE GOT TERRIBLE TASTE IN ROYALTY, RIGHT? DONALD COULDN'T FIGHT A SNEEZE WITH A TISSUE TO HIS BEAK!
"THEY COME EVERY NIGHT, DO THEY? ALWAYS IN GREATER NUMBERS.
"THE BEASTIES EAT YER HOMES AND RETREAT, YET, MORE AND MORE OF YOU ARE MISSIN'..."
...WHILE THE MONSTER POPULATION KEEPS GROWIN'!
BIG DEAL! HAVE YOU SEEN THE SIZE OF THESE LITTLE GUYS?
AT THEIR HEIGHT, A FROG LOOKS LIKE A JAPANESE MOVIE MONSTER. I MEAN, HOW BIG COULD THEIR "MONSTERS" BE?
BY THE WAY, HAVE YOU TRIED THE PUMPKIN SPICE LATTE? REALLY DELICIOUS, I RECOMMEND IT.

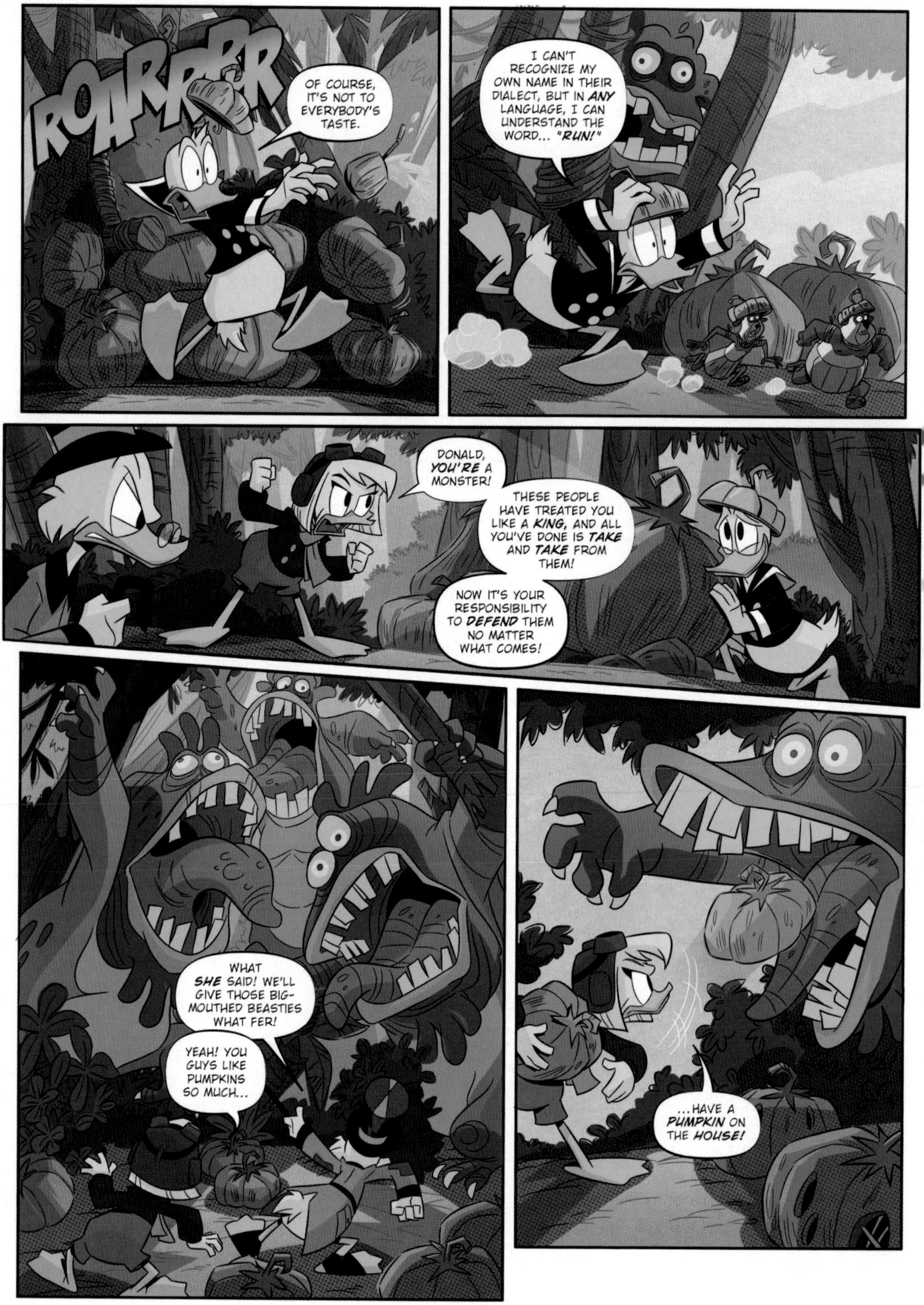
ROARRRR
OF COURSE, IT'S NOT TO EVERYBODY'S TASTE.
I CAN'T RECOGNIZE MY OWN NAME IN THEIR DIALECT, BUT IN ANY LANGUAGE, I CAN UNDERSTAND THE WORD... "RUN!"
DONALD, YOU'RE A MONSTER!
THESE PEOPLE HAVE TREATED YOU LIKE A KING, AND ALL YOU'VE DONE IS TAKE AND TAKE FROM THEM!
NOW IT'S YOUR RESPONSIBILITY TO DEFEND THEM NO MATTER WHAT COMES!
WHAT SHE SAID! WE'LL GIVE THOSE BIG-MOUTHED BEASTIES WHAT FER!
YEAH! YOU GUYS LIKE PUMPKINS SO MUCH...
...HAVE A PUMPKIN ON THE HOUSE!

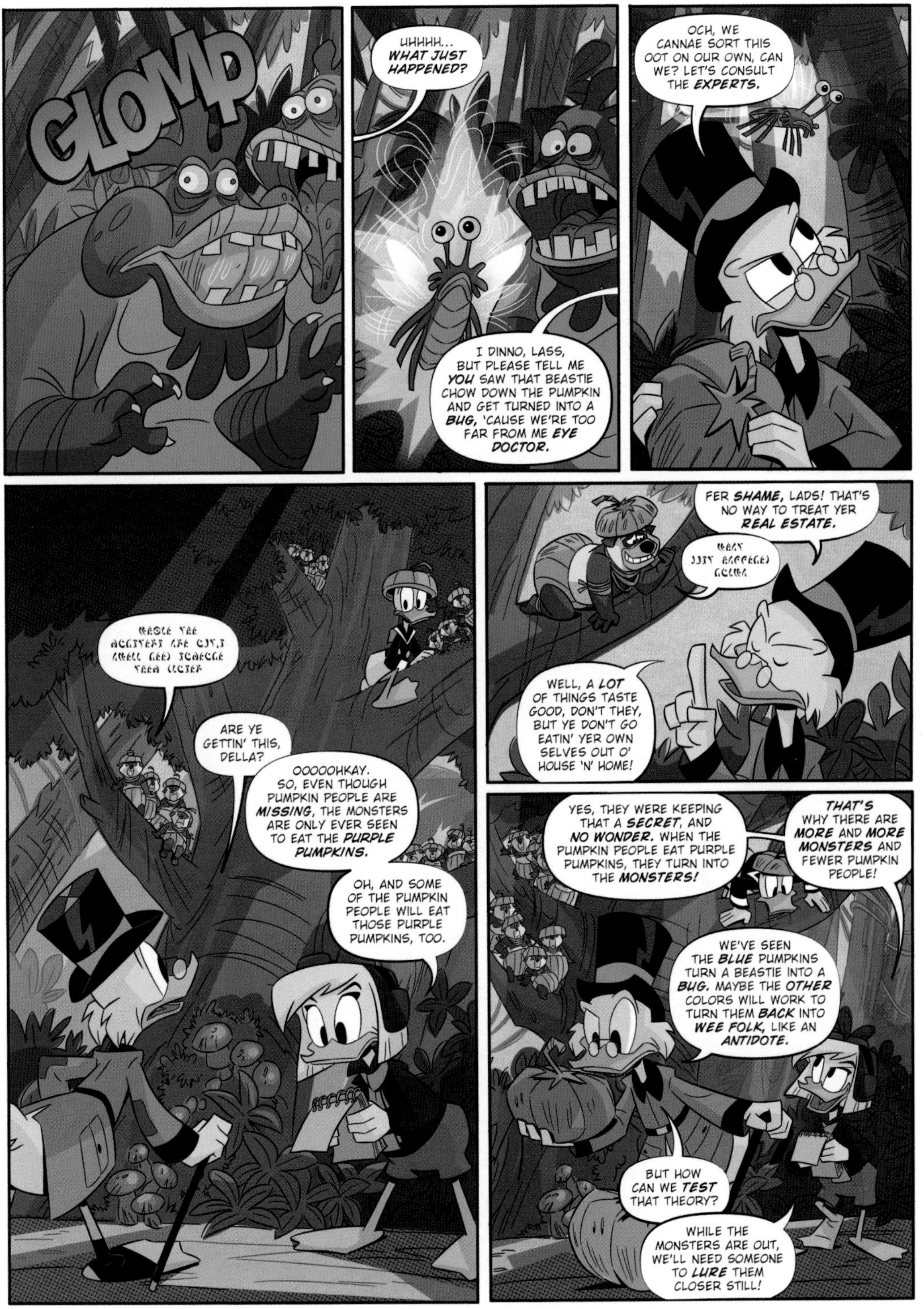
GLOMP
UHHHH... WHAT JUST HAPPENED?
I DINNO, LASS, BUT PLEASE TELL ME YOU SAW THAT BEASTIE CHOW DOWN THE PUMPKIN AND GET TURNED INTO A BUG, 'CAUSE WE'RE TOO FAR FROM ME EYE DOCTOR.
OCH, WE CANNAE SORT THIS OOT ON OUR OWN, CAN WE? LET'S CONSULT THE EXPERTS.
ARE YE GETTIN' THIS, DELLA?
OOOOOHKAY. SO, EVEN THOUGH PUMPKIN PEOPLE ARE MISSING, THE MONSTERS ARE ONLY EVER SEEN TO EAT THE PURPLE PUMPKINS.
OH, AND SOME OF THE PUMPKIN PEOPLE WILL EAT THOSE PURPLE PUMPKINS, TOO.
FER SHAME, LADS! THAT'S NO WAY TO TREAT YER REAL ESTATE.
WELL, A LOT OF THINGS TASTE GOOD, DON'T THEY, BUT YE DON'T GO EATIN' YER OWN SELVES OUT O' HOUSE 'N' HOME!
YES, THEY WERE KEEPING THAT A SECRET, AND NO WONDER. WHEN THE PUMPKIN PEOPLE EAT PURPLE PUMPKINS, THEY TURN INTO THE MONSTERS!
THAT'S WHY THERE ARE MORE AND MORE MONSTERS AND FEWER PUMPKIN PEOPLE!
WE'VE SEEN THE BLUE PUMPKINS TURN A BEASTIE INTO A BUG. MAYBE THE OTHER COLORS WILL WORK TO TURN THEM BACK INTO WEE FOLK, LIKE AN ANTIDOTE.
BUT HOW CAN WE TEST THAT THEORY?
WHILE THE MONSTERS ARE OUT, WE'LL NEED SOMEONE TO LURE THEM CLOSER STILL!

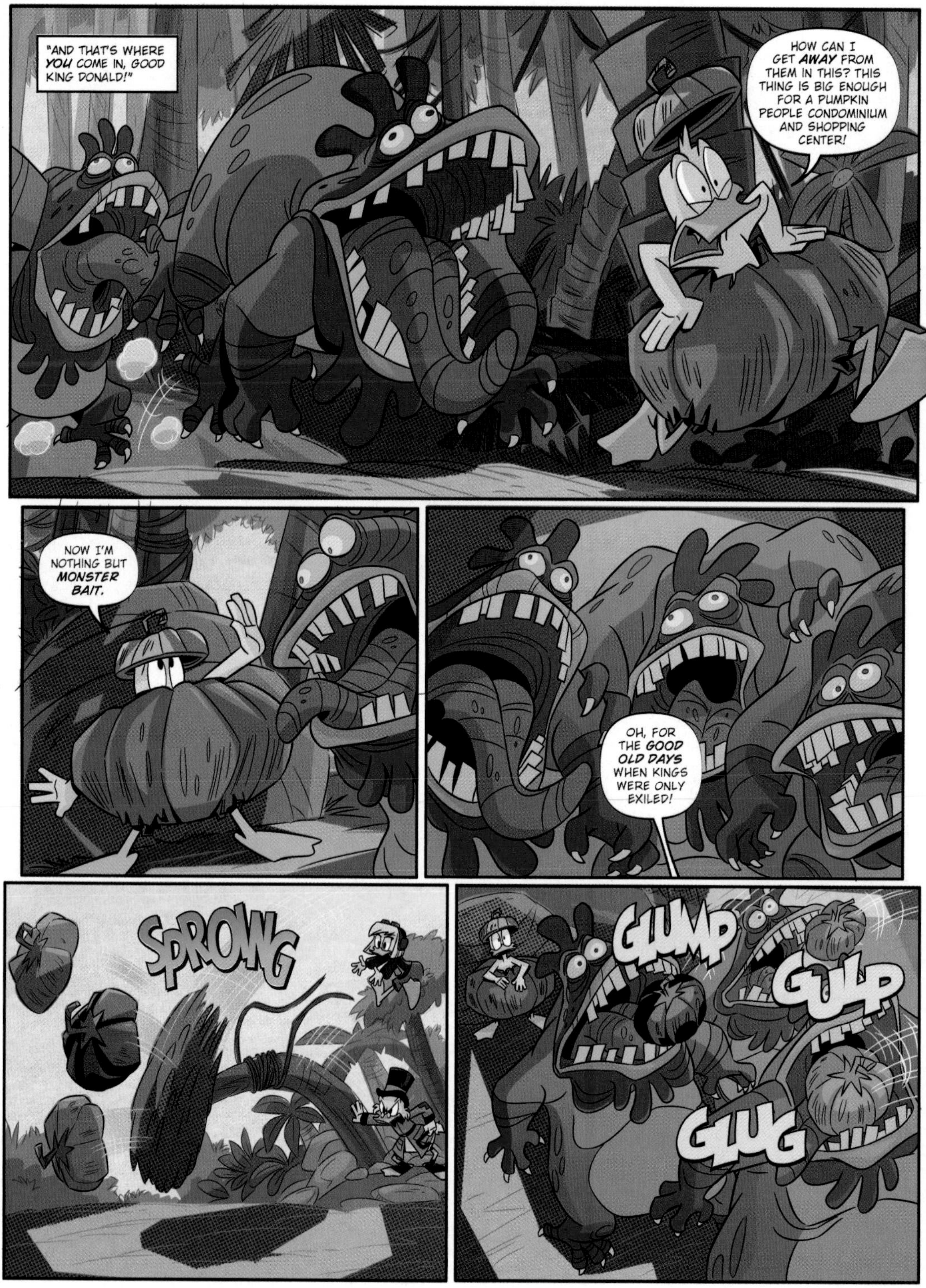
"AND THAT'S WHERE *YOU* COME IN, GOOD KING DONALD!"
HOW CAN I GET *AWAY* FROM THEM IN THIS? THIS THING IS BIG ENOUGH FOR A PUMPKIN PEOPLE CONDOMINIUM AND SHOPPING CENTER!
NOW I'M NOTHING BUT *MONSTER BAIT.*
OH, FOR THE *GOOD OLD DAYS* WHEN KINGS WERE ONLY EXILED!
SPROING
GLUMP
GULP
GLUG

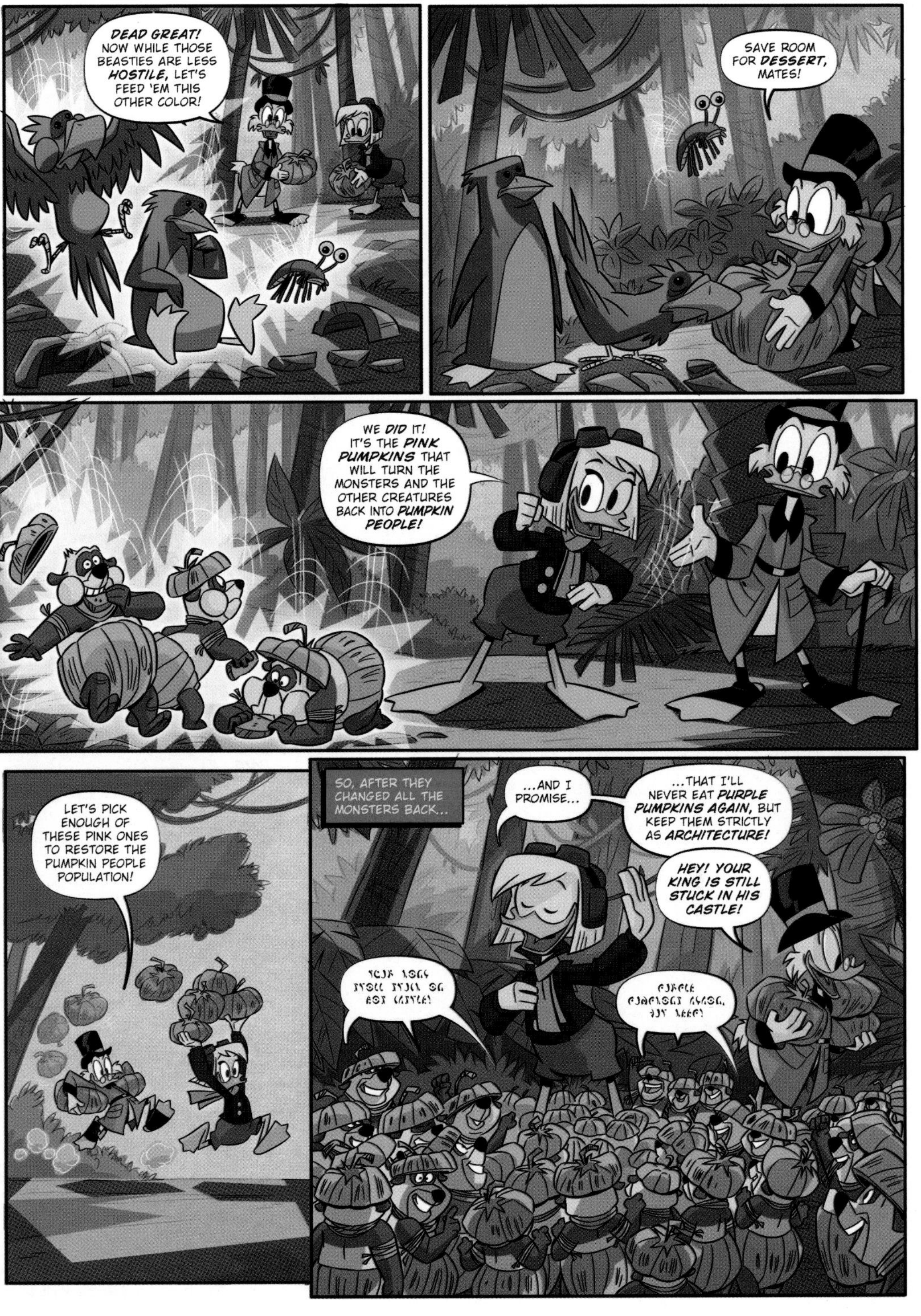
DEAD GREAT! NOW WHILE THOSE BEASTIES ARE LESS HOSTILE, LET'S FEED 'EM THIS OTHER COLOR!
SAVE ROOM FOR DESSERT, MATES!
WE DID IT! IT'S THE PINK PUMPKINS THAT WILL TURN THE MONSTERS AND THE OTHER CREATURES BACK INTO PUMPKIN PEOPLE!
LET'S PICK ENOUGH OF THESE PINK ONES TO RESTORE THE PUMPKIN PEOPLE POPULATION!
SO, AFTER THEY CHANGED ALL THE MONSTERS BACK...
...AND I PROMISE...
...THAT I'LL NEVER EAT PURPLE PUMPKINS AGAIN, BUT KEEP THEM STRICTLY AS ARCHITECTURE!
HEY! YOUR KING IS STILL STUCK IN HIS CASTLE!

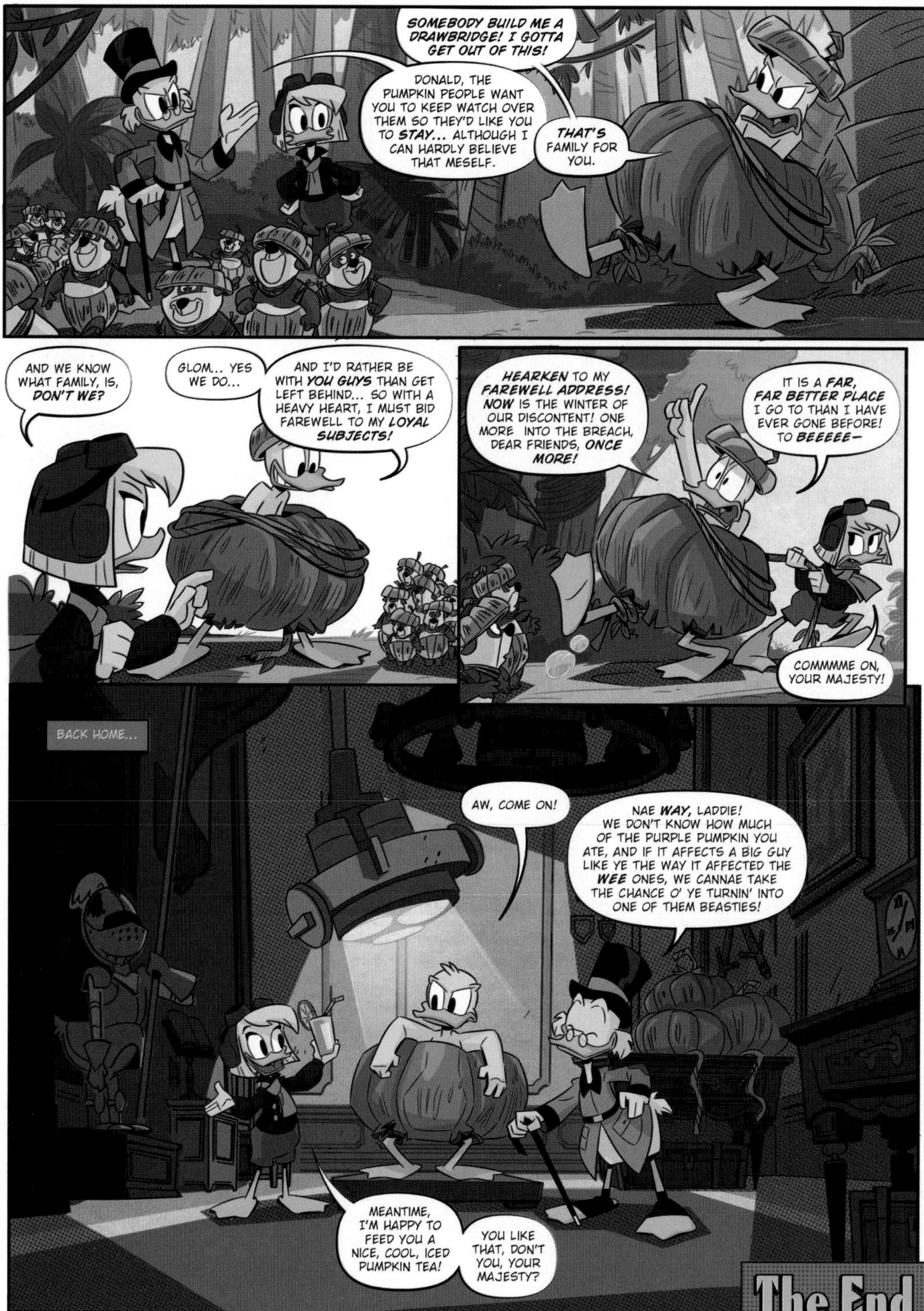
SOMEBODY BUILD ME A DRAWBRIDGE! I GOTTA GET OUT OF THIS!
DONALD, THE PUMPKIN PEOPLE WANT YOU TO KEEP WATCH OVER THEM SO THEY'D LIKE YOU TO STAY... ALTHOUGH I CAN HARDLY BELIEVE THAT MESELF.
THAT'S FAMILY FOR YOU.
AND WE KNOW WHAT FAMILY, IS, DON'T WE?
GLOM... YES WE DO...
AND I'D RATHER BE WITH YOU GUYS THAN GET LEFT BEHIND... SO WITH A HEAVY HEART, I MUST BID FAREWELL TO MY LOYAL SUBJECTS!
HEARKEN TO MY FAREWELL ADDRESS! NOW IS THE WINTER OF OUR DISCONTENT! ONE MORE INTO THE BREACH, DEAR FRIENDS, ONCE MORE!
IT IS A FAR, FAR BETTER PLACE I GO TO THAN I HAVE EVER GONE BEFORE! TO BEEEEE—
COMMMME ON, YOUR MAJESTY!
BACK HOME...
AW, COME ON!
NAE WAY, LADDIE! WE DON'T KNOW HOW MUCH OF THE PURPLE PUMPKIN YOU ATE, AND IF IT AFFECTS A BIG GUY LIKE YE THE WAY IT AFFECTED THE WEE ONES, WE CANNAE TAKE THE CHANCE O' YE TURNIN' INTO ONE OF THEM BEASTIES!
MEANTIME, I'M HAPPY TO FEED YOU A NICE, COOL, ICED PUMPKIN TEA!
YOU LIKE THAT, DON'T YOU, YOUR MAJESTY?
The End

Disney DuckTales

HAPPY, HAPPY VALLEY!

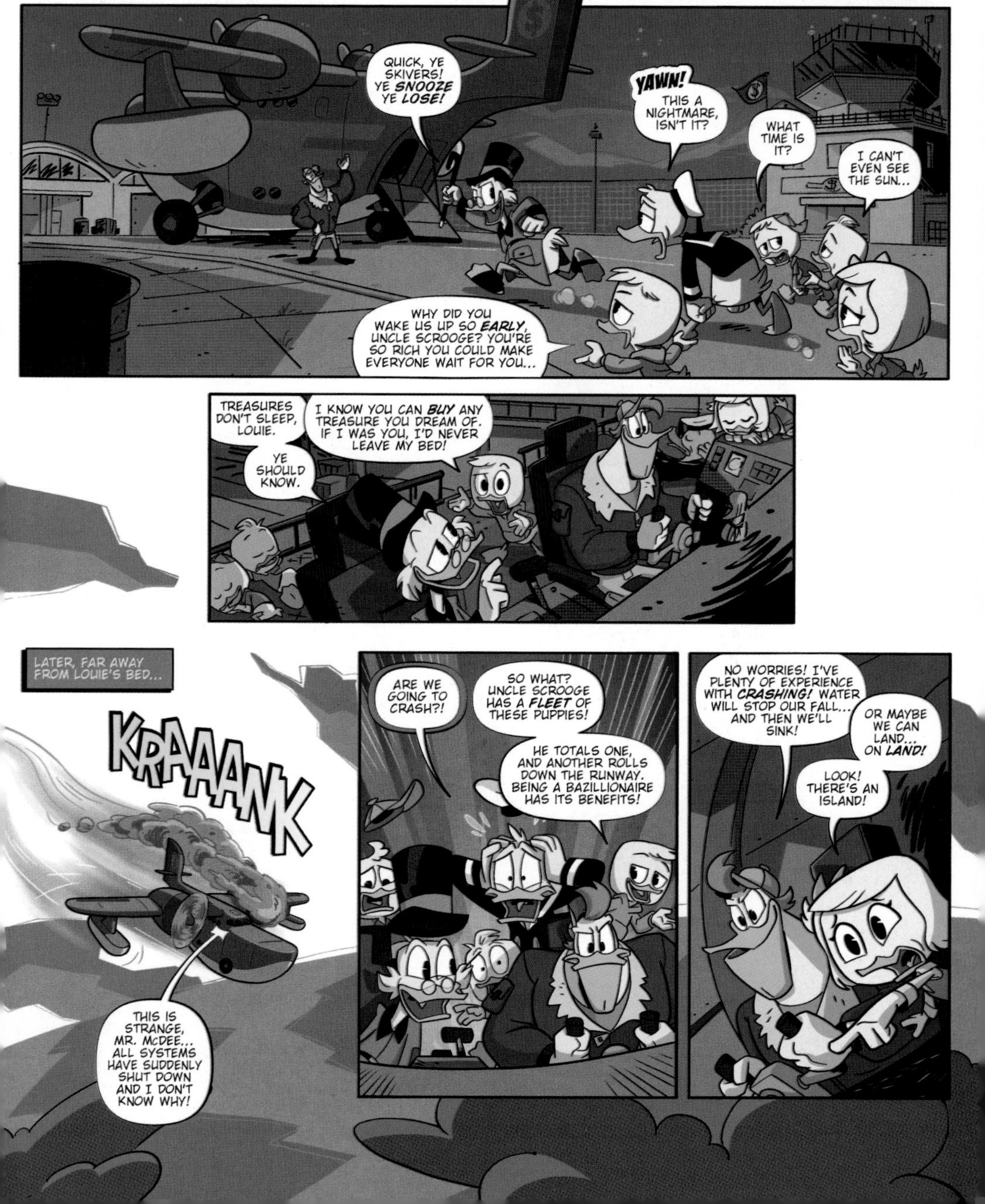

QUICK, YE SKIVERS! YE SNOOZE YE LOSE!
YAWN! THIS A NIGHTMARE, ISN'T IT?
WHAT TIME IS IT?
I CAN'T EVEN SEE THE SUN...
WHY DID YOU WAKE US UP SO EARLY, UNCLE SCROOGE? YOU'RE SO RICH YOU COULD MAKE EVERYONE WAIT FOR YOU...
TREASURES DON'T SLEEP, LOUIE.
I KNOW YOU CAN BUY ANY TREASURE YOU DREAM OF. IF I WAS YOU, I'D NEVER LEAVE MY BED!
YE SHOULD KNOW.
LATER, FAR AWAY FROM LOUIE'S BED...
KRAAAANK
THIS IS STRANGE, MR. McDEE... ALL SYSTEMS HAVE SUDDENLY SHUT DOWN AND I DON'T KNOW WHY!
ARE WE GOING TO CRASH?!
SO WHAT? UNCLE SCROOGE HAS A FLEET OF THESE PUPPIES!
HE TOTALS ONE, AND ANOTHER ROLLS DOWN THE RUNWAY. BEING A BAZILLIONAIRE HAS ITS BENEFITS!
NO WORRIES! I'VE PLENTY OF EXPERIENCE WITH CRASHING! WATER WILL STOP OUR FALL... AND THEN WE'LL SINK!
OR MAYBE WE CAN LAND... ON LAND!
LOOK! THERE'S AN ISLAND!

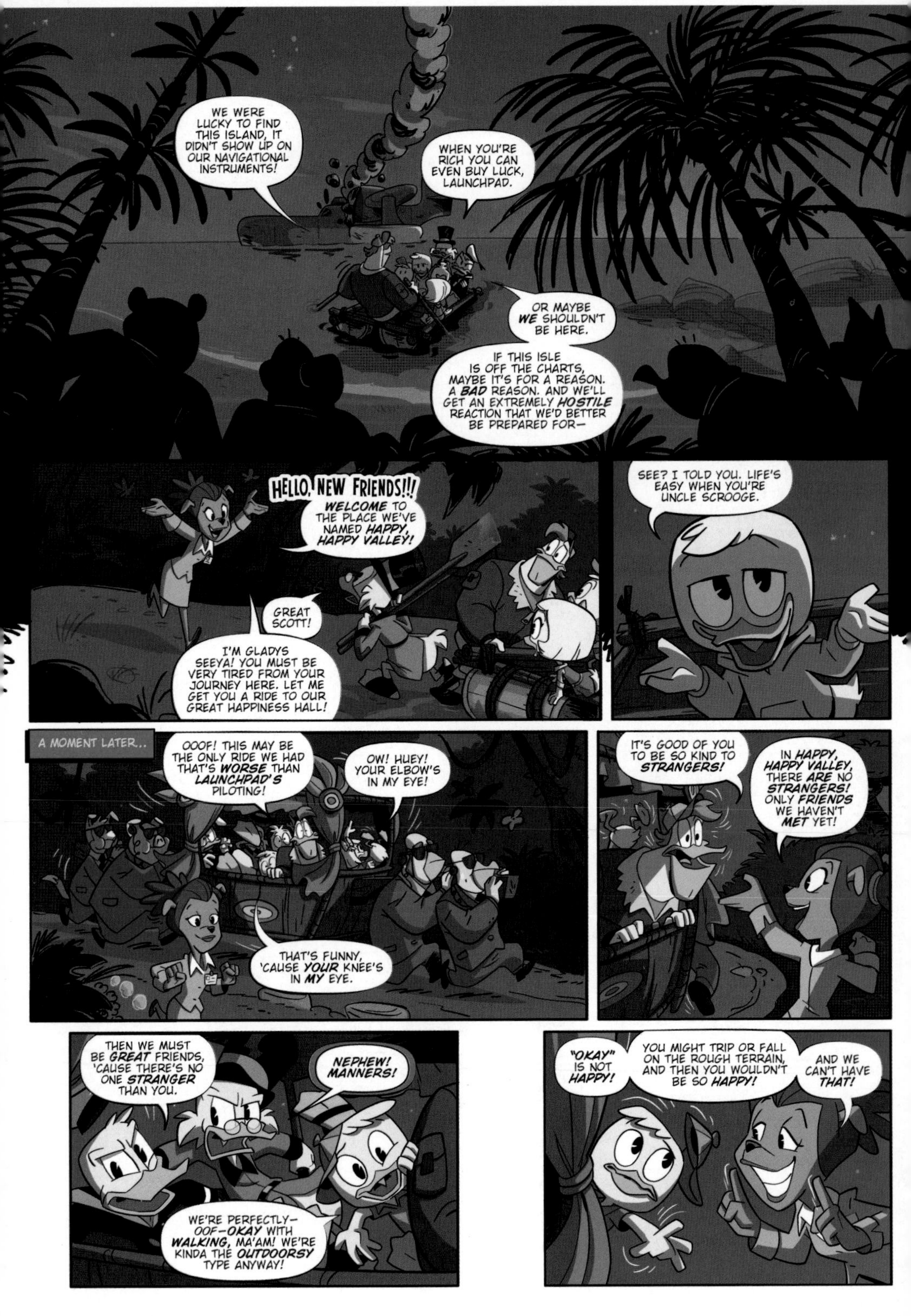
WE WERE LUCKY TO FIND THIS ISLAND, IT DIDN'T SHOW UP ON OUR NAVIGATIONAL INSTRUMENTS!
WHEN YOU'RE RICH YOU CAN EVEN BUY LUCK, LAUNCHPAD.
OR MAYBE WE SHOULDN'T BE HERE.
IF THIS ISLE IS OFF THE CHARTS, MAYBE IT'S FOR A REASON. A BAD REASON. AND WE'LL GET AN EXTREMELY HOSTILE REACTION THAT WE'D BETTER BE PREPARED FOR—
HELLO, NEW FRIENDS!!!
WELCOME TO THE PLACE WE'VE NAMED HAPPY, HAPPY VALLEY!
GREAT SCOTT!
I'M GLADYS SEEYA! YOU MUST BE VERY TIRED FROM YOUR JOURNEY HERE. LET ME GET YOU A RIDE TO OUR GREAT HAPPINESS HALL!
SEE? I TOLD YOU. LIFE'S EASY WHEN YOU'RE UNCLE SCROOGE.
A MOMENT LATER...
OOOF! THIS MAY BE THE ONLY RIDE WE HAD THAT'S WORSE THAN LAUNCHPAD'S PILOTING!
OW! HUEY! YOUR ELBOW'S IN MY EYE!
THAT'S FUNNY, 'CAUSE YOUR KNEE'S IN MY EYE.
IT'S GOOD OF YOU TO BE SO KIND TO STRANGERS!
IN HAPPY, HAPPY VALLEY, THERE ARE NO STRANGERS! ONLY FRIENDS WE HAVEN'T MET YET!
THEN WE MUST BE GREAT FRIENDS, 'CAUSE THERE'S NO ONE STRANGER THAN YOU.
NEPHEW! MANNERS!
WE'RE PERFECTLY—OOF—OKAY WITH WALKING, MA'AM! WE'RE KINDA THE OUTDOORSY TYPE ANYWAY!
"OKAY" IS NOT HAPPY!
YOU MIGHT TRIP OR FALL ON THE ROUGH TERRAIN, AND THEN YOU WOULDN'T BE SO HAPPY!
AND WE CAN'T HAVE THAT!

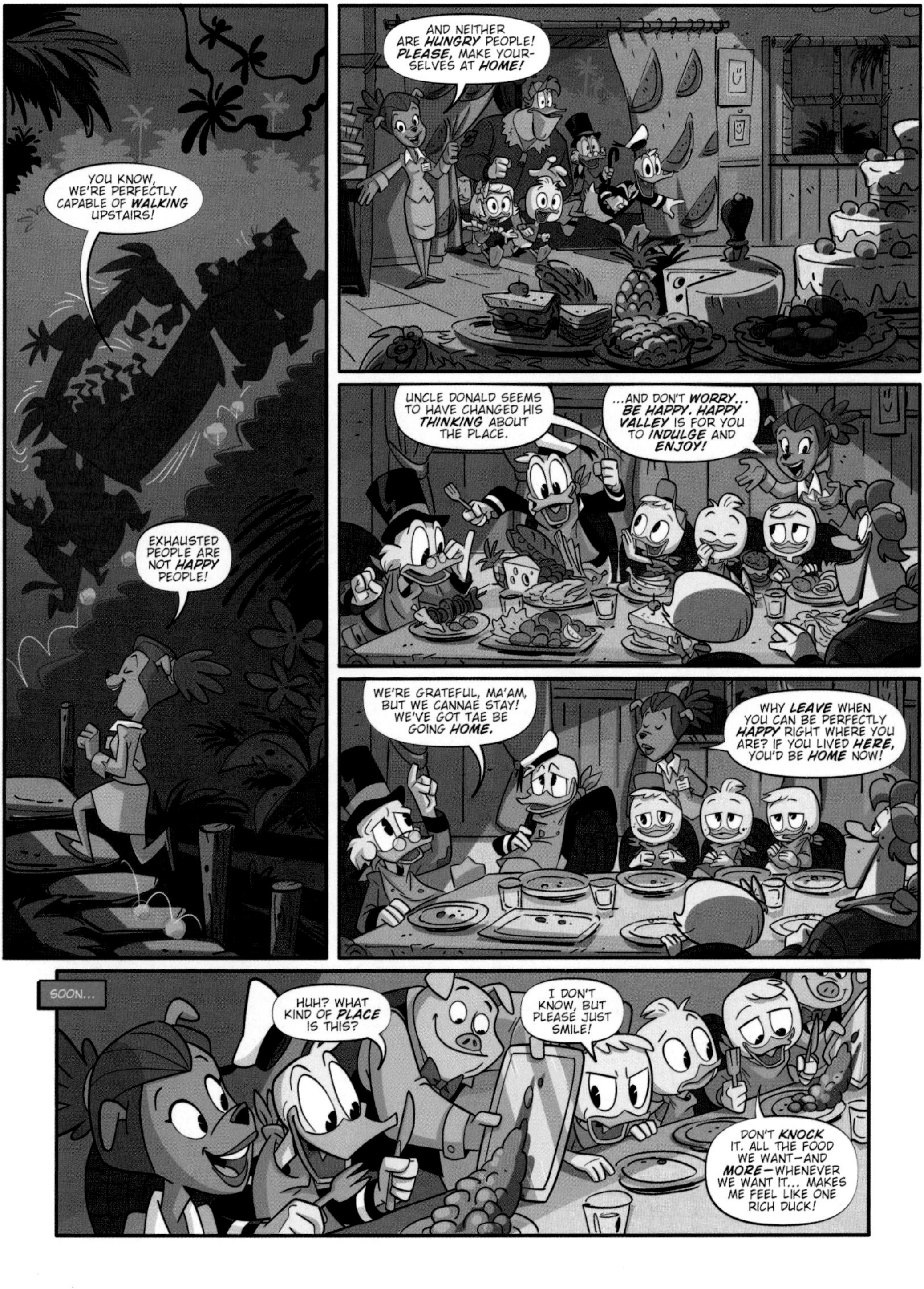
YOU KNOW, WE'RE PERFECTLY CAPABLE OF WALKING UPSTAIRS!
EXHAUSTED PEOPLE ARE NOT HAPPY PEOPLE!
AND NEITHER ARE HUNGRY PEOPLE! PLEASE, MAKE YOURSELVES AT HOME!
UNCLE DONALD SEEMS TO HAVE CHANGED HIS THINKING ABOUT THE PLACE.
...AND DON'T WORRY... BE HAPPY. HAPPY VALLEY IS FOR YOU TO INDULGE AND ENJOY!
WE'RE GRATEFUL, MA'AM, BUT WE CANNAE STAY! WE'VE GOT TAE BE GOING HOME.
WHY LEAVE WHEN YOU CAN BE PERFECTLY HAPPY RIGHT WHERE YOU ARE? IF YOU LIVED HERE, YOU'D BE HOME NOW!
SOON...
HUH? WHAT KIND OF PLACE IS THIS?
I DON'T KNOW, BUT PLEASE JUST SMILE!
DON'T KNOCK IT. ALL THE FOOD WE WANT—AND MORE—WHENEVER WE WANT IT... MAKES ME FEEL LIKE ONE RICH DUCK!

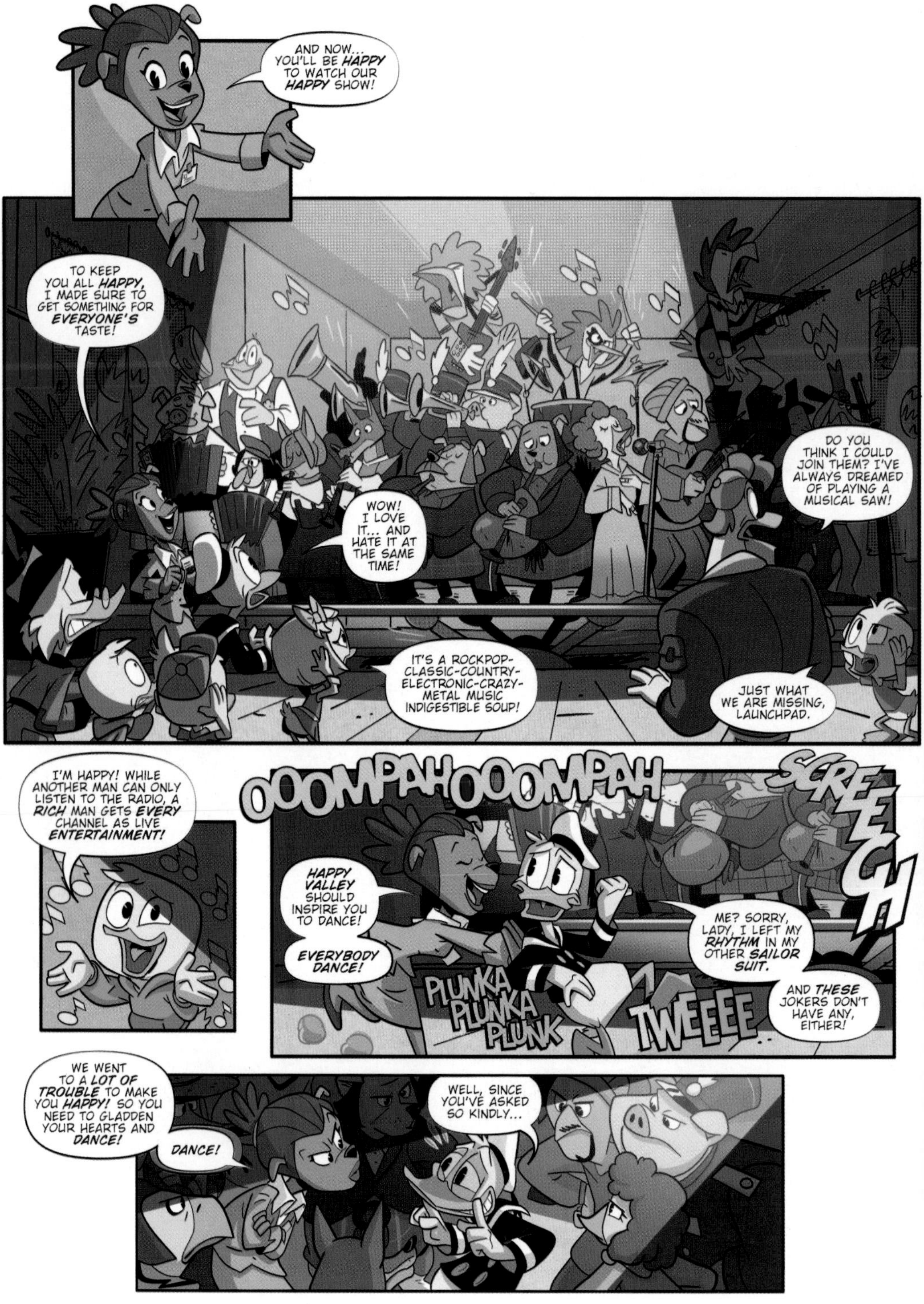
AND NOW... YOU'LL BE HAPPY TO WATCH OUR HAPPY SHOW!
TO KEEP YOU ALL HAPPY, I MADE SURE TO GET SOMETHING FOR EVERYONE'S TASTE!
WOW! I LOVE IT... AND HATE IT AT THE SAME TIME!
DO YOU THINK I COULD JOIN THEM? I'VE ALWAYS DREAMED OF PLAYING A MUSICAL SAW!
IT'S A ROCKPOP-CLASSIC-COUNTRY-ELECTRONIC-CRAZY-METAL MUSIC INDIGESTIBLE SOUP!
JUST WHAT WE ARE MISSING, LAUNCHPAD.
I'M HAPPY! WHILE ANOTHER MAN CAN ONLY LISTEN TO THE RADIO, A RICH MAN GETS EVERY CHANNEL AS LIVE ENTERTAINMENT!
OOOMPAHOOOMPAH
SCREEECH
HAPPY VALLEY SHOULD INSPIRE YOU TO DANCE!
EVERYBODY DANCE!
ME? SORRY, LADY, I LEFT MY RHYTHM IN MY OTHER SAILOR SUIT.
PLUNKA PLUNKA PLUNK
TWEEEE
AND THESE JOKERS DON'T HAVE ANY, EITHER!
WE WENT TO A LOT OF TROUBLE TO MAKE YOU HAPPY! SO YOU NEED TO GLADDEN YOUR HEARTS AND DANCE!
DANCE!
WELL, SINCE YOU'VE ASKED SO KINDLY...

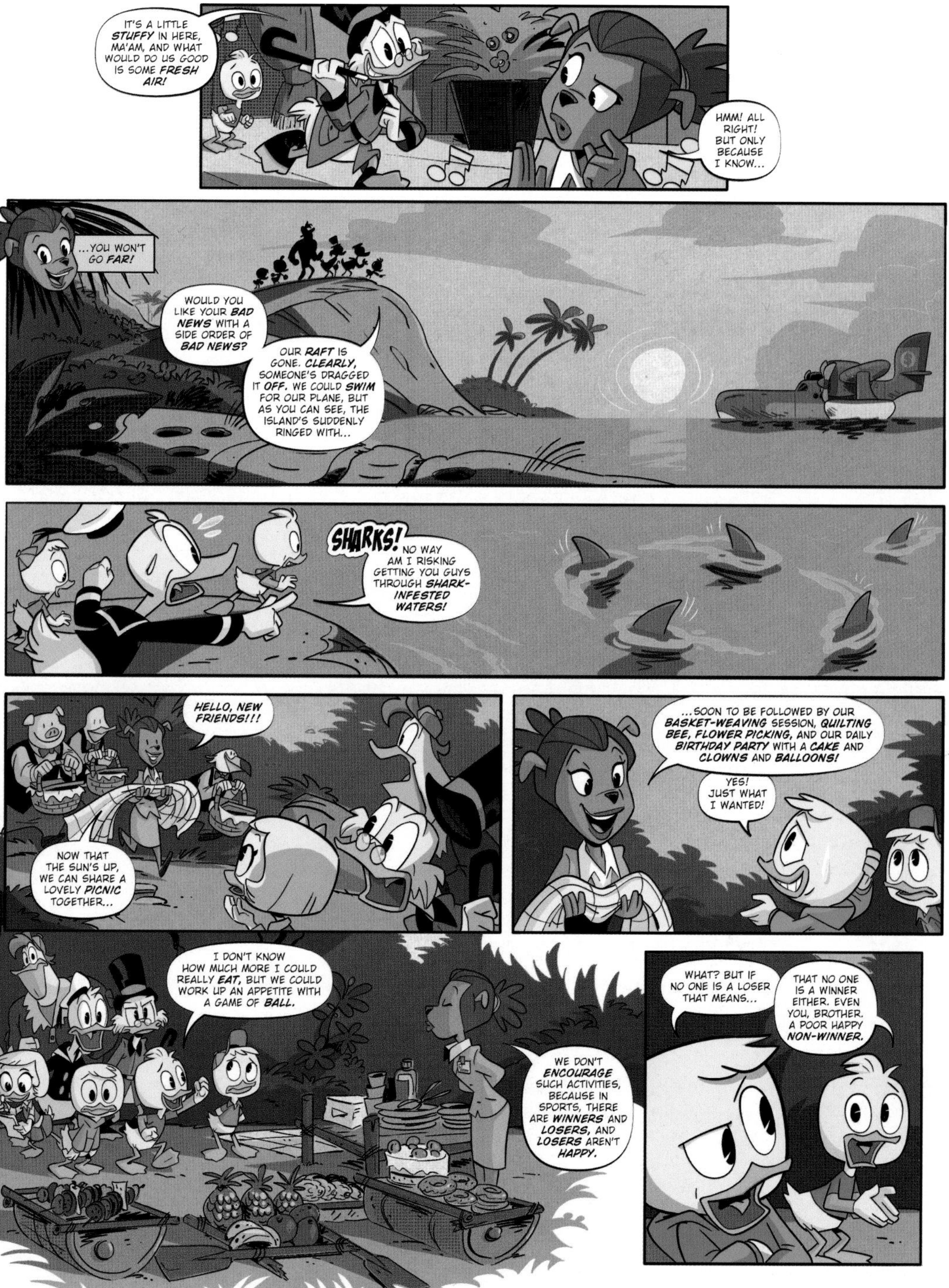

IT'S A LITTLE STUFFY IN HERE, MA'AM, AND WHAT WOULD DO US GOOD IS SOME FRESH AIR!
HMM! ALL RIGHT! BUT ONLY BECAUSE I KNOW...
...YOU WON'T GO FAR!
WOULD YOU LIKE YOUR BAD NEWS WITH A SIDE ORDER OF BAD NEWS?
OUR RAFT IS GONE. CLEARLY, SOMEONE'S DRAGGED IT OFF. WE COULD SWIM FOR OUR PLANE, BUT AS YOU CAN SEE, THE ISLAND'S SUDDENLY RINGED WITH...
SHARKS!
NO WAY AM I RISKING GETTING YOU GUYS THROUGH SHARK-INFESTED WATERS!
HELLO, NEW FRIENDS!!!
NOW THAT THE SUN'S UP, WE CAN SHARE A LOVELY PICNIC TOGETHER...
...SOON TO BE FOLLOWED BY OUR BASKET-WEAVING SESSION, QUILTING BEE, FLOWER PICKING, AND OUR DAILY BIRTHDAY PARTY WITH A CAKE AND CLOWNS AND BALLOONS!
YES! JUST WHAT I WANTED!
I DON'T KNOW HOW MUCH MORE I COULD REALLY EAT, BUT WE COULD WORK UP AN APPETITE WITH A GAME OF BALL.
WE DON'T ENCOURAGE SUCH ACTIVITIES, BECAUSE IN SPORTS, THERE ARE WINNERS AND LOSERS, AND LOSERS AREN'T HAPPY.
WHAT? BUT IF NO ONE IS A LOSER THAT MEANS...
THAT NO ONE IS A WINNER EITHER. EVEN YOU, BROTHER. A POOR HAPPY NON-WINNER.

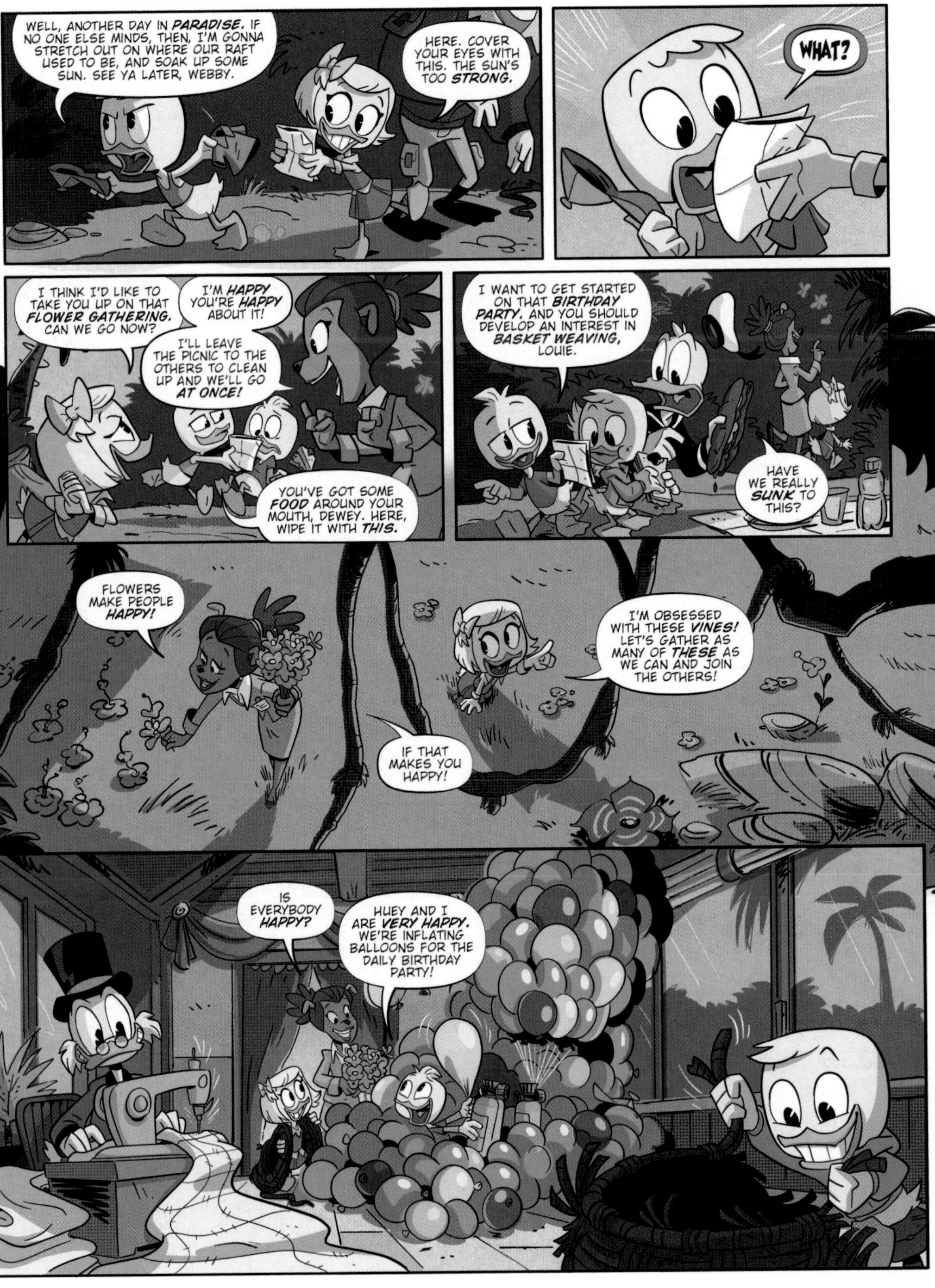
WELL, ANOTHER DAY IN PARADISE. IF NO ONE ELSE MINDS, THEN, I'M GONNA STRETCH OUT ON WHERE OUR RAFT USED TO BE, AND SOAK UP SOME SUN. SEE YA LATER, WEBBY.
HERE. COVER YOUR EYES WITH THIS. THE SUN'S TOO STRONG.
WHAT?
I THINK I'D LIKE TO TAKE YOU UP ON THAT FLOWER GATHERING. CAN WE GO NOW?
I'M HAPPY YOU'RE HAPPY ABOUT IT!
I'LL LEAVE THE PICNIC TO THE OTHERS TO CLEAN UP AND WE'LL GO AT ONCE!
YOU'VE GOT SOME FOOD AROUND YOUR MOUTH, DEWEY. HERE, WIPE IT WITH THIS.
I WANT TO GET STARTED ON THAT BIRTHDAY PARTY. AND YOU SHOULD DEVELOP AN INTEREST IN BASKET WEAVING, LOUIE.
HAVE WE REALLY SUNK TO THIS?
FLOWERS MAKE PEOPLE HAPPY!
I'M OBSESSED WITH THESE VINES! LET'S GATHER AS MANY OF THESE AS WE CAN AND JOIN THE OTHERS!
IF THAT MAKES YOU HAPPY!
IS EVERYBODY HAPPY?
HUEY AND I ARE VERY HAPPY. WE'RE INFLATING BALLOONS FOR THE DAILY BIRTHDAY PARTY!

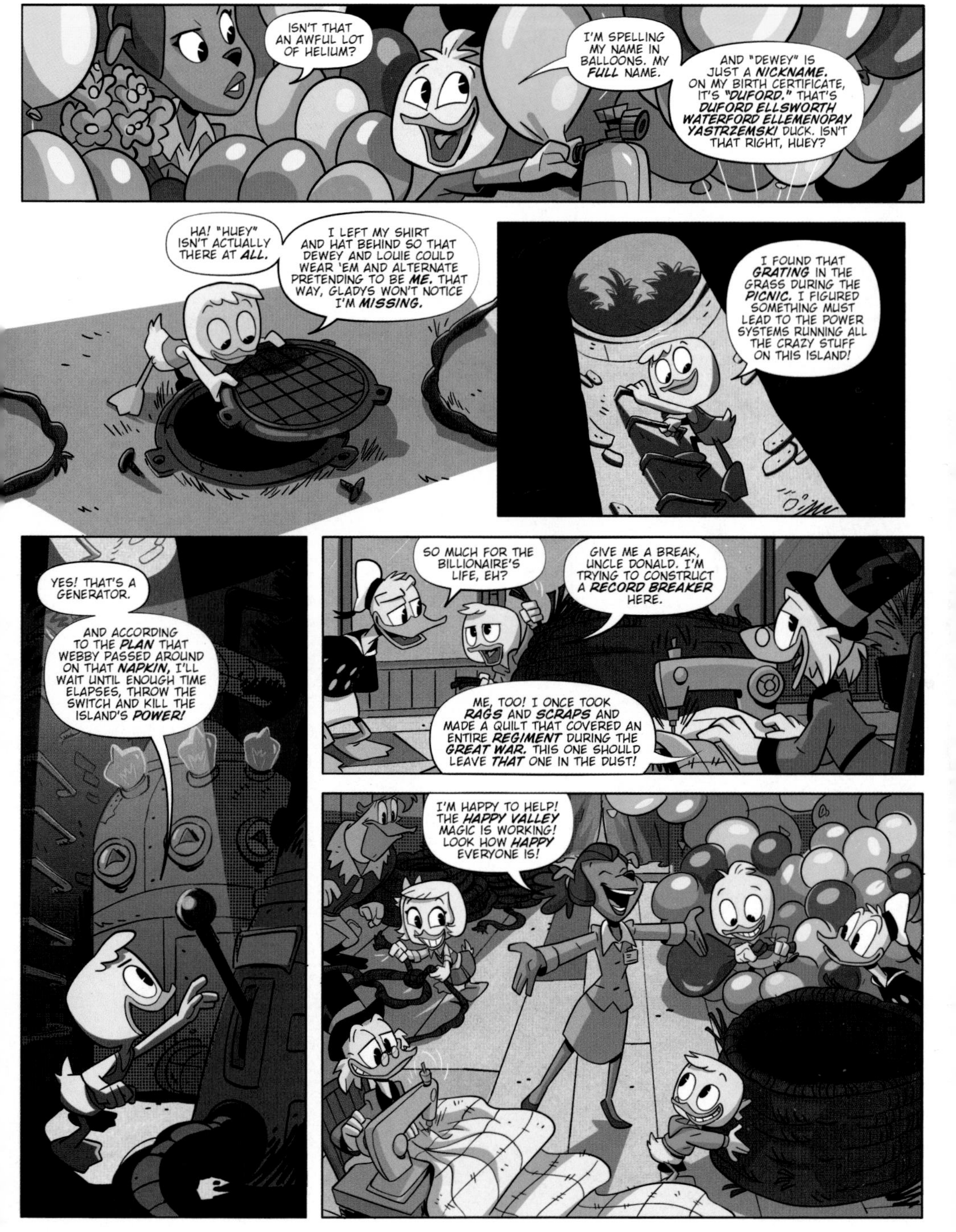
ISN'T THAT AN AWFUL LOT OF HELIUM?
I'M SPELLING MY NAME IN BALLOONS. MY FULL NAME.
AND "DEWEY" IS JUST A NICKNAME. ON MY BIRTH CERTIFICATE, IT'S "DUFORD." THAT'S DUFORD ELLSWORTH WATERFORD ELLEMENOPAY YASTRZEMSKI DUCK. ISN'T THAT RIGHT, HUEY?
HA! "HUEY" ISN'T ACTUALLY THERE AT ALL.
I LEFT MY SHIRT AND HAT BEHIND SO THAT DEWEY AND LOUIE COULD WEAR 'EM AND ALTERNATE PRETENDING TO BE ME. THAT WAY, GLADYS WON'T NOTICE I'M MISSING.
I FOUND THAT GRATING IN THE GRASS DURING THE PICNIC. I FIGURED SOMETHING MUST LEAD TO THE POWER SYSTEMS RUNNING ALL THE CRAZY STUFF ON THIS ISLAND!
YES! THAT'S A GENERATOR.
AND ACCORDING TO THE PLAN THAT WEBBY PASSED AROUND ON THAT NAPKIN, I'LL WAIT UNTIL ENOUGH TIME ELAPSES, THROW THE SWITCH AND KILL THE ISLAND'S POWER!
SO MUCH FOR THE BILLIONAIRE'S LIFE, EH?
GIVE ME A BREAK, UNCLE DONALD. I'M TRYING TO CONSTRUCT A RECORD BREAKER HERE.
ME, TOO! I ONCE TOOK RAGS AND SCRAPS AND MADE A QUILT THAT COVERED AN ENTIRE REGIMENT DURING THE GREAT WAR. THIS ONE SHOULD LEAVE THAT ONE IN THE DUST!
I'M HAPPY TO HELP! THE HAPPY VALLEY MAGIC IS WORKING! LOOK HOW HAPPY EVERYONE IS!

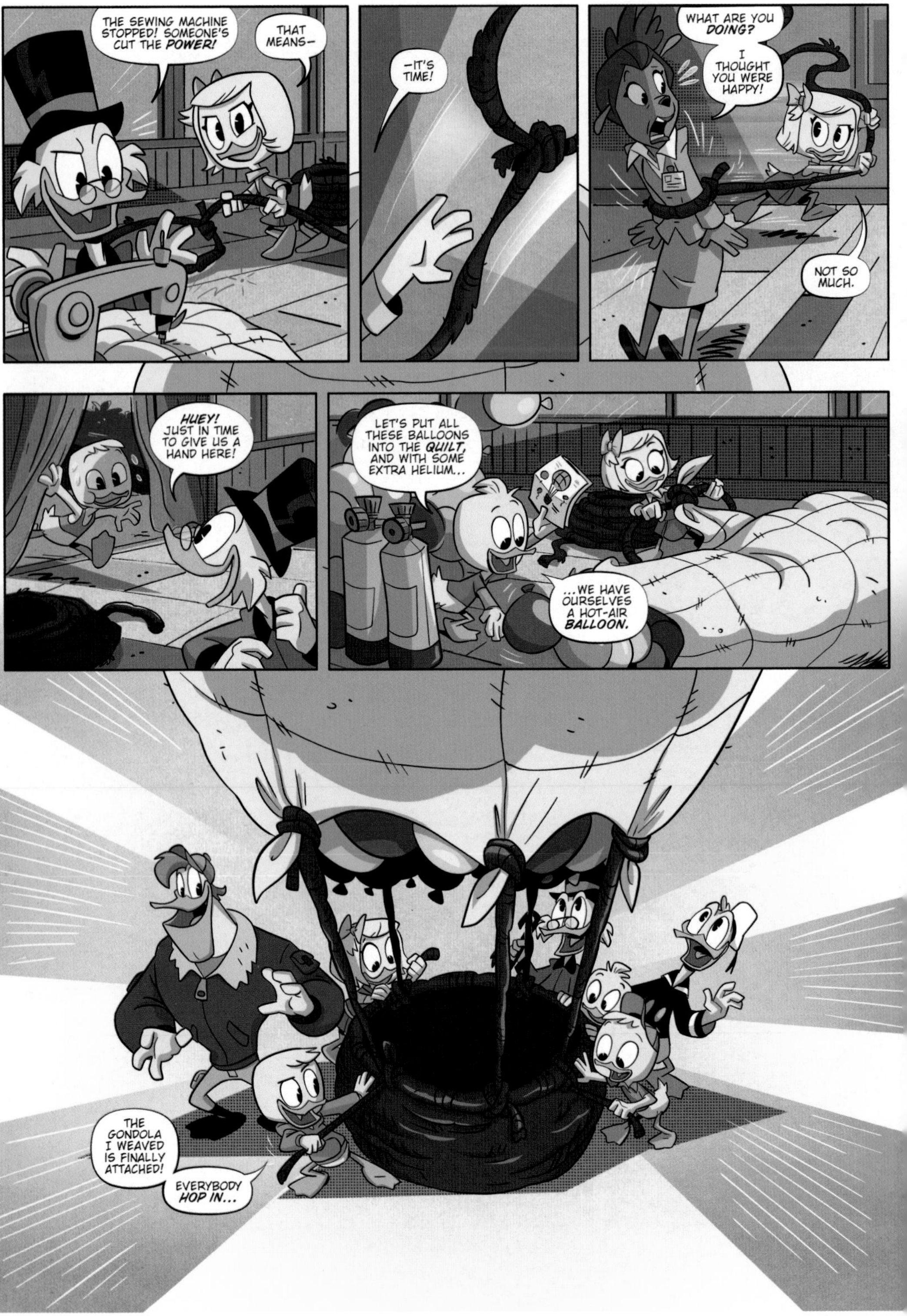

THE SEWING MACHINE STOPPED! SOMEONE'S CUT THE POWER!
THAT MEANS—
—IT'S TIME!
WHAT ARE YOU DOING?
I THOUGHT YOU WERE HAPPY!
NOT SO MUCH.
HUEY! JUST IN TIME TO GIVE US A HAND HERE!
LET'S PUT ALL THESE BALLOONS INTO THE QUILT, AND WITH SOME EXTRA HELIUM...
...WE HAVE OURSELVES A HOT-AIR BALLOON.
THE GONDOLA I WEAVED IS FINALLY ATTACHED!
EVERYBODY HOP IN...

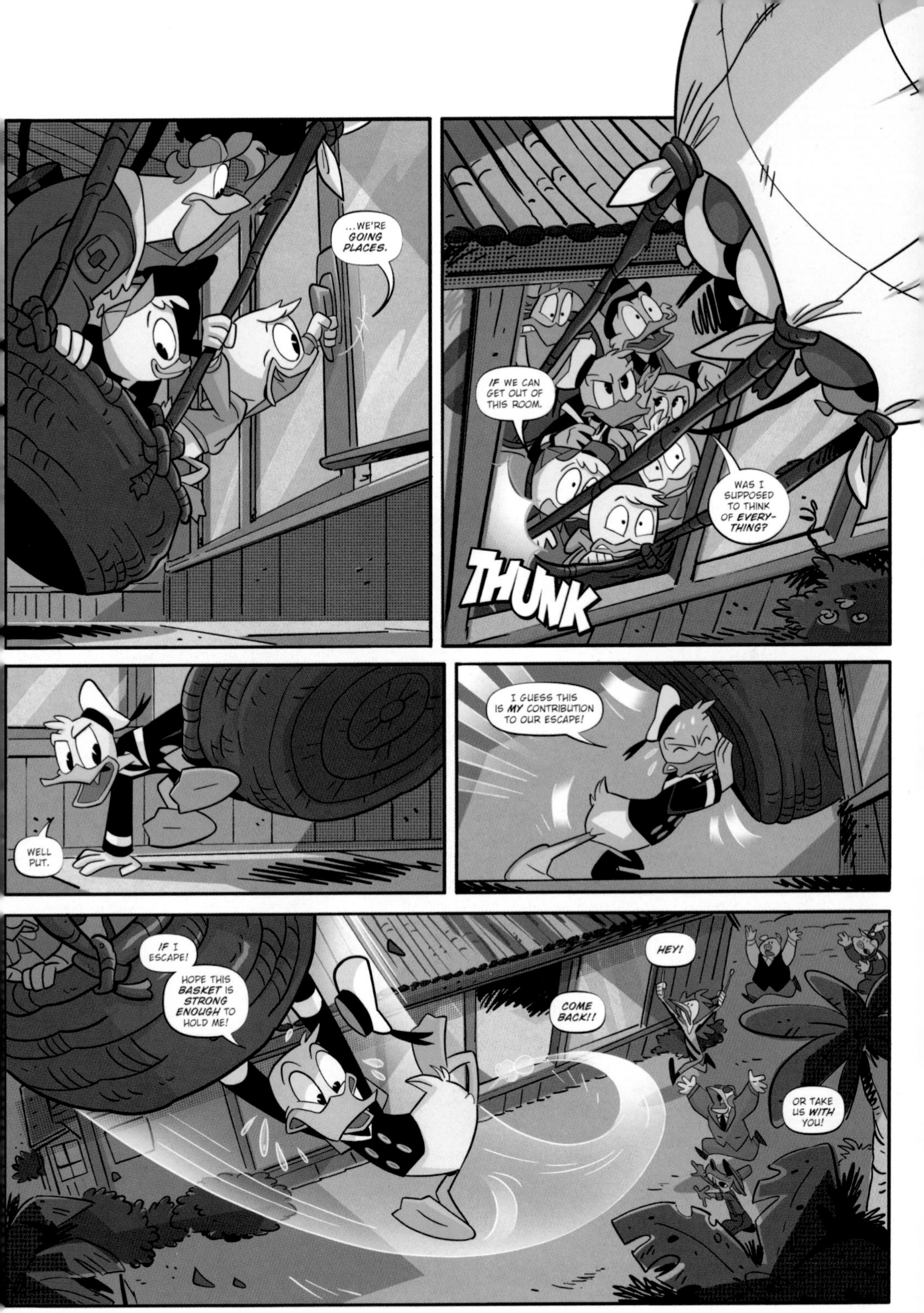
...WE'RE GOING PLACES.
IF WE CAN GET OUT OF THIS ROOM.
WAS I SUPPOSED TO THINK OF EVERY-THING?
THUNK
WELL PUT.
I GUESS THIS IS MY CONTRIBUTION TO OUR ESCAPE!
IF I ESCAPE!
HOPE THIS BASKET IS STRONG ENOUGH TO HOLD ME!
HEY!
COME BACK!!
OR TAKE US WITH YOU!

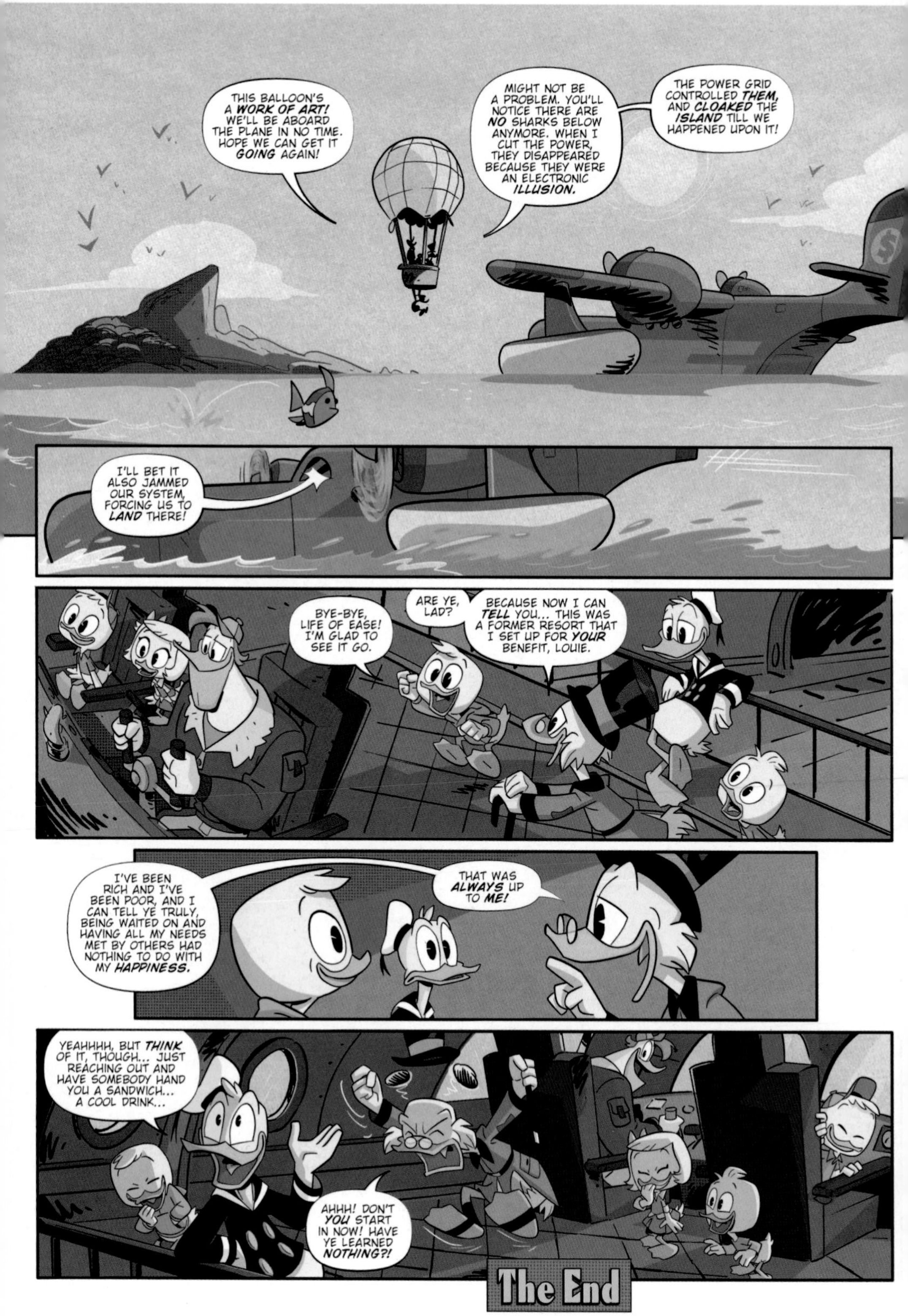
THIS BALLOON'S A WORK OF ART! WE'LL BE ABOARD THE PLANE IN NO TIME. HOPE WE CAN GET IT GOING AGAIN!
MIGHT NOT BE A PROBLEM. YOU'LL NOTICE THERE ARE NO SHARKS BELOW ANYMORE. WHEN I CUT THE POWER, THEY DISAPPEARED BECAUSE THEY WERE AN ELECTRONIC ILLUSION.
THE POWER GRID CONTROLLED THEM, AND CLOAKED THE ISLAND TILL WE HAPPENED UPON IT!
I'LL BET IT ALSO JAMMED OUR SYSTEM, FORCING US TO LAND THERE!
BYE-BYE, LIFE OF EASE! I'M GLAD TO SEE IT GO.
ARE YE, LAD?
BECAUSE NOW I CAN TELL YOU... THIS WAS A FORMER RESORT THAT I SET UP FOR YOUR BENEFIT, LOUIE.
I'VE BEEN RICH AND I'VE BEEN POOR, AND I CAN TELL YE TRULY, BEING WAITED ON AND HAVING ALL MY NEEDS MET BY OTHERS HAD NOTHING TO DO WITH MY HAPPINESS.
THAT WAS ALWAYS UP TO ME!
YEAHHHH, BUT THINK OF IT, THOUGH... JUST REACHING OUT AND HAVE SOMEBODY HAND YOU A SANDWICH... A COOL DRINK...
AHHH! DON'T YOU START IN NOW! HAVE YE LEARNED NOTHING?!
The End

Disney DuckTales

FIGHT!

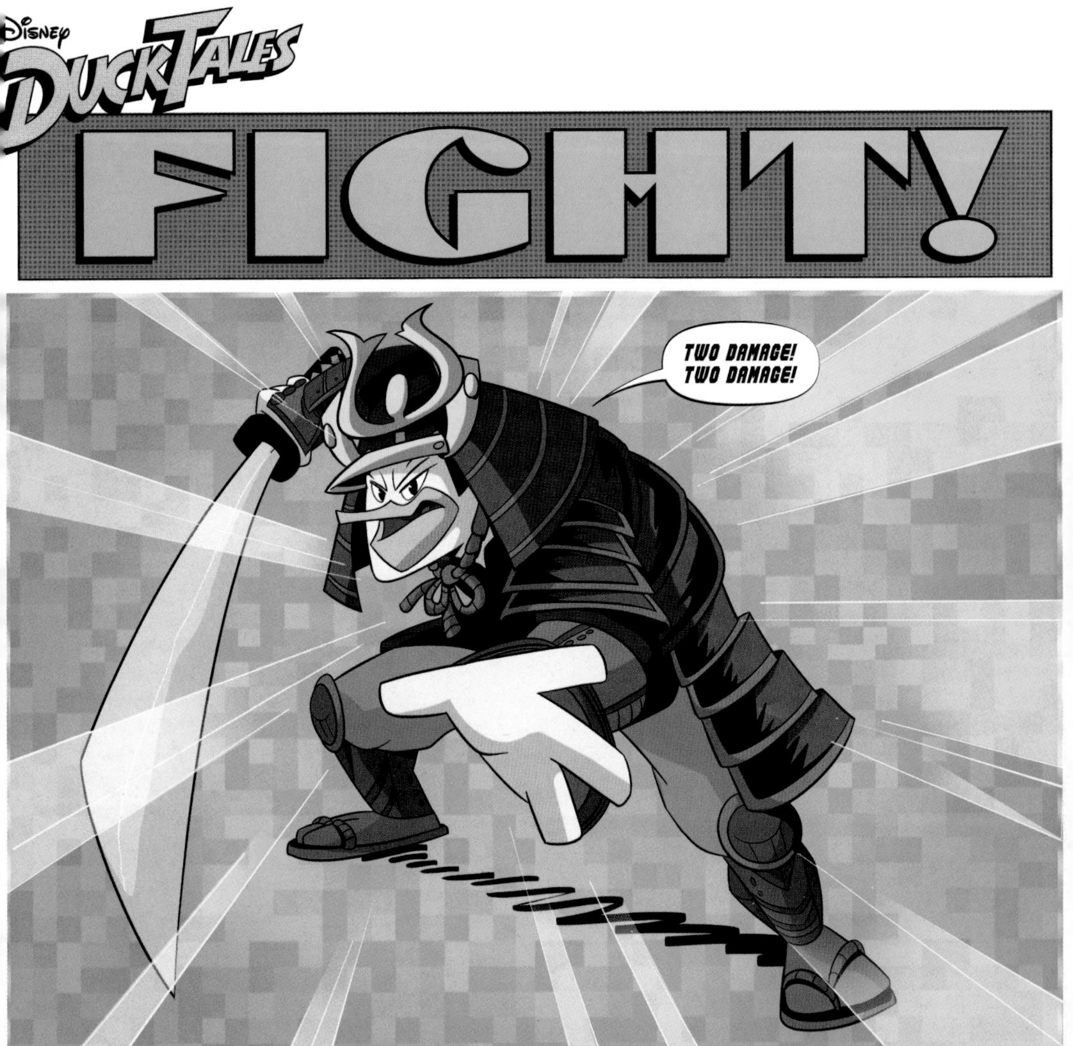
TWO DAMAGE! TWO DAMAGE!

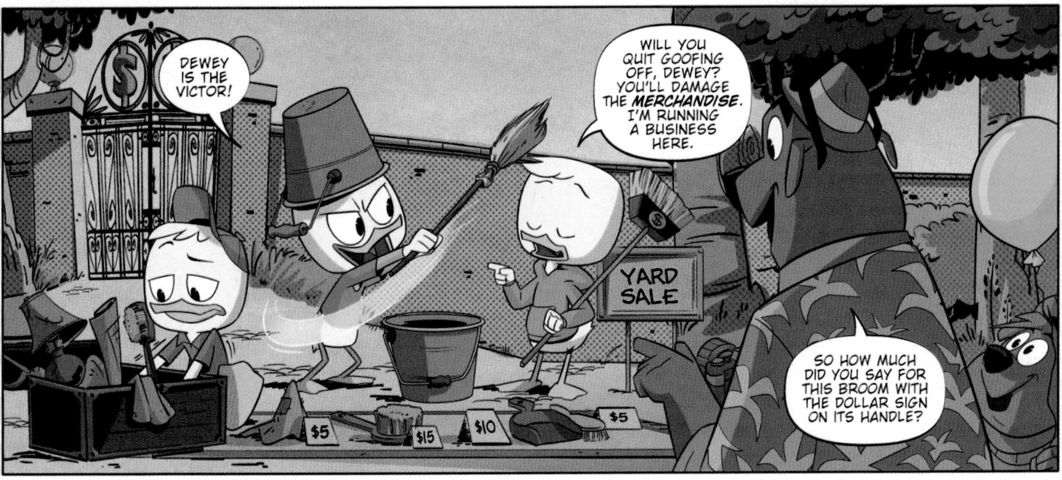
DEWEY IS THE VICTOR!
WILL YOU QUIT GOOFING OFF, DEWEY? YOU'LL DAMAGE THE MERCHANDISE. I'M RUNNING A BUSINESS HERE.
YARD SALE
$5
$15
$10
$5
SO HOW MUCH DID YOU SAY FOR THIS BROOM WITH THE DOLLAR SIGN ON ITS HANDLE?

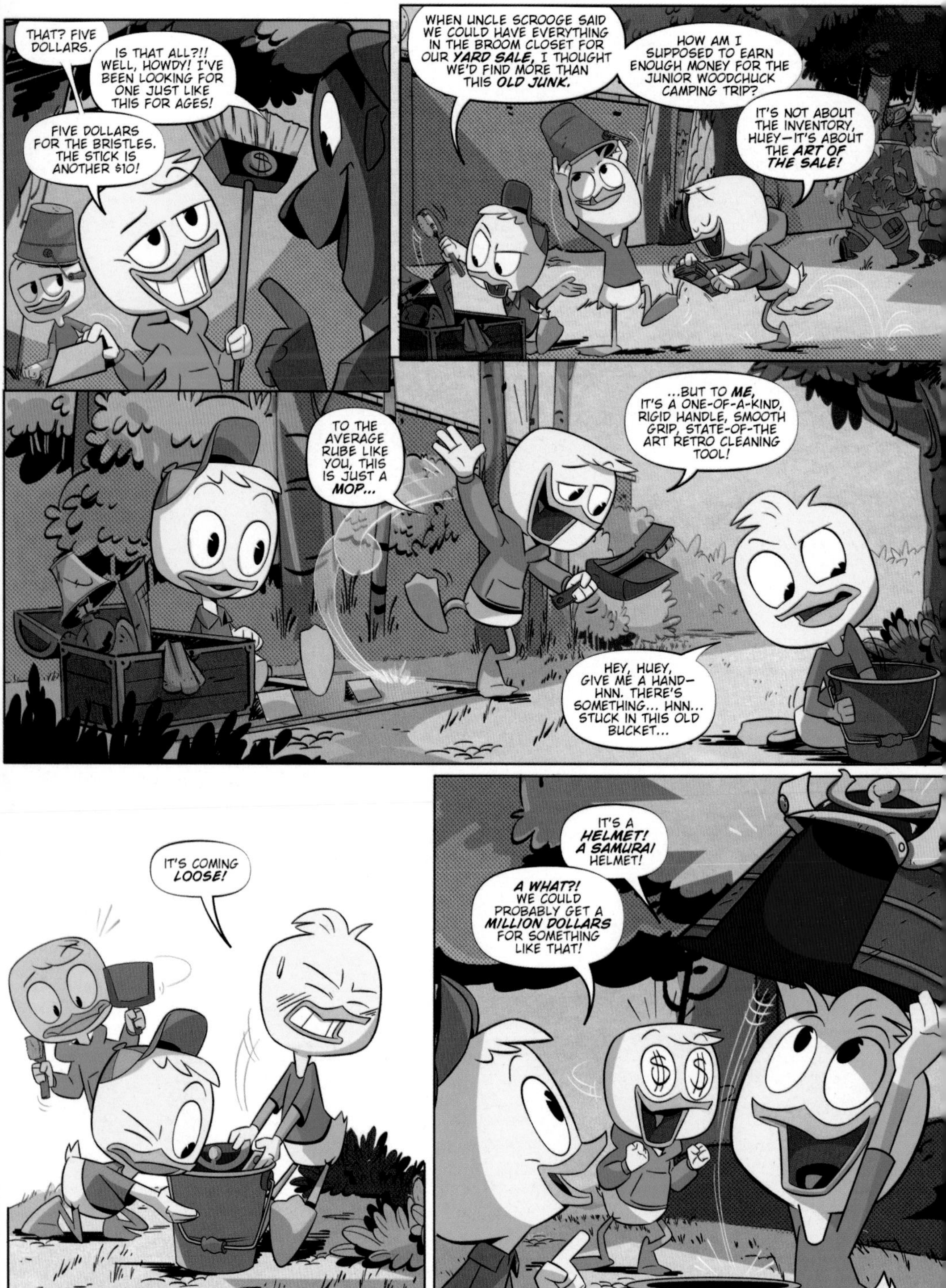
THAT? FIVE DOLLARS.
IS THAT ALL?!! WELL, HOWDY! I'VE BEEN LOOKING FOR ONE JUST LIKE THIS FOR AGES!
FIVE DOLLARS FOR THE BRISTLES. THE STICK IS ANOTHER $10!
WHEN UNCLE SCROOGE SAID WE COULD HAVE EVERYTHING IN THE BROOM CLOSET FOR OUR YARD SALE, I THOUGHT WE'D FIND MORE THAN THIS OLD JUNK.
HOW AM I SUPPOSED TO EARN ENOUGH MONEY FOR THE JUNIOR WOODCHUCK CAMPING TRIP?
IT'S NOT ABOUT THE INVENTORY, HUEY—IT'S ABOUT THE ART OF THE SALE!
TO THE AVERAGE RUBE LIKE YOU, THIS IS JUST A MOP...
...BUT TO ME, IT'S A ONE-OF-A-KIND, RIGID HANDLE, SMOOTH GRIP, STATE-OF-THE ART RETRO CLEANING TOOL!
HEY, HUEY, GIVE ME A HAND— HNN. THERE'S SOMETHING... HNN... STUCK IN THIS OLD BUCKET...
IT'S COMING LOOSE!
IT'S A HELMET! A SAMURAI HELMET!
A WHAT?! WE COULD PROBABLY GET A MILLION DOLLARS FOR SOMETHING LIKE THAT!

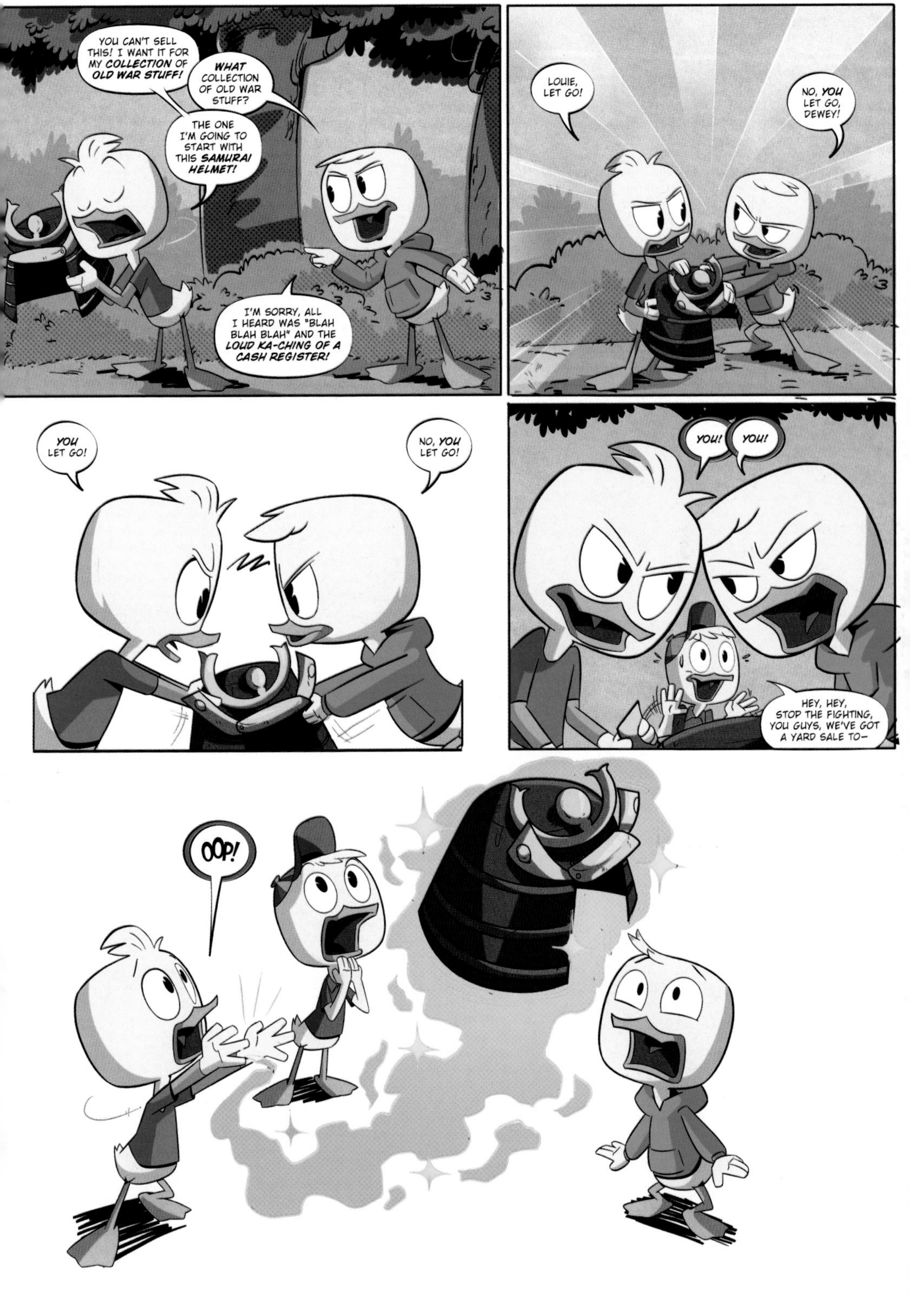
YOU CAN'T SELL THIS! I WANT IT FOR MY COLLECTION OF OLD WAR STUFF!
WHAT COLLECTION OF OLD WAR STUFF?
THE ONE I'M GOING TO START WITH THIS SAMURAI HELMET!
I'M SORRY, ALL I HEARD WAS "BLAH BLAH BLAH" AND THE LOUD KA-CHING OF A CASH REGISTER!
LOUIE, LET GO!
NO, YOU LET GO, DEWEY!
YOU LET GO!
NO, YOU LET GO!
YOU!
YOU!
HEY, HEY, STOP THE FIGHTING, YOU GUYS, WE'VE GOT A YARD SALE TO—
OOP!

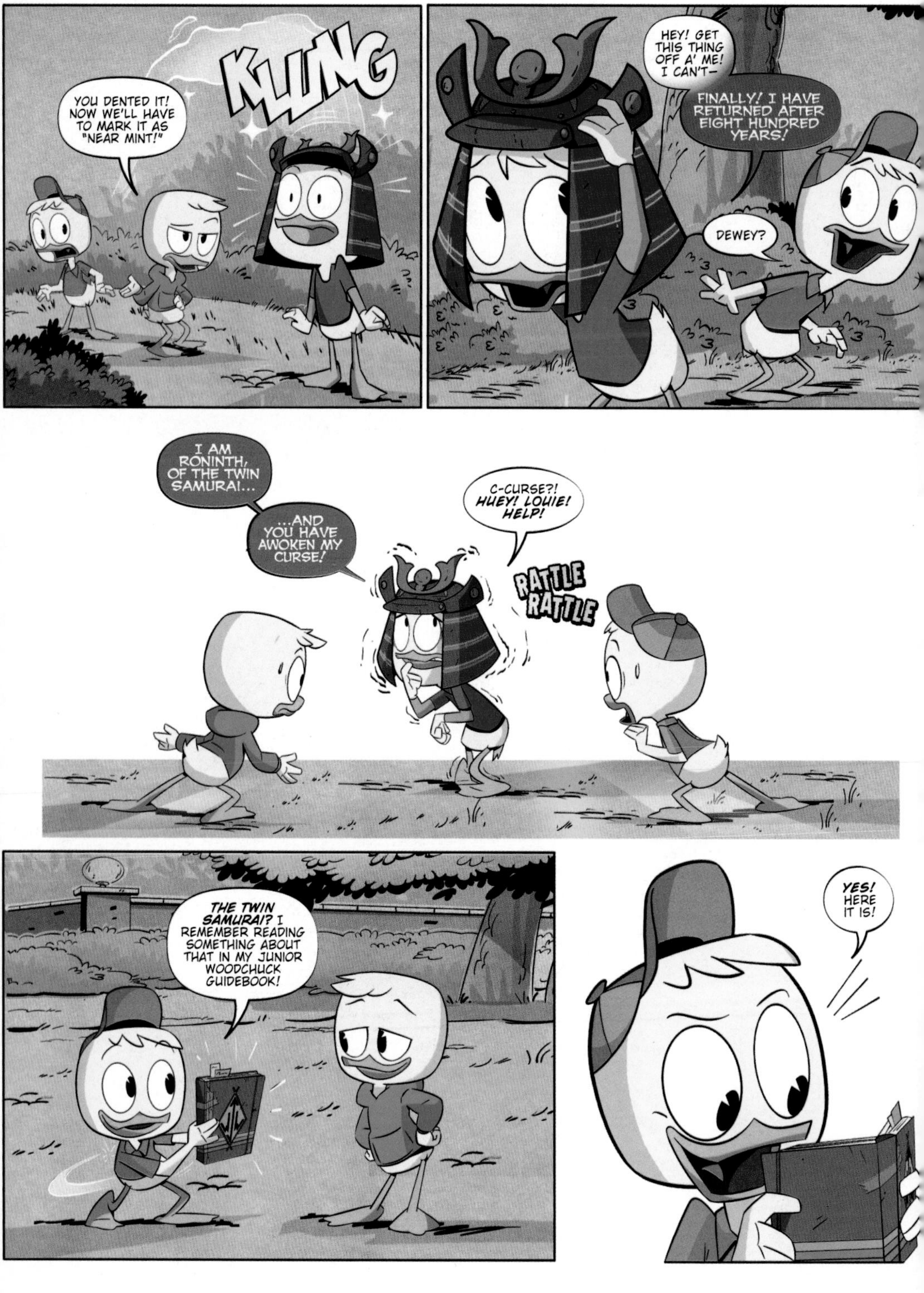
KLUNG
YOU DENTED IT! NOW WE'LL HAVE TO MARK IT AS "NEAR MINT!"
HEY! GET THIS THING OFF A' ME! I CAN'T—
FINALLY! I HAVE RETURNED AFTER EIGHT HUNDRED YEARS!
DEWEY?
I AM RONINTH, OF THE TWIN SAMURAI...
...AND YOU HAVE AWOKEN MY CURSE!
C-CURSE?! HUEY! LOUIE! HELP!
RATTLE RATTLE
THE TWIN SAMURAI? I REMEMBER READING SOMETHING ABOUT THAT IN MY JUNIOR WOODCHUCK GUIDEBOOK!
YES! HERE IT IS!

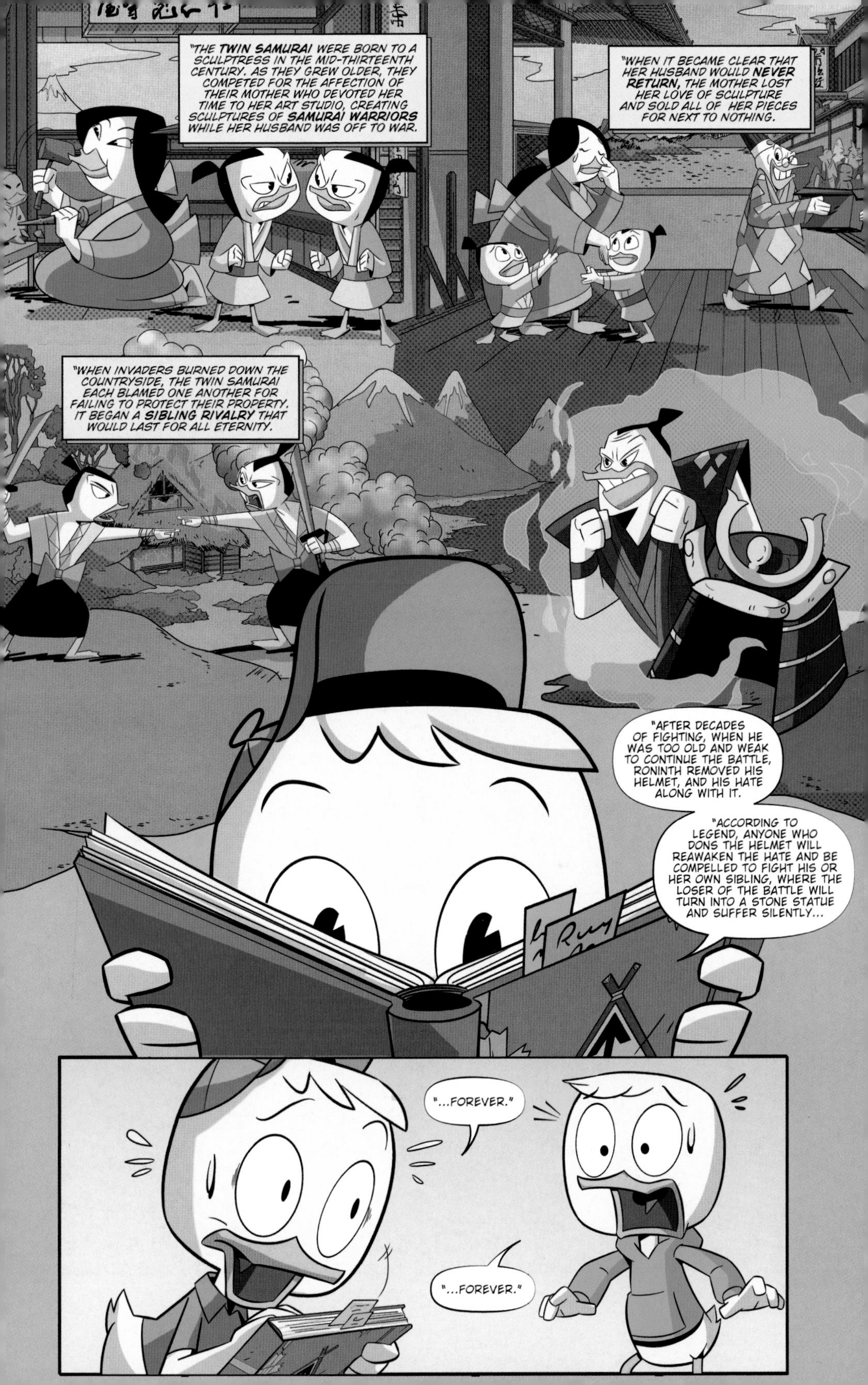
"THE TWIN SAMURAI WERE BORN TO A SCULPTRESS IN THE MID-THIRTEENTH CENTURY. AS THEY GREW OLDER, THEY COMPETED FOR THE AFFECTION OF THEIR MOTHER WHO DEVOTED HER TIME TO HER ART STUDIO, CREATING SCULPTURES OF SAMURAI WARRIORS WHILE HER HUSBAND WAS OFF TO WAR.
"WHEN IT BECAME CLEAR THAT HER HUSBAND WOULD NEVER RETURN, THE MOTHER LOST HER LOVE OF SCULPTURE AND SOLD ALL OF HER PIECES FOR NEXT TO NOTHING.
"WHEN INVADERS BURNED DOWN THE COUNTRYSIDE, THE TWIN SAMURAI EACH BLAMED ONE ANOTHER FOR FAILING TO PROTECT THEIR PROPERTY. IT BEGAN A SIBLING RIVALRY THAT WOULD LAST FOR ALL ETERNITY.
"AFTER DECADES OF FIGHTING, WHEN HE WAS TOO OLD AND WEAK TO CONTINUE THE BATTLE, RONINTH REMOVED HIS HELMET, AND HIS HATE ALONG WITH IT.
"ACCORDING TO LEGEND, ANYONE WHO DONS THE HELMET WILL REAWAKEN THE HATE AND BE COMPELLED TO FIGHT HIS OR HER OWN SIBLING, WHERE THE LOSER OF THE BATTLE WILL TURN INTO A STONE STATUE AND SUFFER SILENTLY...
"...FOREVER."
"...FOREVER."

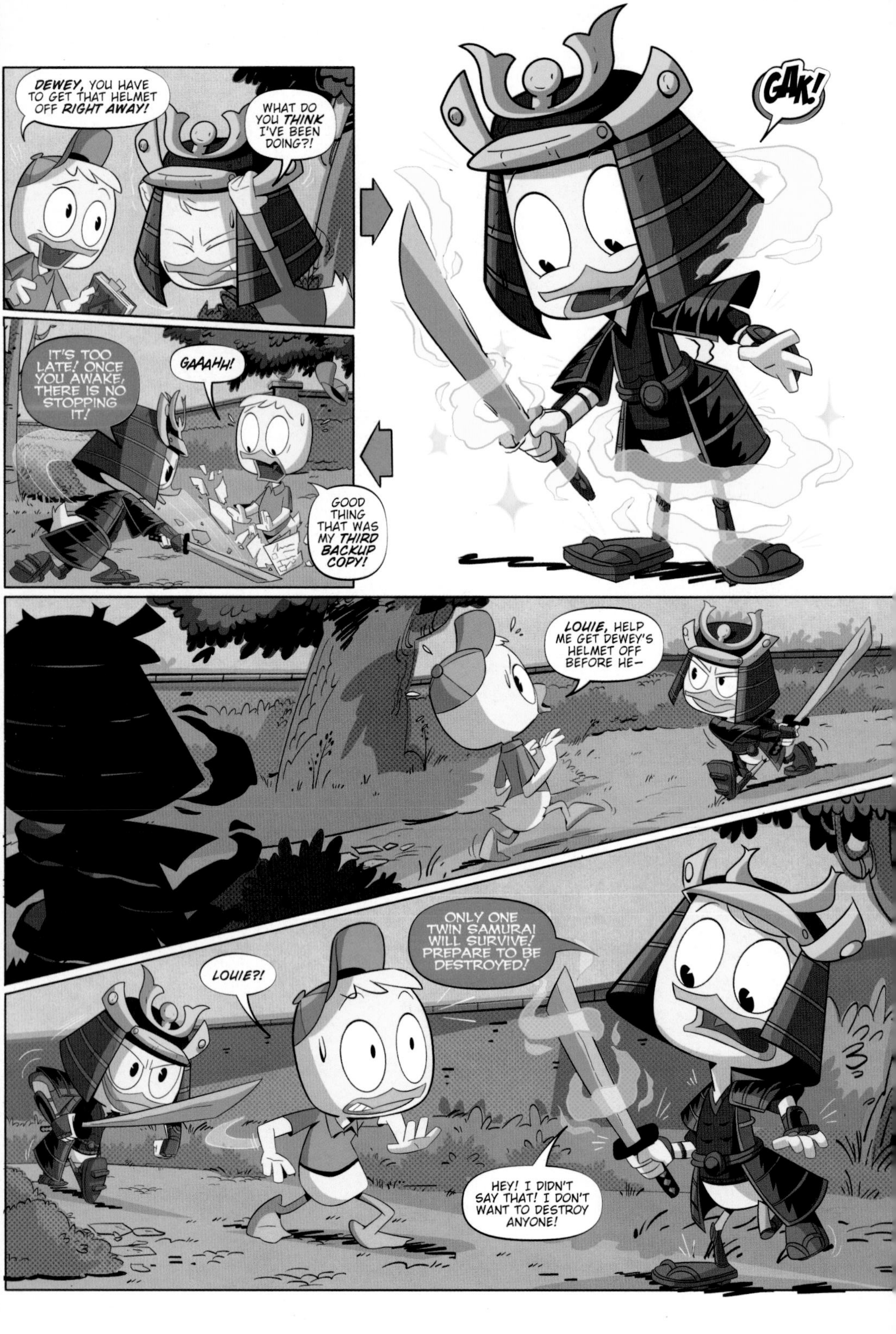

DEWEY, YOU HAVE TO GET THAT HELMET OFF RIGHT AWAY!
WHAT DO YOU THINK I'VE BEEN DOING?!
GAK!
IT'S TOO LATE! ONCE YOU AWAKE, THERE IS NO STOPPING IT!
GAAAHH!
GOOD THING THAT WAS MY THIRD BACKUP COPY!
LOUIE, HELP ME GET DEWEY'S HELMET OFF BEFORE HE—
ONLY ONE TWIN SAMURAI WILL SURVIVE! PREPARE TO BE DESTROYED!
LOUIE?!
HEY! I DIDN'T SAY THAT! I DON'T WANT TO DESTROY ANYONE!

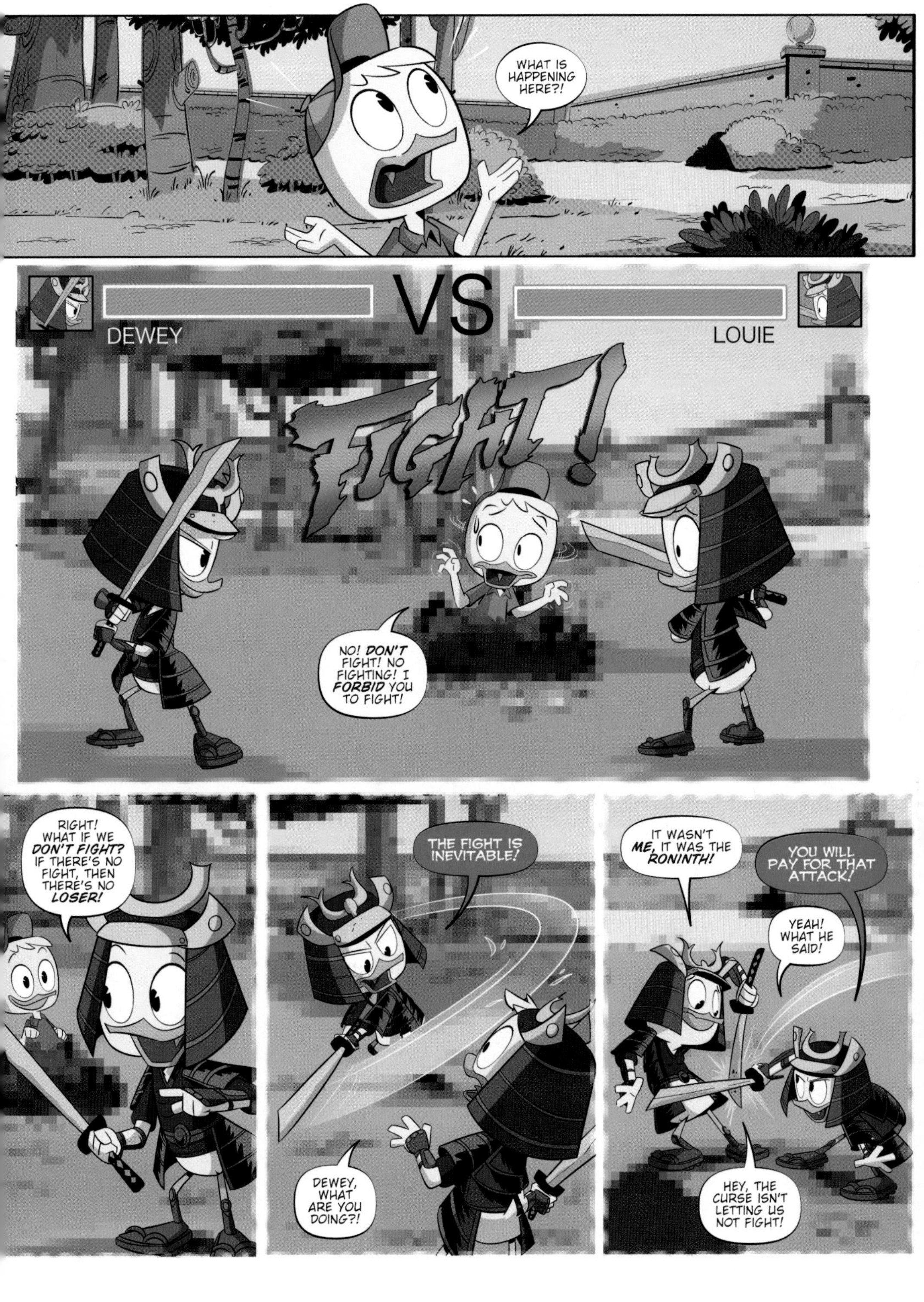
WHAT IS HAPPENING HERE?!
DEWEY
VS
LOUIE
FIGHT!
NO! DON'T FIGHT! NO FIGHTING! I FORBID YOU TO FIGHT!
RIGHT! WHAT IF WE DON'T FIGHT? IF THERE'S NO FIGHT, THEN THERE'S NO LOSER!
THE FIGHT IS INEVITABLE!
DEWEY, WHAT ARE YOU DOING?!
IT WASN'T ME, IT WAS THE RONINTH!
YOU WILL PAY FOR THAT ATTACK!
YEAH! WHAT HE SAID!
HEY, THE CURSE ISN'T LETTING US NOT FIGHT!

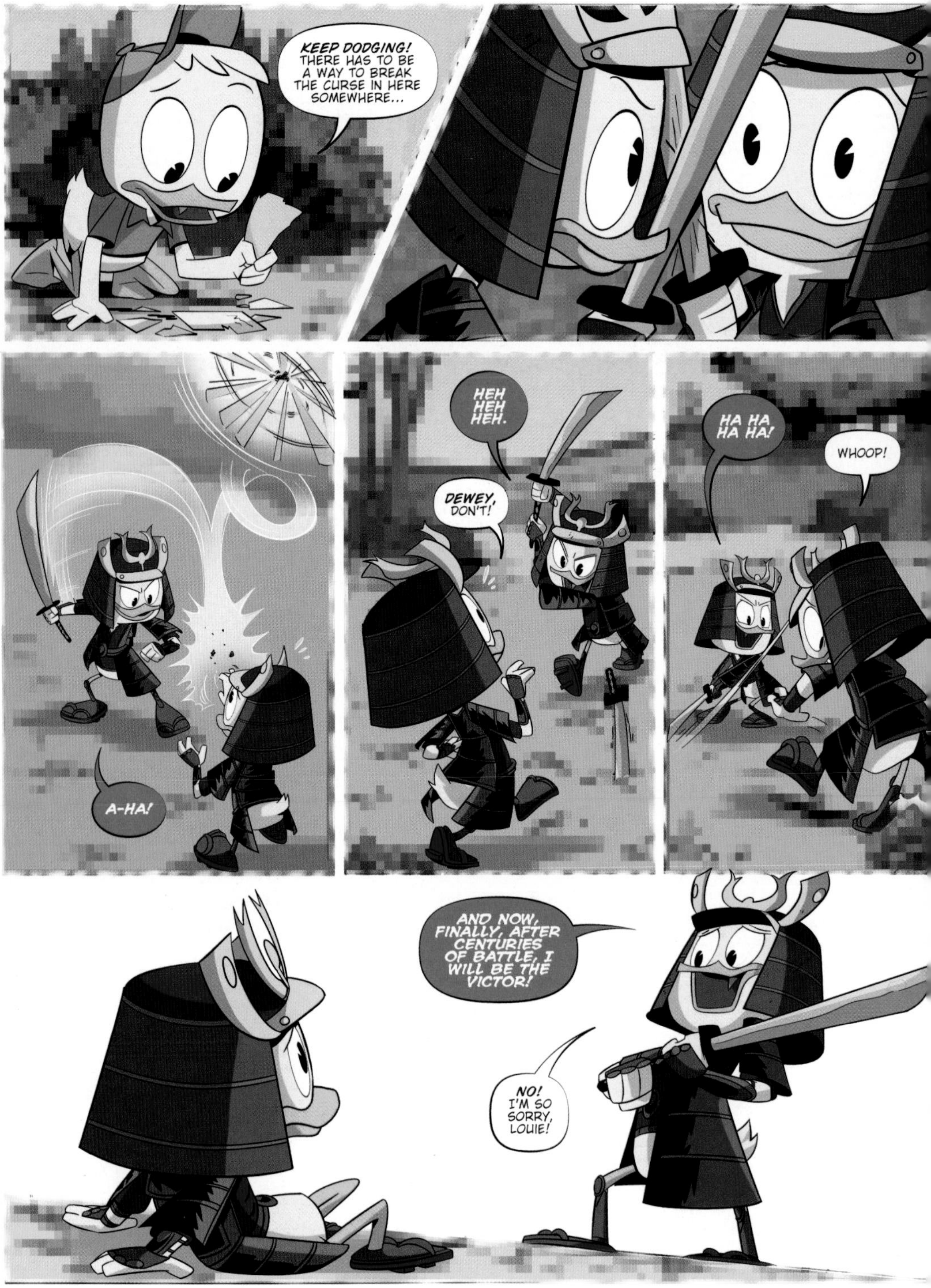
KEEP DODGING! THERE HAS TO BE A WAY TO BREAK THE CURSE IN HERE SOMEWHERE...
A-HA!
HEH HEH HEH.
DEWEY, DON'T!
HA HA HA HA!
WHOOP!
AND NOW, FINALLY, AFTER CENTURIES OF BATTLE, I WILL BE THE VICTOR!
NO! I'M SO SORRY, LOUIE!

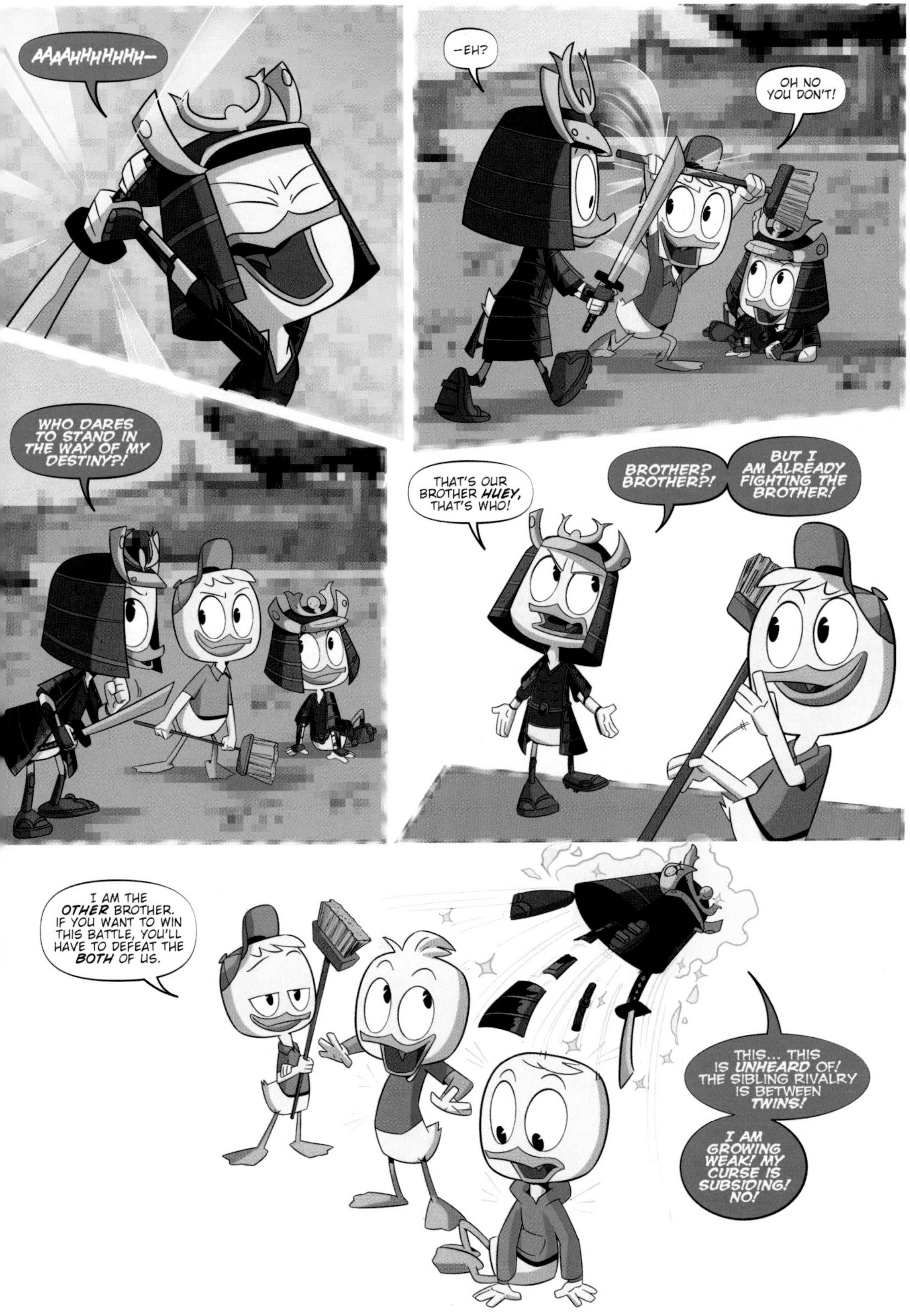
AAAAHHHHHHH—
—EH?
OH NO YOU DON'T!
WHO DARES TO STAND IN THE WAY OF MY DESTINY?!
THAT'S OUR BROTHER HUEY, THAT'S WHO!
BROTHER? BROTHER?!
BUT I AM ALREADY FIGHTING THE BROTHER!
I AM THE OTHER BROTHER. IF YOU WANT TO WIN THIS BATTLE, YOU'LL HAVE TO DEFEAT THE BOTH OF US.
THIS... THIS IS UNHEARD OF! THE SIBLING RIVALRY IS BETWEEN TWINS!
I AM GROWING WEAK! MY CURSE IS SUBSIDING! NO!

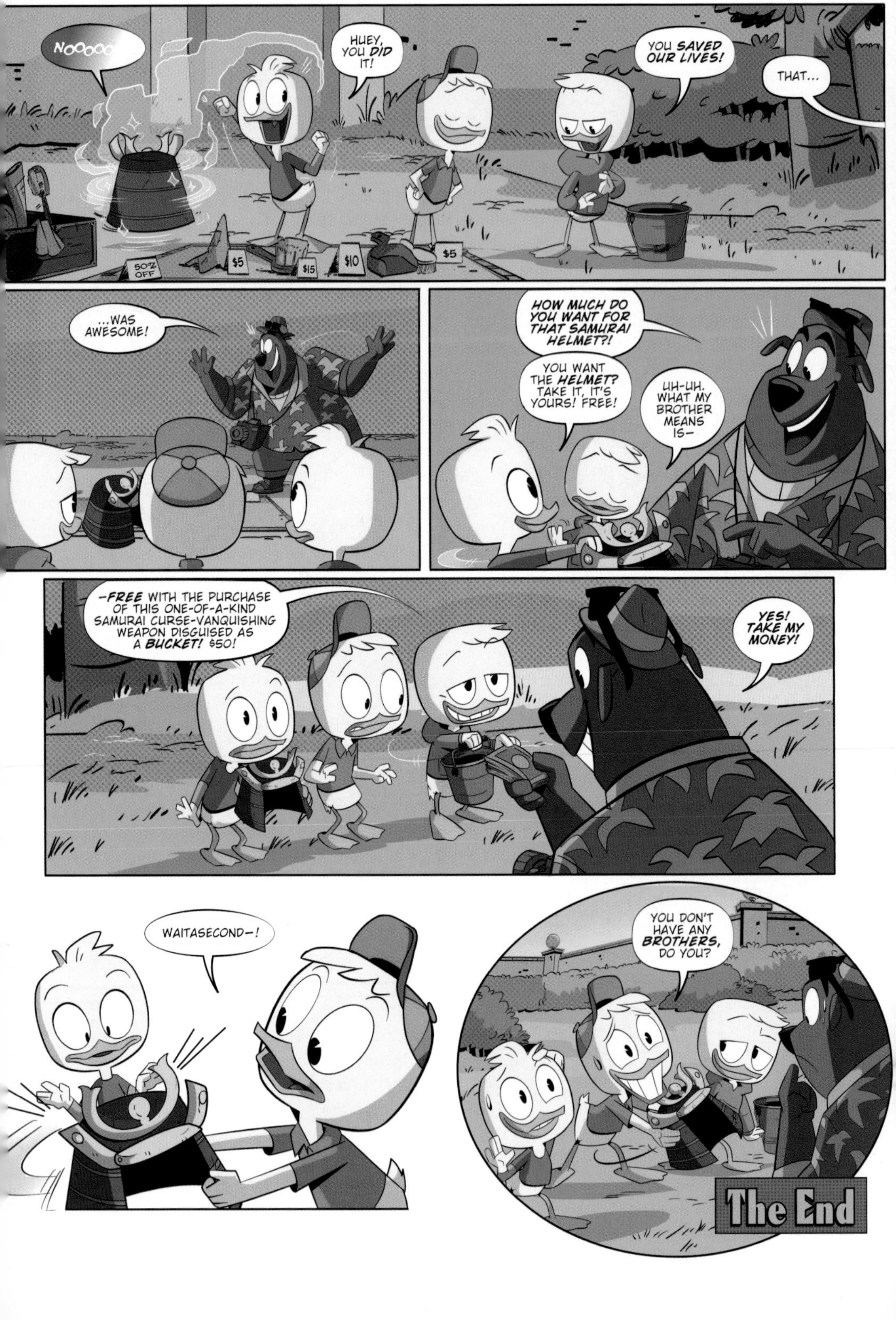
NOOOOO
HUEY, YOU DID IT!
YOU SAVED OUR LIVES!
THAT...
50% OFF
$5
$15
$10
$5
...WAS AWESOME!
HOW MUCH DO YOU WANT FOR THAT SAMURAI HELMET?!
YOU WANT THE HELMET? TAKE IT, IT'S YOURS! FREE!
UH-UH. WHAT MY BROTHER MEANS IS—
—FREE WITH THE PURCHASE OF THIS ONE-OF-A-KIND SAMURAI CURSE-VANQUISHING WEAPON DISGUISED AS A BUCKET! $50!
YES! TAKE MY MONEY!
WAITASECOND—!
YOU DON'T HAVE ANY BROTHERS, DO YOU?
The End

Disney DuckTales

GO, GO, GOLDEN YEARS!

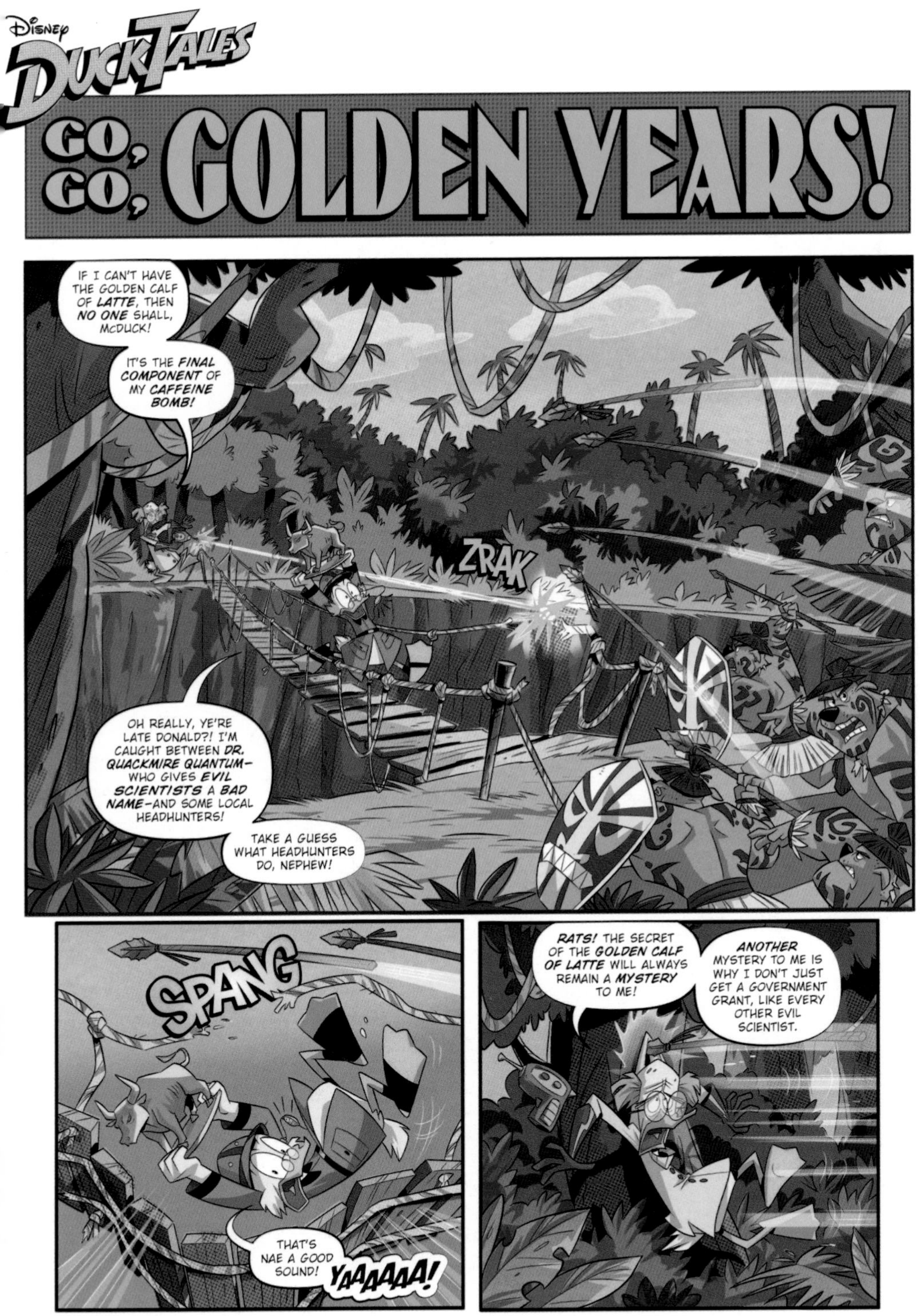

IF I CAN'T HAVE THE GOLDEN CALF OF LATTE, THEN NO ONE SHALL, McDUCK!
IT'S THE FINAL COMPONENT OF MY CAFFEINE BOMB!
ZRAK
OH REALLY, YE'RE LATE DONALD?! I'M CAUGHT BETWEEN DR. QUACKMIRE QUANTUM—WHO GIVES EVIL SCIENTISTS A BAD NAME—AND SOME LOCAL HEADHUNTERS!
TAKE A GUESS WHAT HEADHUNTERS DO, NEPHEW!
SPANG
THAT'S NAE A GOOD SOUND!
YAAAAAA!
RATS! THE SECRET OF THE GOLDEN CALF OF LATTE WILL ALWAYS REMAIN A MYSTERY TO ME!
ANOTHER MYSTERY TO ME IS WHY I DON'T JUST GET A GOVERNMENT GRANT, LIKE EVERY OTHER EVIL SCIENTIST.

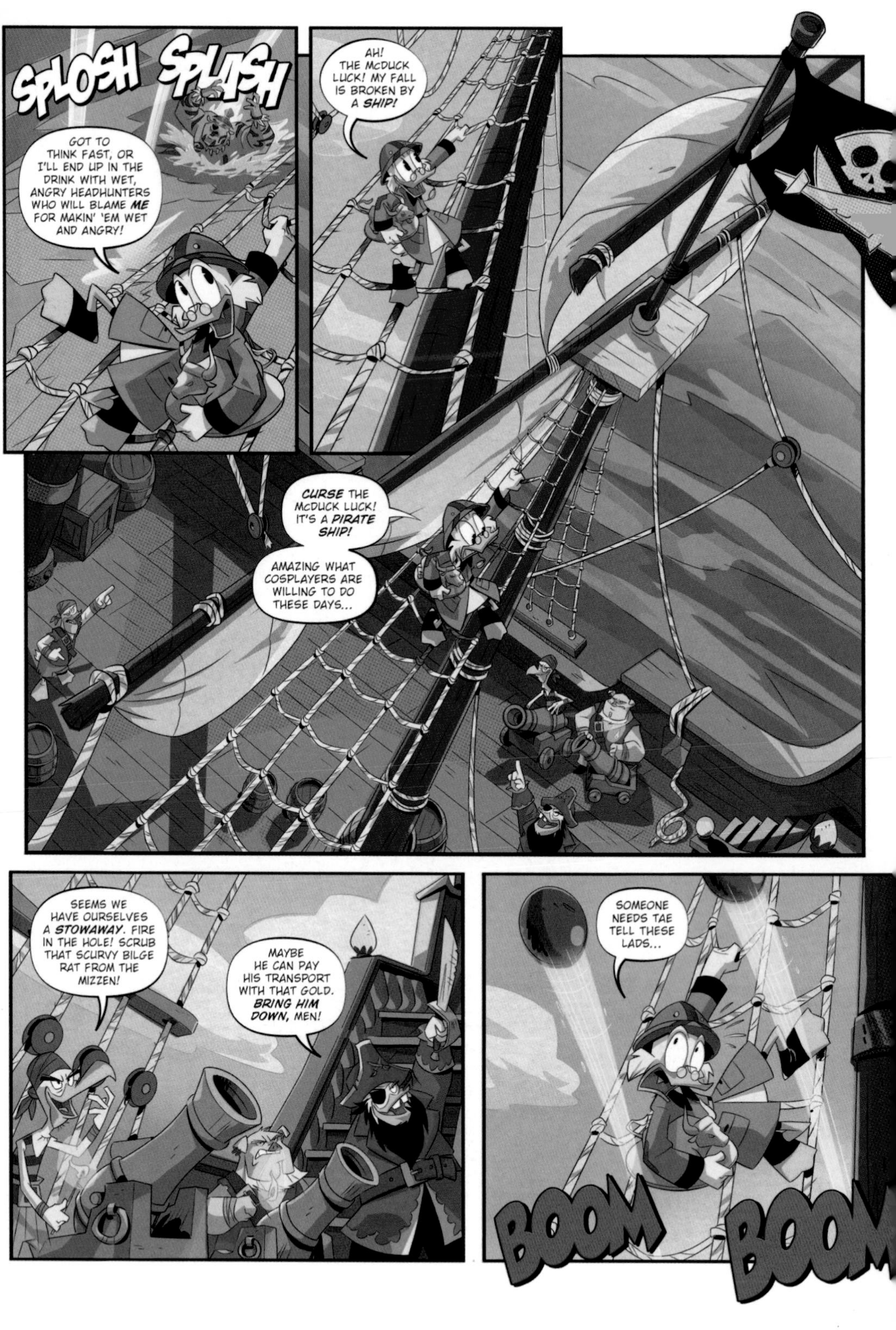
SPLOSH SPLISH
GOT TO THINK FAST, OR I'LL END UP IN THE DRINK WITH WET, ANGRY HEADHUNTERS WHO WILL BLAME ME FOR MAKIN' 'EM WET AND ANGRY!
AH! THE McDUCK LUCK! MY FALL IS BROKEN BY A SHIP!
CURSE THE McDUCK LUCK! IT'S A PIRATE SHIP!
AMAZING WHAT COSPLAYERS ARE WILLING TO DO THESE DAYS...
SEEMS WE HAVE OURSELVES A STOWAWAY. FIRE IN THE HOLE! SCRUB THAT SCURVY BILGE RAT FROM THE MIZZEN!
MAYBE HE CAN PAY HIS TRANSPORT WITH THAT GOLD. BRING HIM DOWN, MEN!
SOMEONE NEEDS TAE TELL THESE LADS...
BOOM
BOOM

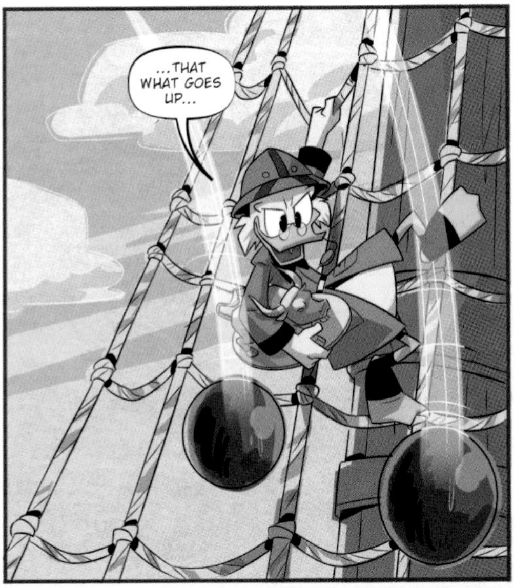
...THAT WHAT GOES UP...

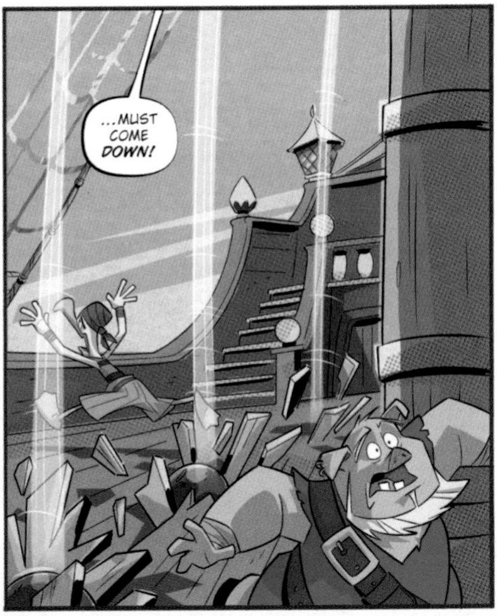
...MUST COME DOWN!

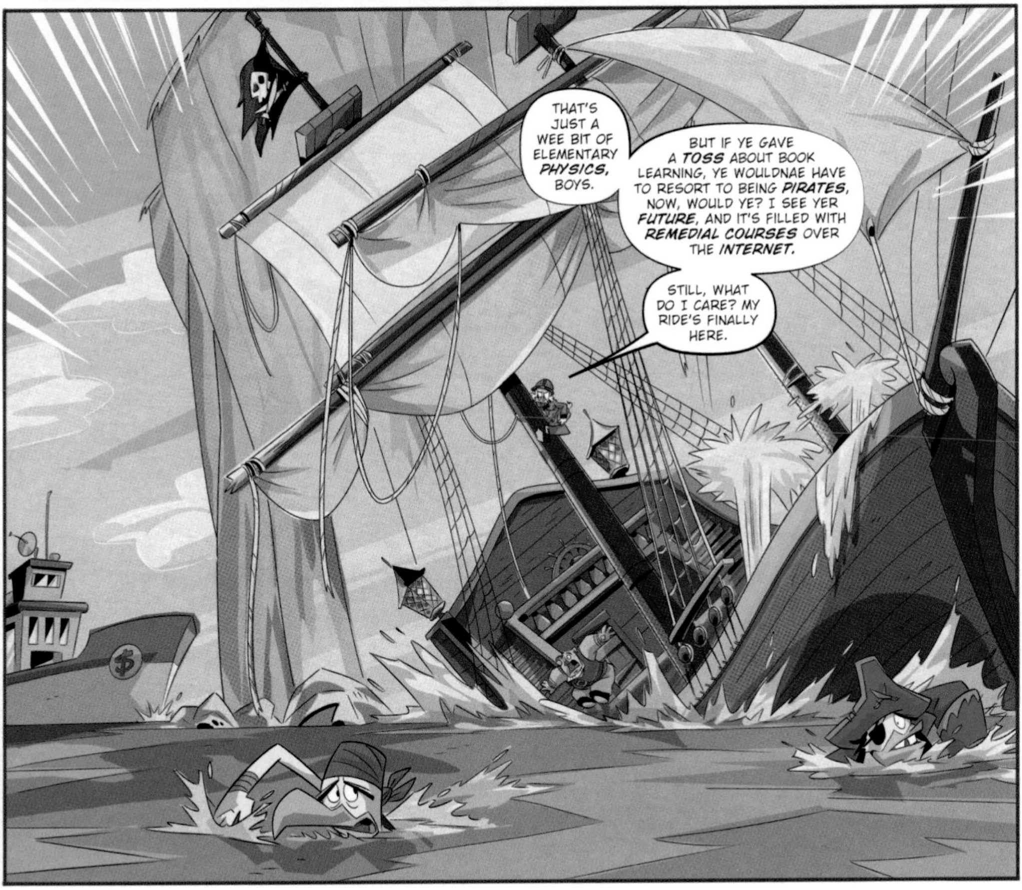
THAT'S JUST A WEE BIT OF ELEMENTARY PHYSICS, BOYS.
BUT IF YE GAVE A TOSS ABOUT BOOK LEARNING, YE WOULDNAE HAVE TO RESORT TO BEING PIRATES, NOW, WOULD YE? I SEE YER FUTURE, AND IT'S FILLED WITH REMEDIAL COURSES OVER THE INTERNET.
STILL, WHAT DO I CARE? MY RIDE'S FINALLY HERE.

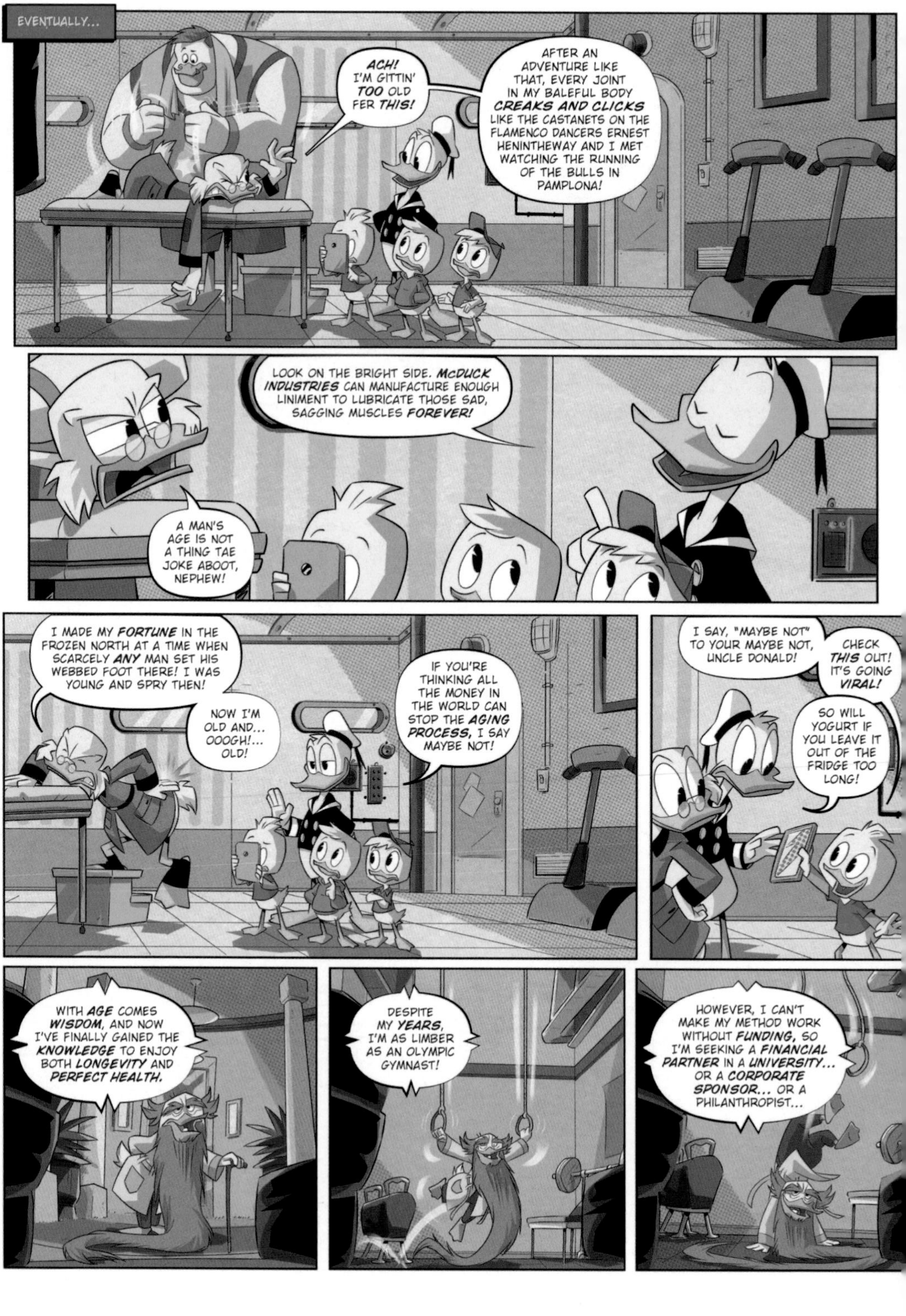
EVENTUALLY...
ACH! I'M GITTIN' TOO OLD FER THIS!
AFTER AN ADVENTURE LIKE THAT, EVERY JOINT IN MY BALEFUL BODY CREAKS AND CLICKS LIKE THE CASTANETS ON THE FLAMENCO DANCERS ERNEST HENINTHEWAY AND I MET WATCHING THE RUNNING OF THE BULLS IN PAMPLONA!
LOOK ON THE BRIGHT SIDE. McDUCK INDUSTRIES CAN MANUFACTURE ENOUGH LINIMENT TO LUBRICATE THOSE SAD, SAGGING MUSCLES FOREVER!
A MAN'S AGE IS NOT A THING TAE JOKE ABOOT, NEPHEW!
I MADE MY FORTUNE IN THE FROZEN NORTH AT A TIME WHEN SCARCELY ANY MAN SET HIS WEBBED FOOT THERE! I WAS YOUNG AND SPRY THEN!
NOW I'M OLD AND... OOOGH!... OLD!
IF YOU'RE THINKING ALL THE MONEY IN THE WORLD CAN STOP THE AGING PROCESS, I SAY MAYBE NOT!
I SAY, "MAYBE NOT" TO YOUR MAYBE NOT, UNCLE DONALD!
CHECK THIS OUT! IT'S GOING VIRAL!
SO WILL YOGURT IF YOU LEAVE IT OUT OF THE FRIDGE TOO LONG!
WITH AGE COMES WISDOM, AND NOW I'VE FINALLY GAINED THE KNOWLEDGE TO ENJOY BOTH LONGEVITY AND PERFECT HEALTH.
DESPITE MY YEARS, I'M AS LIMBER AS AN OLYMPIC GYMNAST!
HOWEVER, I CAN'T MAKE MY METHOD WORK WITHOUT FUNDING, SO I'M SEEKING A FINANCIAL PARTNER IN A UNIVERSITY... OR A CORPORATE SPONSOR... OR A PHILANTHROPIST...

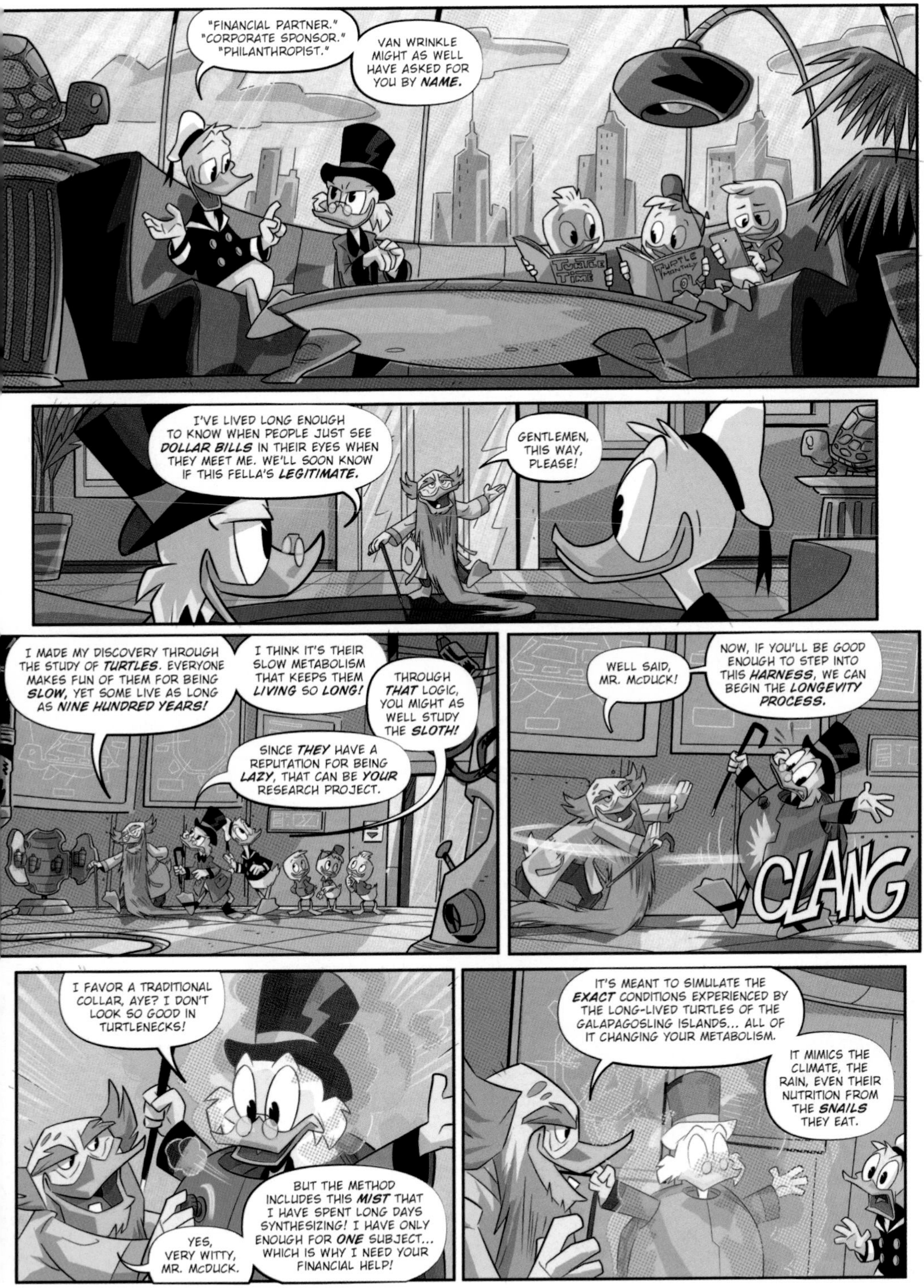
"FINANCIAL PARTNER." "CORPORATE SPONSOR." "PHILANTHROPIST."
VAN WRINKLE MIGHT AS WELL HAVE ASKED FOR YOU BY NAME.
TURTLE TIME
TURTLE MONTHLY
I'VE LIVED LONG ENOUGH TO KNOW WHEN PEOPLE JUST SEE DOLLAR BILLS IN THEIR EYES WHEN THEY MEET ME. WE'LL SOON KNOW IF THIS FELLA'S LEGITIMATE.
GENTLEMEN, THIS WAY, PLEASE!
I MADE MY DISCOVERY THROUGH THE STUDY OF TURTLES. EVERYONE MAKES FUN OF THEM FOR BEING SLOW, YET SOME LIVE AS LONG AS NINE HUNDRED YEARS!
I THINK IT'S THEIR SLOW METABOLISM THAT KEEPS THEM LIVING SO LONG!
THROUGH THAT LOGIC, YOU MIGHT AS WELL STUDY THE SLOTH!
SINCE THEY HAVE A REPUTATION FOR BEING LAZY, THAT CAN BE YOUR RESEARCH PROJECT.
WELL SAID, MR. McDUCK!
NOW, IF YOU'LL BE GOOD ENOUGH TO STEP INTO THIS HARNESS, WE CAN BEGIN THE LONGEVITY PROCESS.
CLANG
I FAVOR A TRADITIONAL COLLAR, AYE? I DON'T LOOK SO GOOD IN TURTLENECKS!
YES, VERY WITTY, MR. McDUCK.
BUT THE METHOD INCLUDES THIS MIST THAT I HAVE SPENT LONG DAYS SYNTHESIZING! I HAVE ONLY ENOUGH FOR ONE SUBJECT... WHICH IS WHY I NEED YOUR FINANCIAL HELP!
IT'S MEANT TO SIMULATE THE EXACT CONDITIONS EXPERIENCED BY THE LONG-LIVED TURTLES OF THE GALAPAGOSLING ISLANDS... ALL OF IT CHANGING YOUR METABOLISM.
IT MIMICS THE CLIMATE, THE RAIN, EVEN THEIR NUTRITION FROM THE SNAILS THEY EAT.

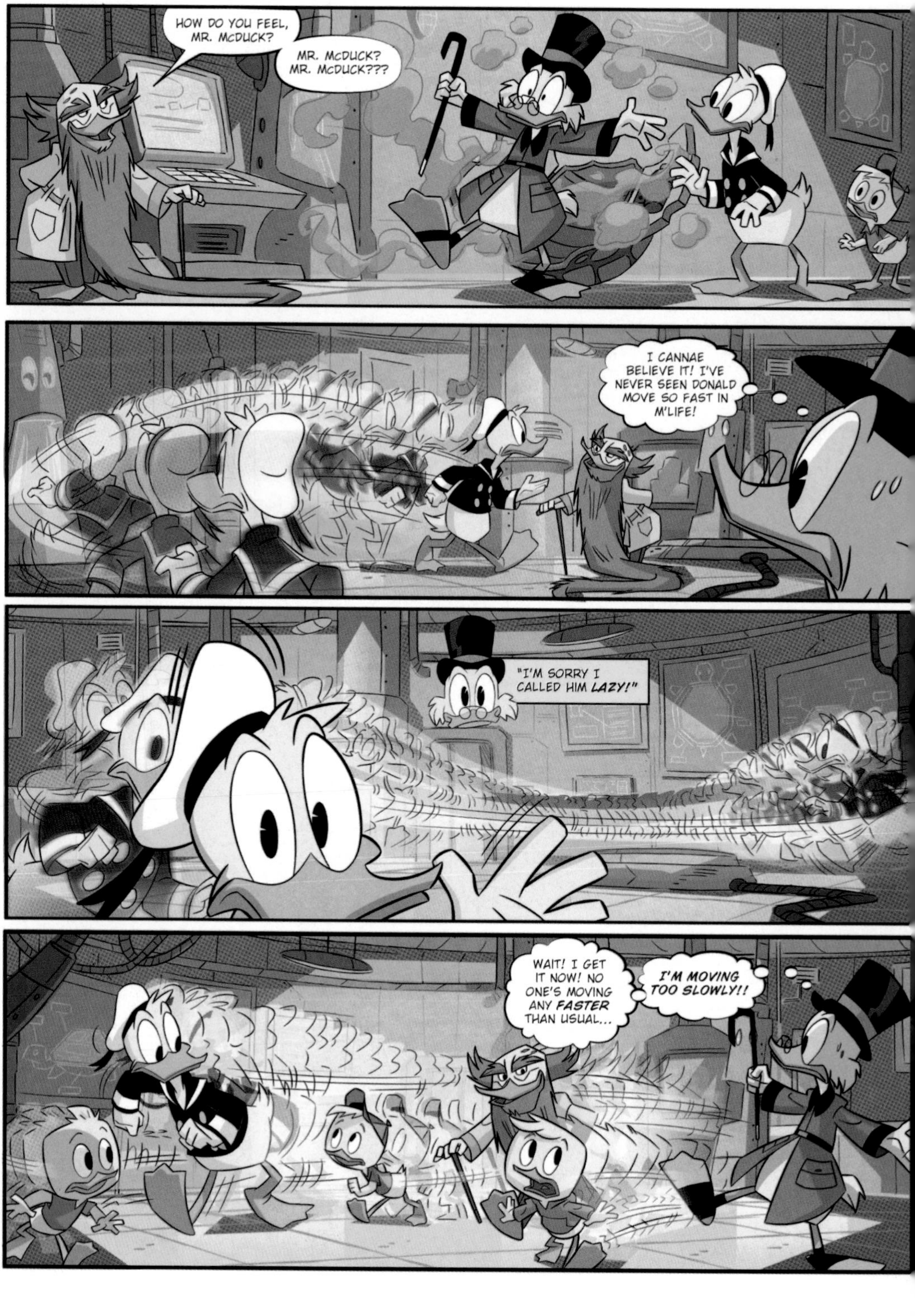
HOW DO YOU FEEL, MR. McDUCK?
MR. McDUCK? MR. McDUCK???
I CANNAE BELIEVE IT! I'VE NEVER SEEN DONALD MOVE SO FAST IN M'LIFE!
"I'M SORRY I CALLED HIM LAZY!"
WAIT! I GET IT NOW! NO ONE'S MOVING ANY FASTER THAN USUAL...
I'M MOVING TOO SLOWLY!!

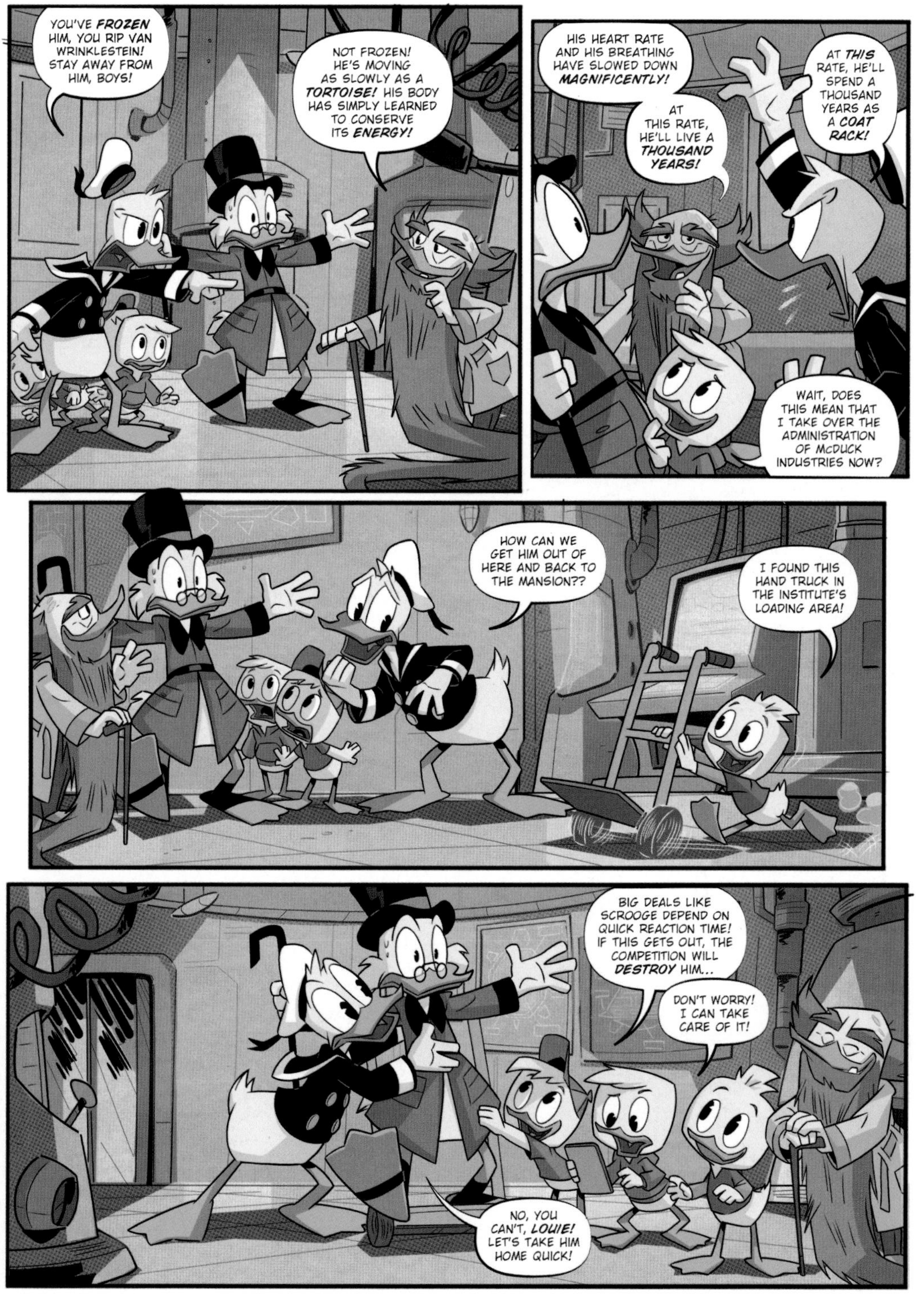
YOU'VE FROZEN HIM, YOU RIP VAN WRINKLESTEIN! STAY AWAY FROM HIM, BOYS!
NOT FROZEN! HE'S MOVING AS SLOWLY AS A TORTOISE! HIS BODY HAS SIMPLY LEARNED TO CONSERVE ITS ENERGY!
HIS HEART RATE AND HIS BREATHING HAVE SLOWED DOWN MAGNIFICENTLY!
AT THIS RATE, HE'LL LIVE A THOUSAND YEARS!
AT THIS RATE, HE'LL SPEND A THOUSAND YEARS AS A COAT RACK!
WAIT, DOES THIS MEAN THAT I TAKE OVER THE ADMINISTRATION OF McDUCK INDUSTRIES NOW?
HOW CAN WE GET HIM OUT OF HERE AND BACK TO THE MANSION??
I FOUND THIS HAND TRUCK IN THE INSTITUTE'S LOADING AREA!
BIG DEALS LIKE SCROOGE DEPEND ON QUICK REACTION TIME! IF THIS GETS OUT, THE COMPETITION WILL DESTROY HIM...
DON'T WORRY! I CAN TAKE CARE OF IT!
NO, YOU CAN'T, LOUIE! LET'S TAKE HIM HOME QUICK!

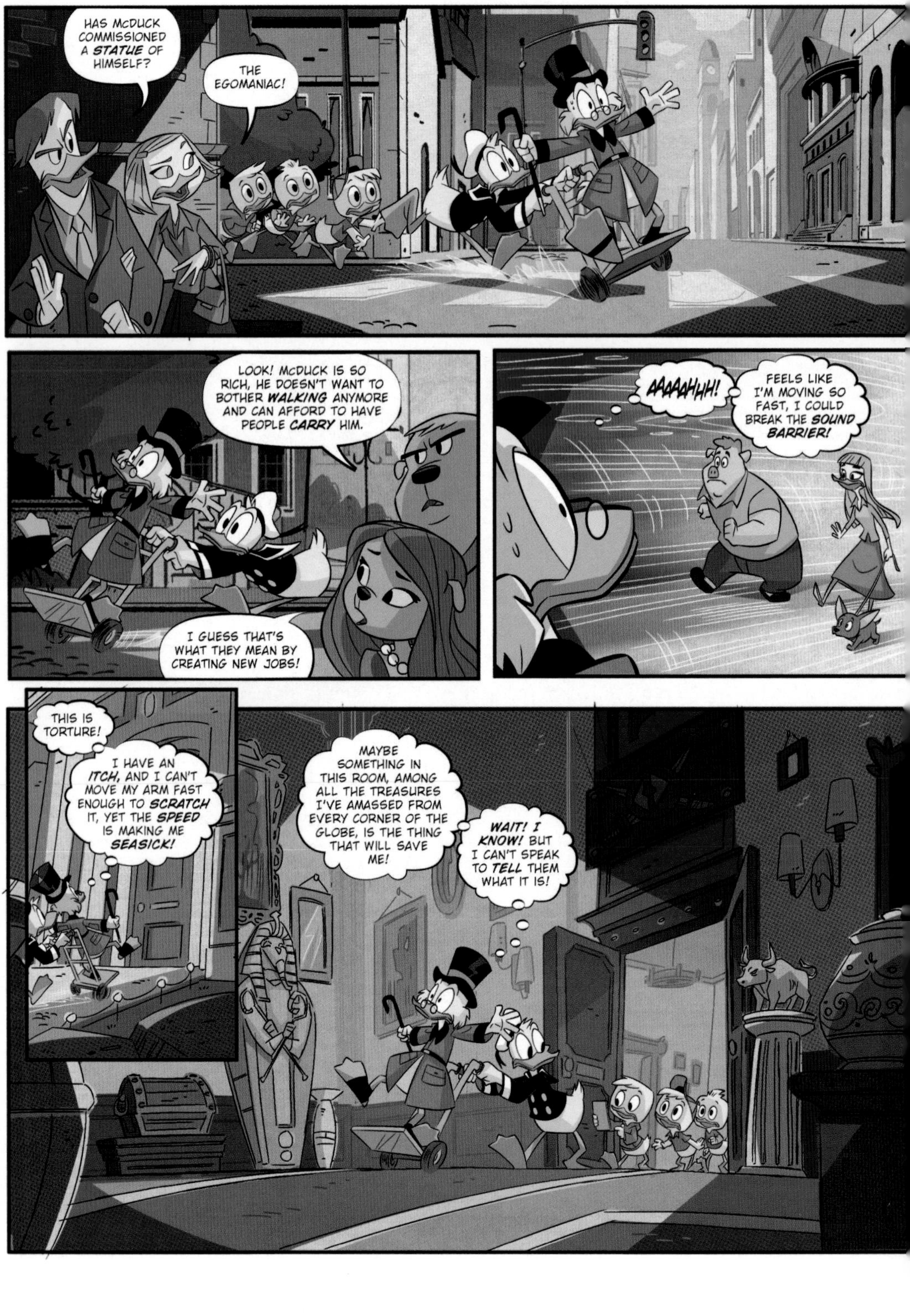
HAS McDUCK COMMISSIONED A STATUE OF HIMSELF?
THE EGOMANIAC!
LOOK! McDUCK IS SO RICH, HE DOESN'T WANT TO BOTHER WALKING ANYMORE AND CAN AFFORD TO HAVE PEOPLE CARRY HIM.
I GUESS THAT'S WHAT THEY MEAN BY CREATING NEW JOBS!
AAAAAHHH!
FEELS LIKE I'M MOVING SO FAST, I COULD BREAK THE SOUND BARRIER!
THIS IS TORTURE!
I HAVE AN ITCH, AND I CAN'T MOVE MY ARM FAST ENOUGH TO SCRATCH IT, YET THE SPEED IS MAKING ME SEASICK!
MAYBE SOMETHING IN THIS ROOM, AMONG ALL THE TREASURES I'VE AMASSED FROM EVERY CORNER OF THE GLOBE, IS THE THING THAT WILL SAVE ME!
WAIT! I KNOW! BUT I CAN'T SPEAK TO TELL THEM WHAT IT IS!

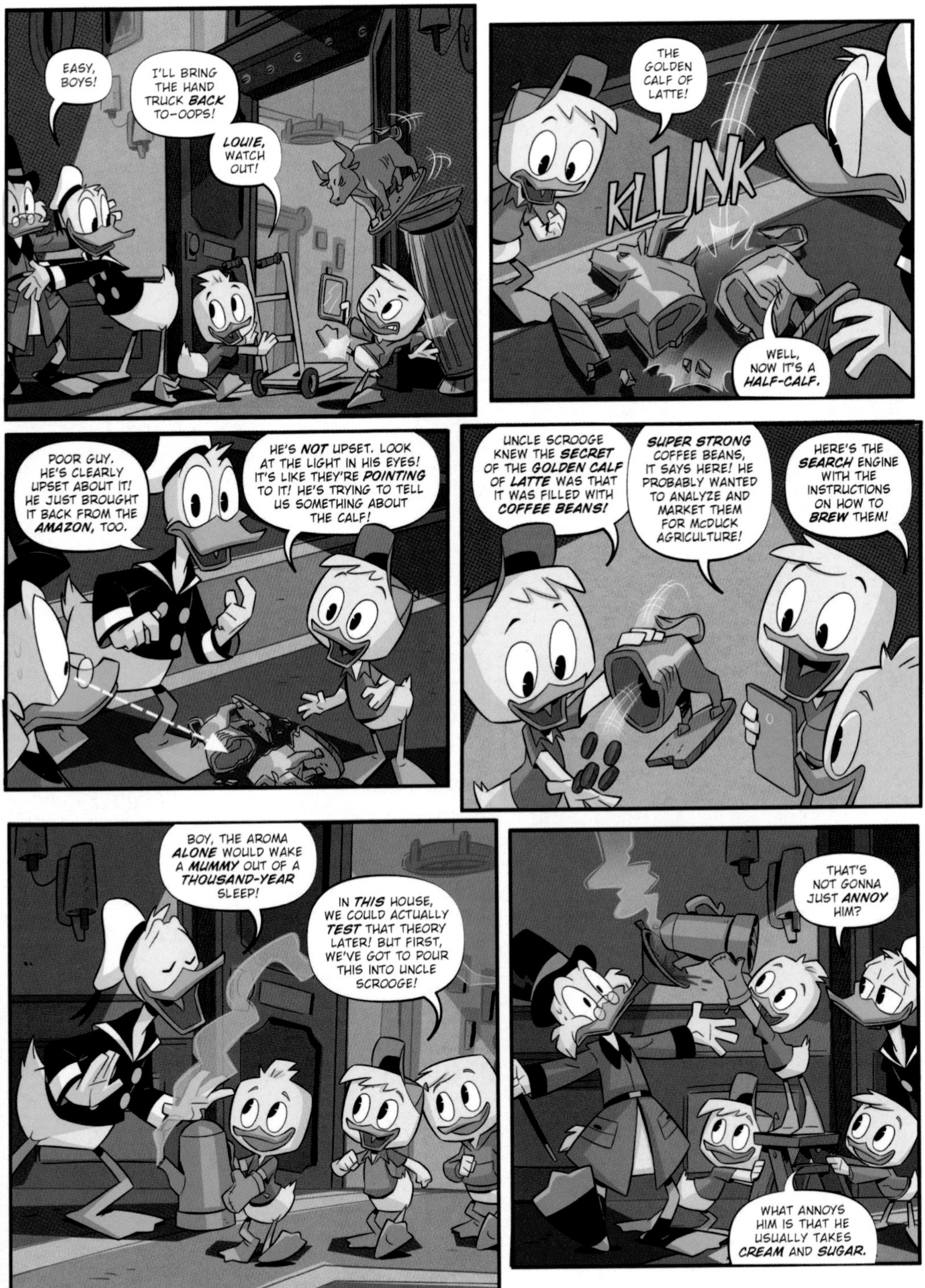
EASY, BOYS!
I'LL BRING THE HAND TRUCK BACK TO—OOPS!
LOUIE, WATCH OUT!
THE GOLDEN CALF OF LATTE!
KLUNK
WELL, NOW IT'S A HALF-CALF.
POOR GUY. HE'S CLEARLY UPSET ABOUT IT! HE JUST BROUGHT IT BACK FROM THE AMAZON, TOO.
HE'S NOT UPSET. LOOK AT THE LIGHT IN HIS EYES! IT'S LIKE THEY'RE POINTING TO IT! HE'S TRYING TO TELL US SOMETHING ABOUT THE CALF!
UNCLE SCROOGE KNEW THE SECRET OF THE GOLDEN CALF OF LATTE WAS THAT IT WAS FILLED WITH COFFEE BEANS!
SUPER STRONG COFFEE BEANS, IT SAYS HERE! HE PROBABLY WANTED TO ANALYZE AND MARKET THEM FOR McDUCK AGRICULTURE!
HERE'S THE SEARCH ENGINE WITH THE INSTRUCTIONS ON HOW TO BREW THEM!
BOY, THE AROMA ALONE WOULD WAKE A MUMMY OUT OF A THOUSAND-YEAR SLEEP!
IN THIS HOUSE, WE COULD ACTUALLY TEST THAT THEORY LATER! BUT FIRST, WE'VE GOT TO POUR THIS INTO UNCLE SCROOGE!
THAT'S NOT GONNA JUST ANNOY HIM?
WHAT ANNOYS HIM IS THAT HE USUALLY TAKES CREAM AND SUGAR.

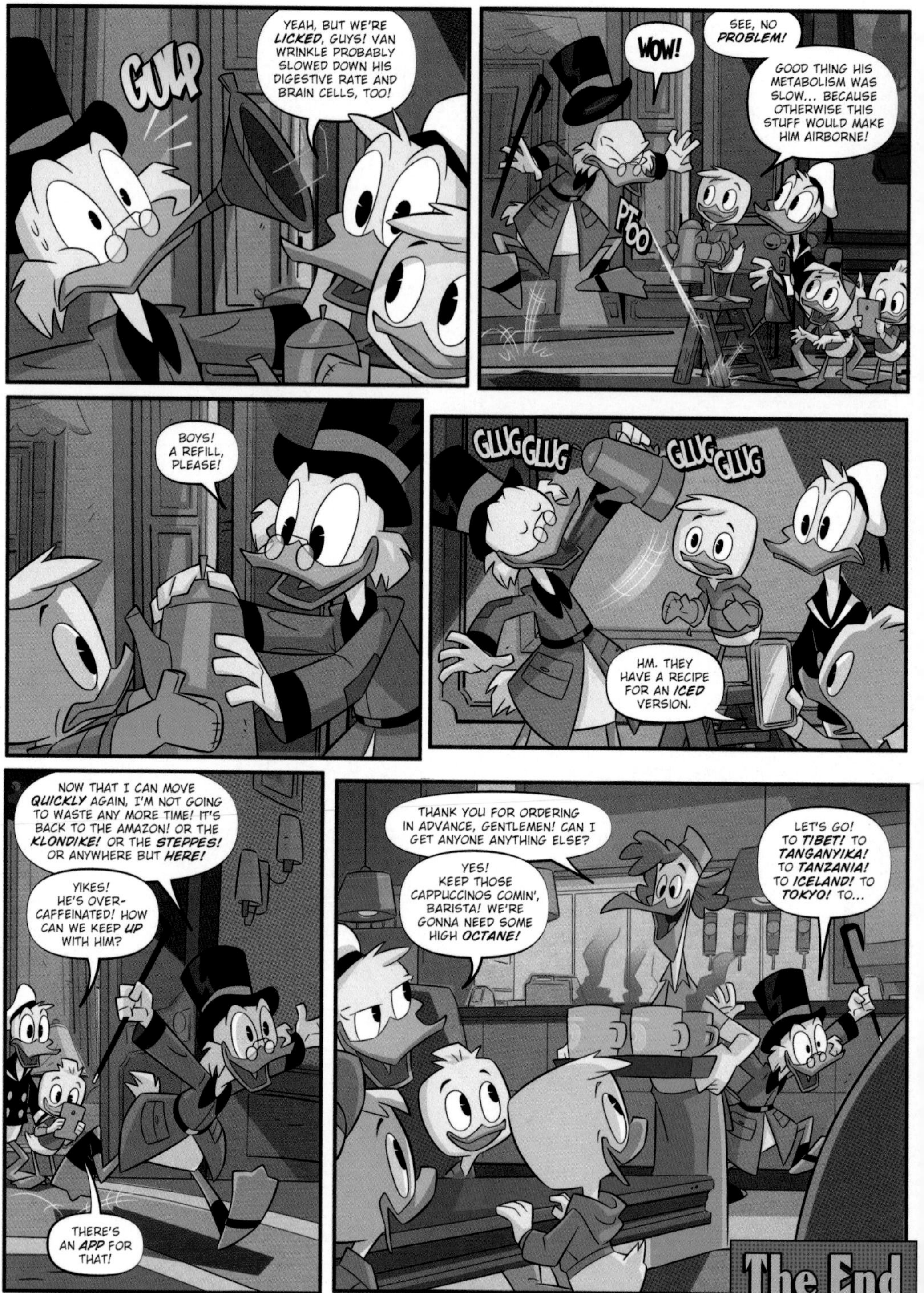
GULP
YEAH, BUT WE'RE LICKED, GUYS! VAN WRINKLE PROBABLY SLOWED DOWN HIS DIGESTIVE RATE AND BRAIN CELLS, TOO!
WOW!
SEE, NO PROBLEM!
GOOD THING HIS METABOLISM WAS SLOW... BECAUSE OTHERWISE THIS STUFF WOULD MAKE HIM AIRBORNE!
PTOO
BOYS! A REFILL, PLEASE!
GLUG GLUG
GLUG GLUG
HM. THEY HAVE A RECIPE FOR AN ICED VERSION.
NOW THAT I CAN MOVE QUICKLY AGAIN, I'M NOT GOING TO WASTE ANY MORE TIME! IT'S BACK TO THE AMAZON! OR THE KLONDIKE! OR THE STEPPES! OR ANYWHERE BUT HERE!
YIKES! HE'S OVER-CAFFEINATED! HOW CAN WE KEEP UP WITH HIM?
THERE'S AN APP FOR THAT!
THANK YOU FOR ORDERING IN ADVANCE, GENTLEMEN! CAN I GET ANYONE ANYTHING ELSE?
YES! KEEP THOSE CAPPUCCINOS COMIN', BARISTA! WE'RE GONNA NEED SOME HIGH OCTANE!
LET'S GO! TO TIBET! TO TANGANYIKA! TO TANZANIA! TO ICELAND! TO TOKYO! TO...
The End

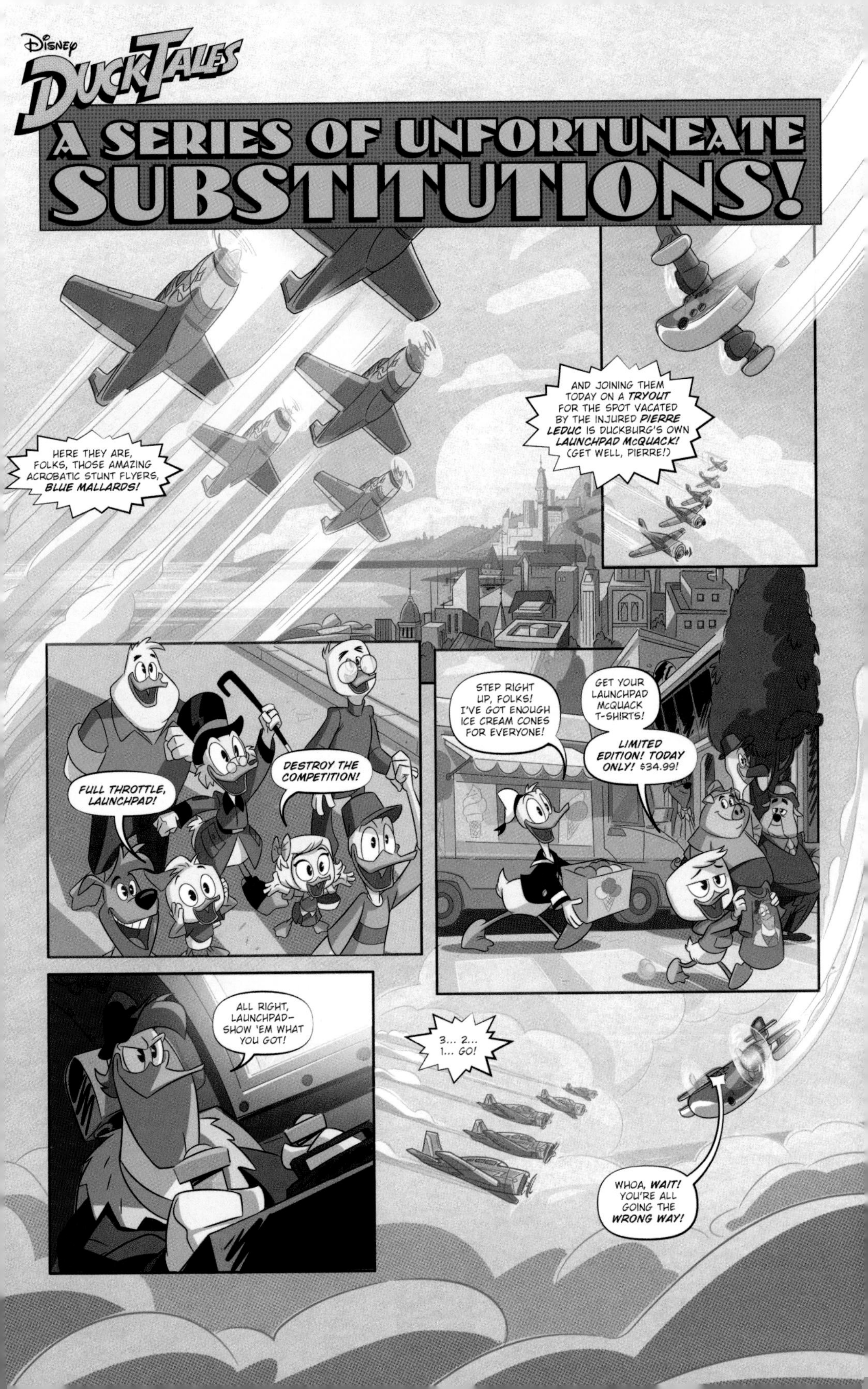
Disney DuckTales
A SERIES OF UNFORTUNEATE SUBSTITUTIONS!
HERE THEY ARE, FOLKS, THOSE AMAZING ACROBATIC STUNT FLYERS, BLUE MALLARDS!
AND JOINING THEM TODAY ON A TRYOUT FOR THE SPOT VACATED BY THE INJURED PIERRE LEDUC IS DUCKBURG'S OWN LAUNCHPAD McQUACK! (GET WELL, PIERRE!)
FULL THROTTLE, LAUNCHPAD!
DESTROY THE COMPETITION!
STEP RIGHT UP, FOLKS! I'VE GOT ENOUGH ICE CREAM CONES FOR EVERYONE!
GET YOUR LAUNCHPAD McQUACK T-SHIRTS!
LIMITED EDITION! TODAY ONLY! $34.99!
ALL RIGHT, LAUNCHPAD– SHOW 'EM WHAT YOU GOT!
3... 2... 1... GO!
WHOA, WAIT! YOU'RE ALL GOING THE WRONG WAY!

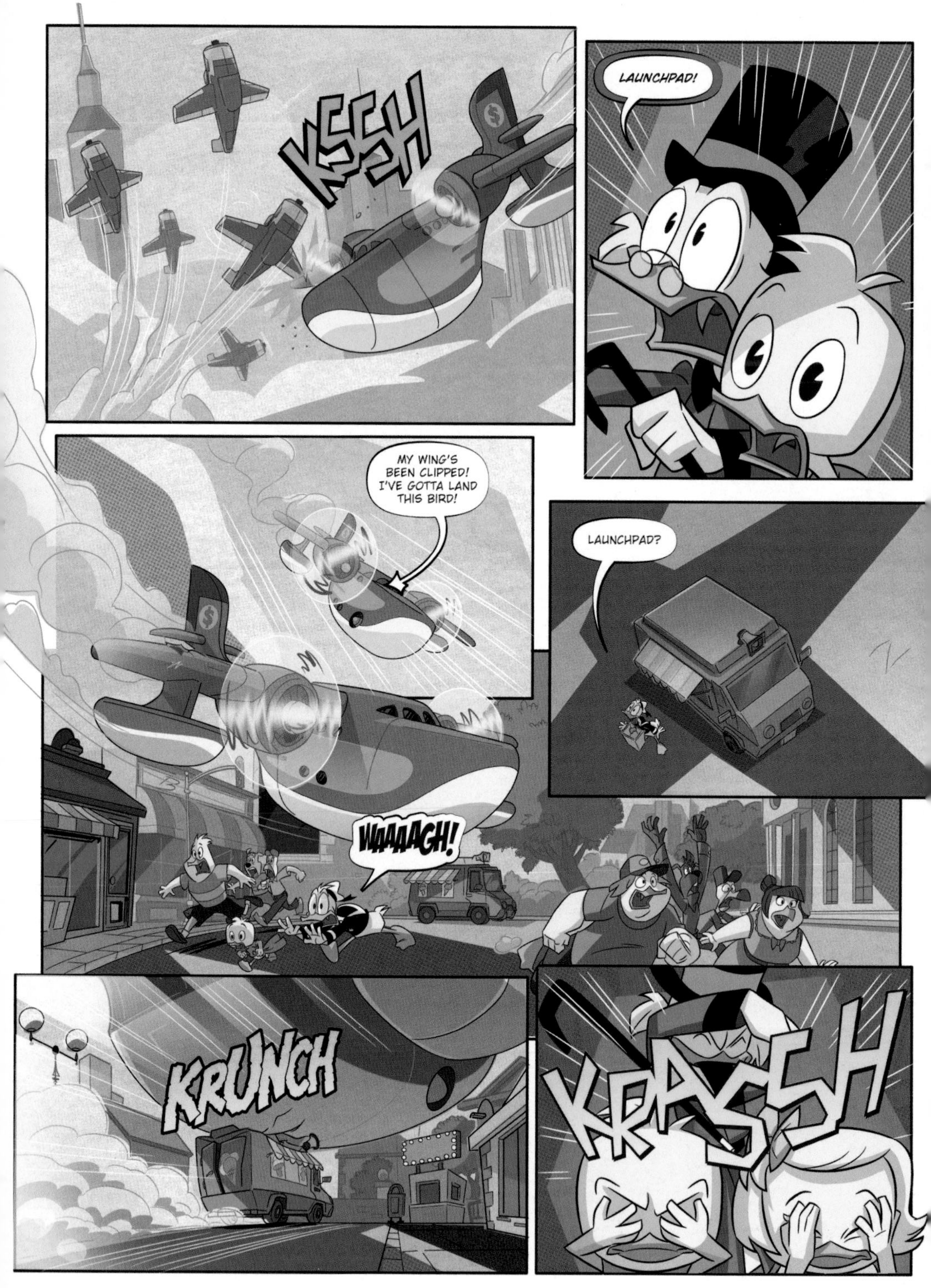
KSSSH
LAUNCHPAD!
MY WING'S BEEN CLIPPED! I'VE GOTTA LAND THIS BIRD!
LAUNCHPAD?
WAAAAGH!
KRUNCH
KRASSH

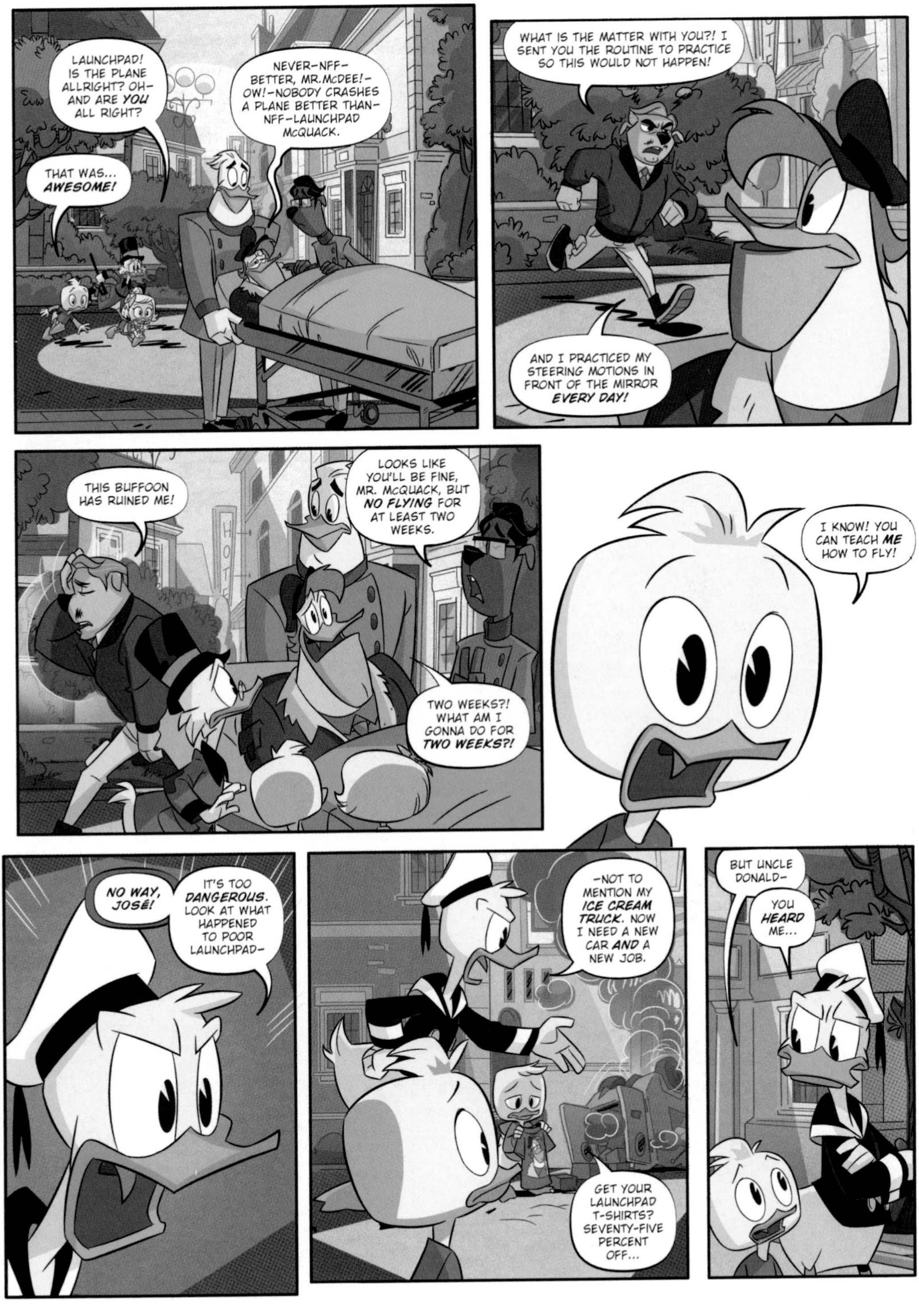

LAUNCHPAD! IS THE PLANE ALLRIGHT? OH— AND ARE **YOU** ALL RIGHT?
THAT WAS... **AWESOME!**
NEVER-NFF- BETTER, MR.McDEE!- OW!-NOBODY CRASHES A PLANE BETTER THAN- NFF-LAUNCHPAD McQUACK.
WHAT IS THE MATTER WITH YOU?! I SENT YOU THE ROUTINE TO PRACTICE SO THIS WOULD NOT HAPPEN!
AND I PRACTICED MY STEERING MOTIONS IN FRONT OF THE MIRROR ***EVERY DAY!***
THIS BUFFOON HAS RUINED ME!
LOOKS LIKE YOU'LL BE FINE, MR. McQUACK, BUT ***NO FLYING*** FOR AT LEAST TWO WEEKS.
TWO WEEKS?! WHAT AM I GONNA DO FOR ***TWO WEEKS?!***
I KNOW! YOU CAN TEACH **ME** HOW TO FLY!
NO WAY, JOSÉ!
IT'S TOO ***DANGEROUS***. LOOK AT WHAT HAPPENED TO POOR LAUNCHPAD-
-NOT TO MENTION MY ***ICE CREAM TRUCK***. NOW I NEED A NEW CAR **AND** A NEW JOB.
GET YOUR LAUNCHPAD T-SHIRTS? SEVENTY-FIVE PERCENT OFF...
BUT UNCLE DONALD-
YOU ***HEARD*** ME...

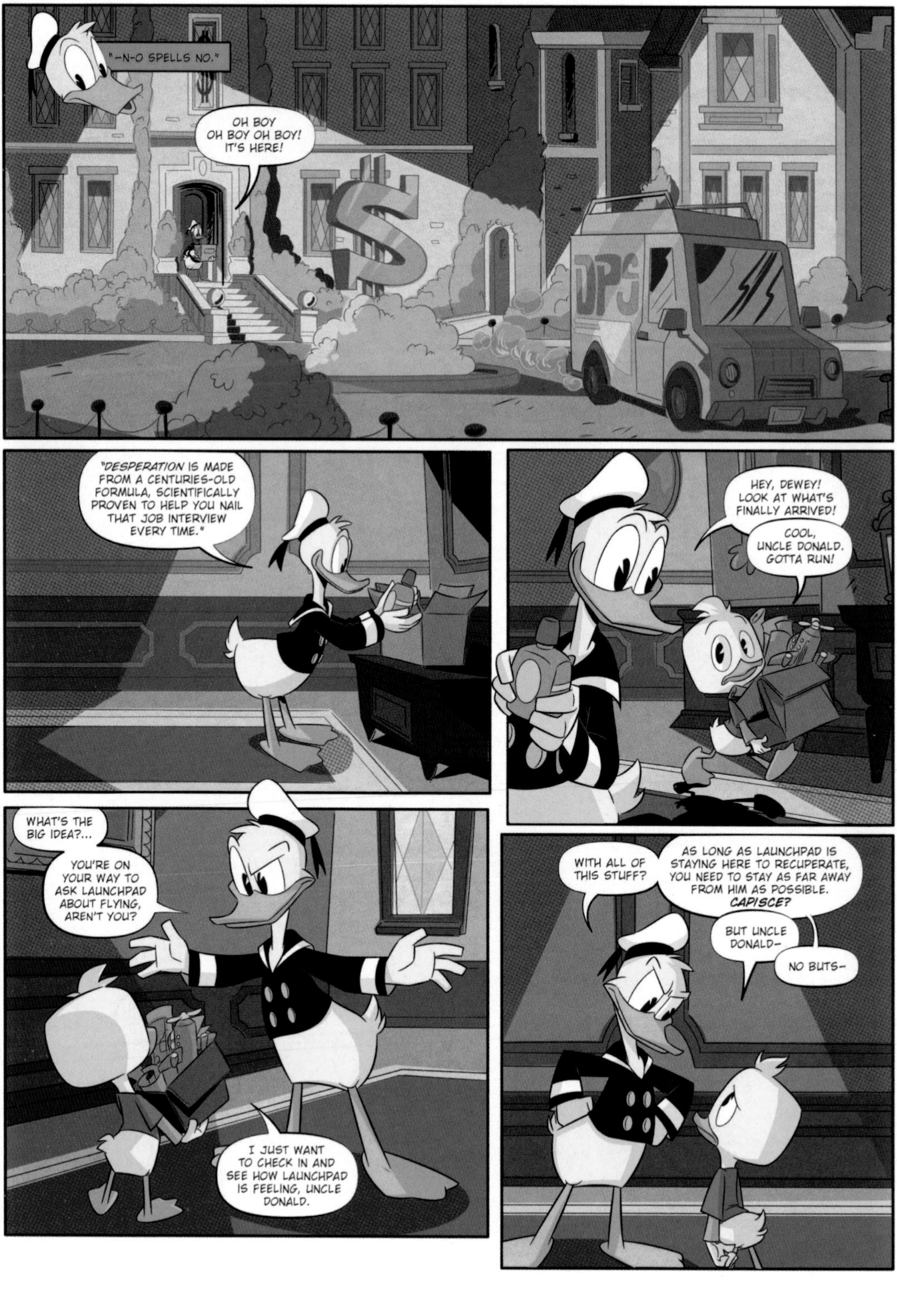
"–N-O SPELLS NO."
OH BOY OH BOY OH BOY! IT'S HERE!
DPS
"DESPERATION IS MADE FROM A CENTURIES-OLD FORMULA, SCIENTIFICALLY PROVEN TO HELP YOU NAIL THAT JOB INTERVIEW EVERY TIME."
HEY, DEWEY! LOOK AT WHAT'S FINALLY ARRIVED!
COOL, UNCLE DONALD. GOTTA RUN!
WHAT'S THE BIG IDEA?...
YOU'RE ON YOUR WAY TO ASK LAUNCHPAD ABOUT FLYING, AREN'T YOU?
I JUST WANT TO CHECK IN AND SEE HOW LAUNCHPAD IS FEELING, UNCLE DONALD.
WITH ALL OF THIS STUFF?
AS LONG AS LAUNCHPAD IS STAYING HERE TO RECUPERATE, YOU NEED TO STAY AS FAR AWAY FROM HIM AS POSSIBLE. CAPISCE?
BUT UNCLE DONALD–
NO BUTS–

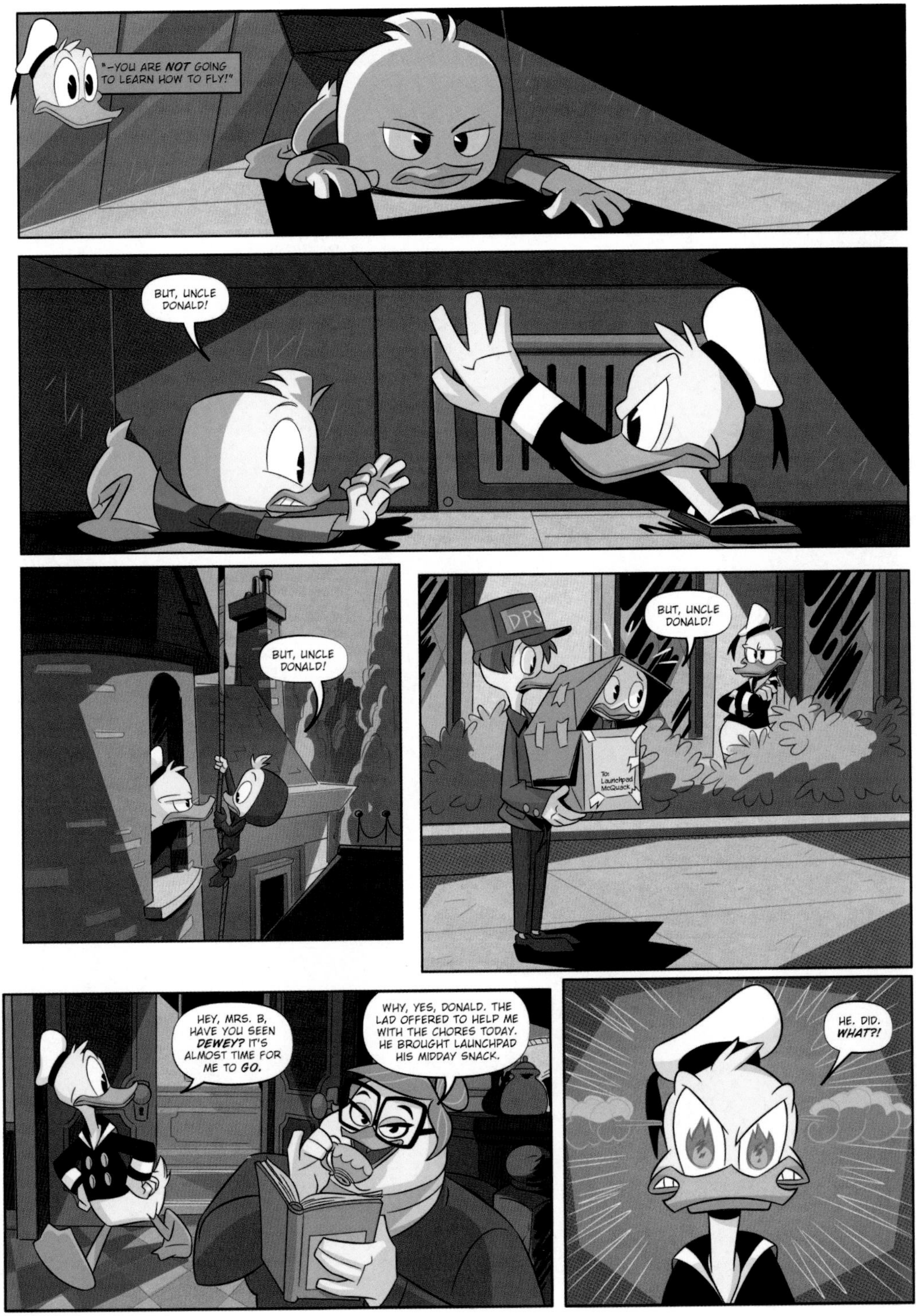
"–YOU ARE NOT GOING TO LEARN HOW TO FLY!"
BUT, UNCLE DONALD!
BUT, UNCLE DONALD!
DPS
BUT, UNCLE DONALD!
To: Launchpad McQuack
HEY, MRS. B, HAVE YOU SEEN DEWEY? IT'S ALMOST TIME FOR ME TO GO.
WHY, YES, DONALD. THE LAD OFFERED TO HELP ME WITH THE CHORES TODAY. HE BROUGHT LAUNCHPAD HIS MIDDAY SNACK.
HE. DID. WHAT?!

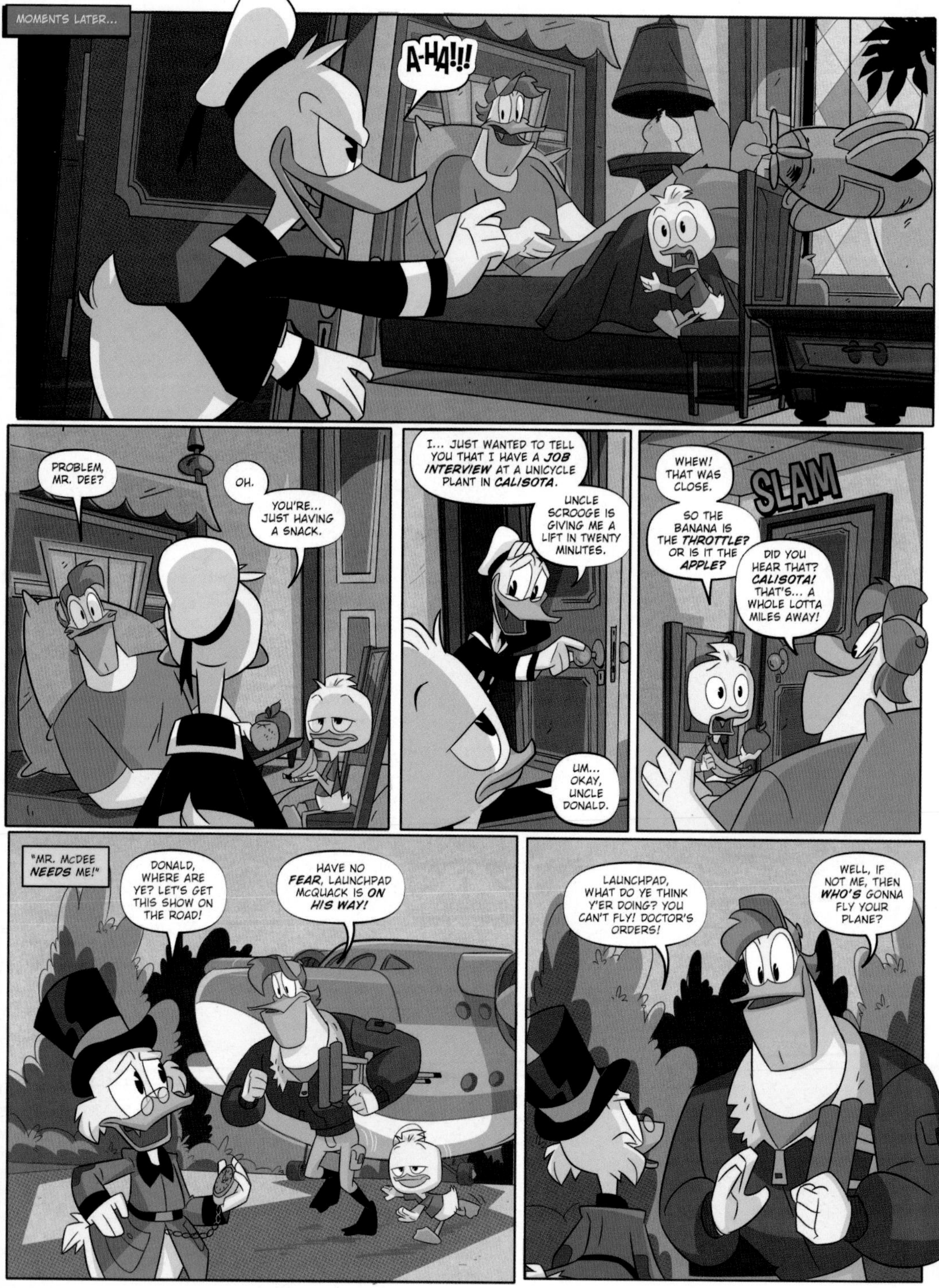
MOMENTS LATER...
A-HA!!!
PROBLEM, MR. DEE?
OH.
YOU'RE... JUST HAVING A SNACK.
I... JUST WANTED TO TELL YOU THAT I HAVE A JOB INTERVIEW AT A UNICYCLE PLANT IN CALISOTA.
UNCLE SCROOGE IS GIVING ME A LIFT IN TWENTY MINUTES.
UM... OKAY, UNCLE DONALD.
SLAM
WHEW! THAT WAS CLOSE.
SO THE BANANA IS THE THROTTLE? OR IS IT THE APPLE?
DID YOU HEAR THAT? CALISOTA! THAT'S... A WHOLE LOTTA MILES AWAY!
"MR. MCDEE NEEDS ME!"
DONALD, WHERE ARE YE? LET'S GET THIS SHOW ON THE ROAD!
HAVE NO FEAR, LAUNCHPAD MCQUACK IS ON HIS WAY!
LAUNCHPAD, WHAT DO YE THINK Y'ER DOING? YOU CAN'T FLY! DOCTOR'S ORDERS!
WELL, IF NOT ME, THEN WHO'S GONNA FLY YOUR PLANE?

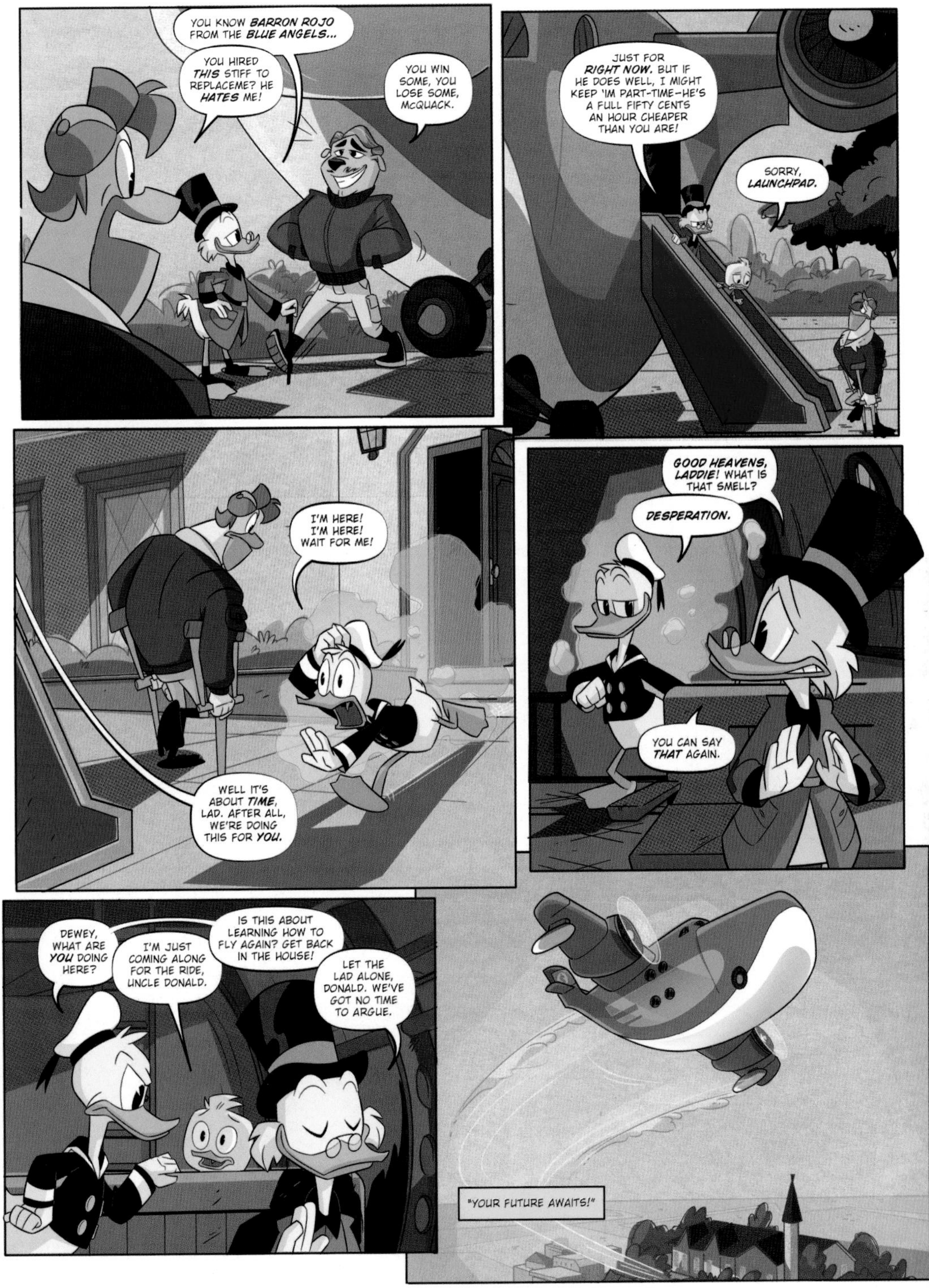
YOU KNOW BARRON ROJO FROM THE BLUE ANGELS...
YOU HIRED THIS STIFF TO REPLACEME? HE HATES ME!
YOU WIN SOME, YOU LOSE SOME, McQUACK.
JUST FOR RIGHT NOW. BUT IF HE DOES WELL, I MIGHT KEEP 'IM PART-TIME—HE'S A FULL FIFTY CENTS AN HOUR CHEAPER THAN YOU ARE!
SORRY, LAUNCHPAD.
I'M HERE! I'M HERE! WAIT FOR ME!
WELL IT'S ABOUT TIME, LAD. AFTER ALL, WE'RE DOING THIS FOR YOU.
GOOD HEAVENS, LADDIE! WHAT IS THAT SMELL?
DESPERATION.
YOU CAN SAY THAT AGAIN.
DEWEY, WHAT ARE YOU DOING HERE?
I'M JUST COMING ALONG FOR THE RIDE, UNCLE DONALD.
IS THIS ABOUT LEARNING HOW TO FLY AGAIN? GET BACK IN THE HOUSE!
LET THE LAD ALONE, DONALD. WE'VE GOT NO TIME TO ARGUE.
"YOUR FUTURE AWAITS!"

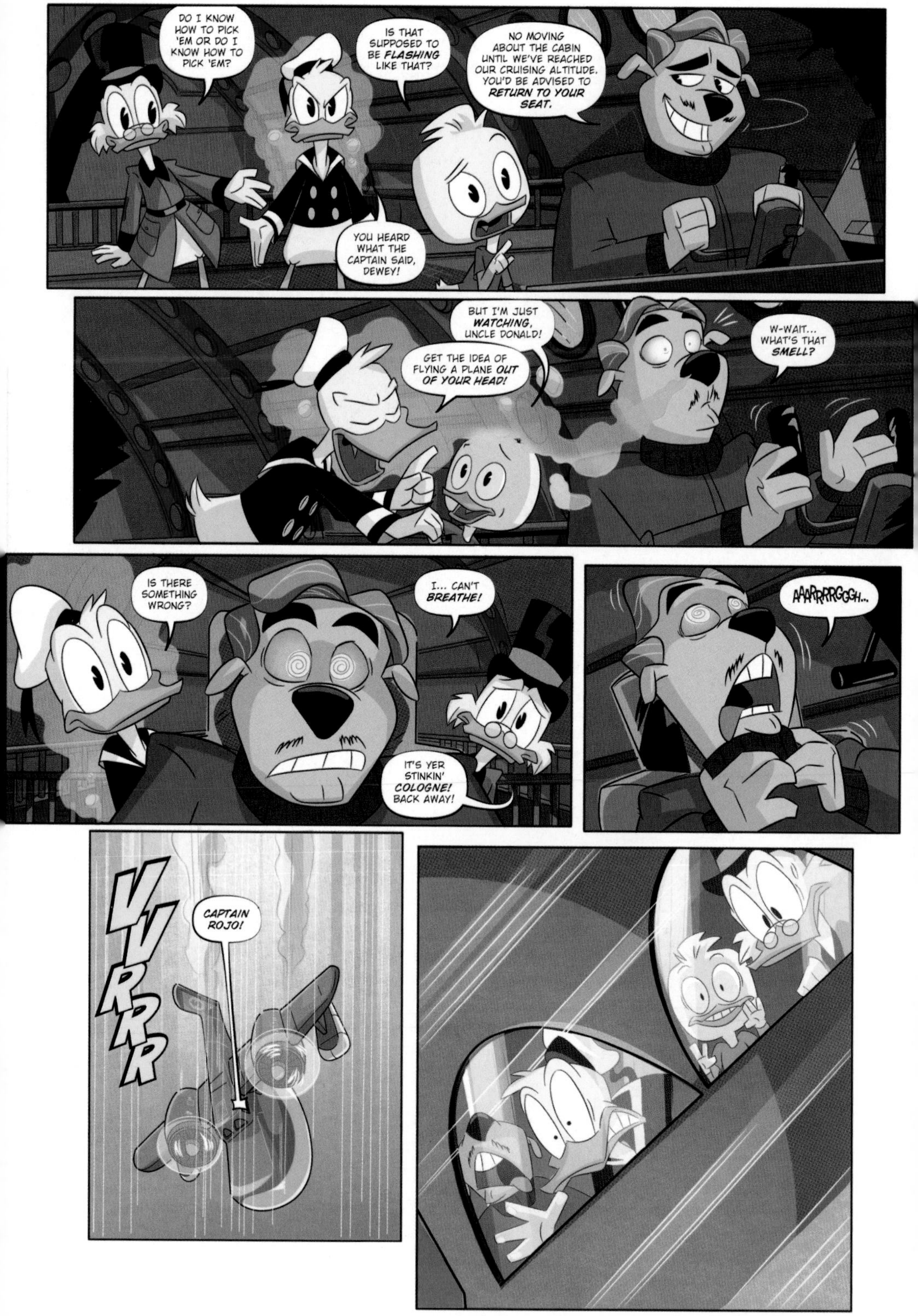

DO I KNOW HOW TO PICK 'EM OR DO I KNOW HOW TO PICK 'EM?
IS THAT SUPPOSED TO BE FLASHING LIKE THAT?
NO MOVING ABOUT THE CABIN UNTIL WE'VE REACHED OUR CRUISING ALTITUDE. YOU'D BE ADVISED TO RETURN TO YOUR SEAT.
YOU HEARD WHAT THE CAPTAIN SAID, DEWEY!
BUT I'M JUST WATCHING, UNCLE DONALD!
GET THE IDEA OF FLYING A PLANE OUT OF YOUR HEAD!
W-WAIT... WHAT'S THAT SMELL?
IS THERE SOMETHING WRONG?
I... CAN'T BREATHE!
IT'S YER STINKIN' COLOGNE! BACK AWAY!
AAARRRRGGGH...
VVRRR
CAPTAIN ROJO!

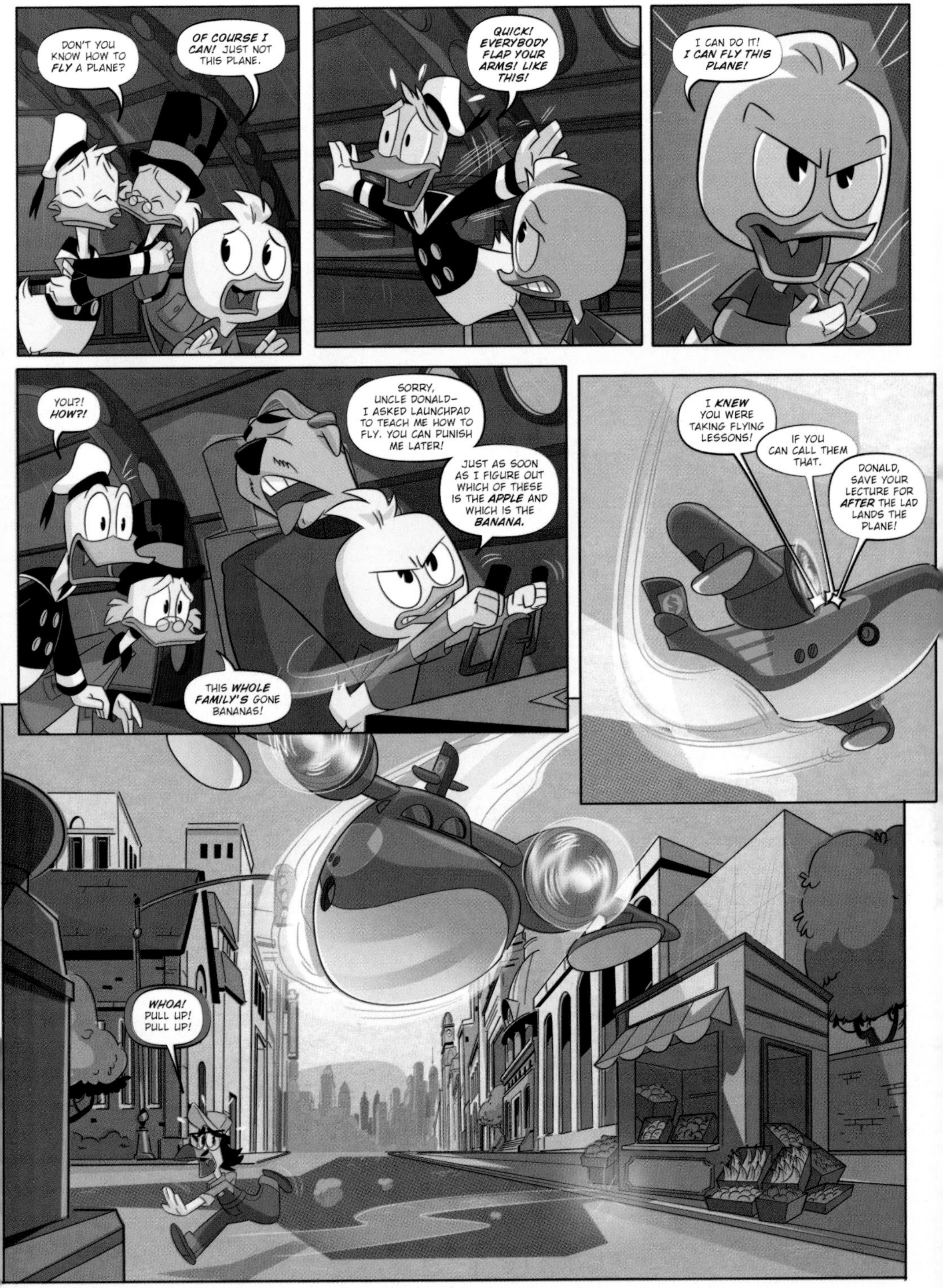
DON'T YOU KNOW HOW TO FLY A PLANE?
OF COURSE I CAN! JUST NOT THIS PLANE.
QUICK! EVERYBODY FLAP YOUR ARMS! LIKE THIS!
I CAN DO IT! I CAN FLY THIS PLANE!
YOU?! HOW?!
SORRY, UNCLE DONALD– I ASKED LAUNCHPAD TO TEACH ME HOW TO FLY. YOU CAN PUNISH ME LATER!
JUST AS SOON AS I FIGURE OUT WHICH OF THESE IS THE APPLE AND WHICH IS THE BANANA.
THIS WHOLE FAMILY'S GONE BANANAS!
I KNEW YOU WERE TAKING FLYING LESSONS!
IF YOU CAN CALL THEM THAT.
DONALD, SAVE YOUR LECTURE FOR AFTER THE LAD LANDS THE PLANE!
WHOA! PULL UP! PULL UP!

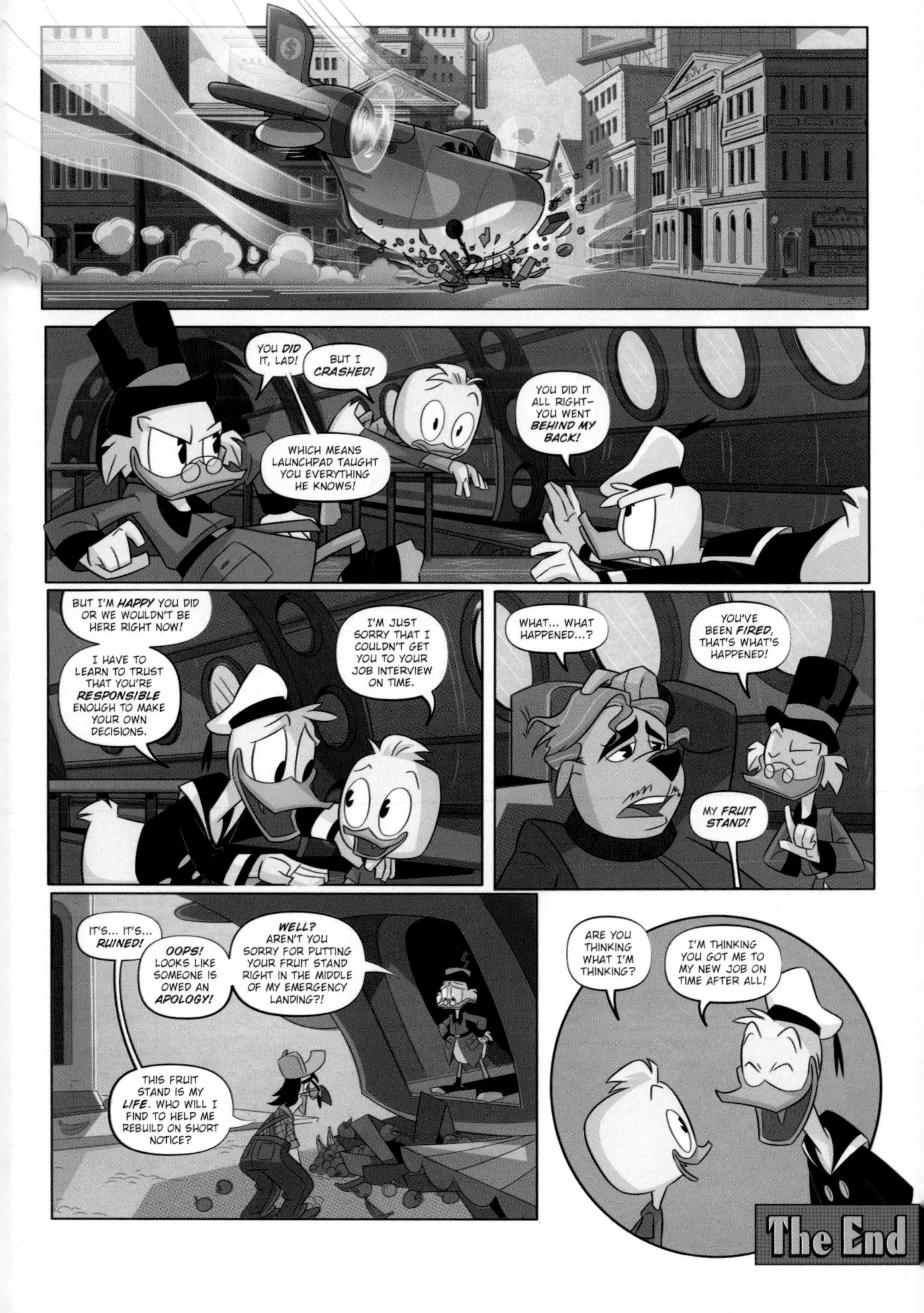
YOU DID IT, LAD!
BUT I CRASHED!
WHICH MEANS LAUNCHPAD TAUGHT YOU EVERYTHING HE KNOWS!
YOU DID IT ALL RIGHT— YOU WENT BEHIND MY BACK!
BUT I'M HAPPY YOU DID OR WE WOULDN'T BE HERE RIGHT NOW!
I HAVE TO LEARN TO TRUST THAT YOU'RE RESPONSIBLE ENOUGH TO MAKE YOUR OWN DECISIONS.
I'M JUST SORRY THAT I COULDN'T GET YOU TO YOUR JOB INTERVIEW ON TIME.
WHAT... WHAT HAPPENED...?
YOU'VE BEEN FIRED, THAT'S WHAT'S HAPPENED!
MY FRUIT STAND!
IT'S... IT'S... RUINED!
OOPS! LOOKS LIKE SOMEONE IS OWED AN APOLOGY!
WELL? AREN'T YOU SORRY FOR PUTTING YOUR FRUIT STAND RIGHT IN THE MIDDLE OF MY EMERGENCY LANDING?!
THIS FRUIT STAND IS MY LIFE. WHO WILL I FIND TO HELP ME REBUILD ON SHORT NOTICE?
ARE YOU THINKING WHAT I'M THINKING?
I'M THINKING YOU GOT ME TO MY NEW JOB ON TIME AFTER ALL!
The End

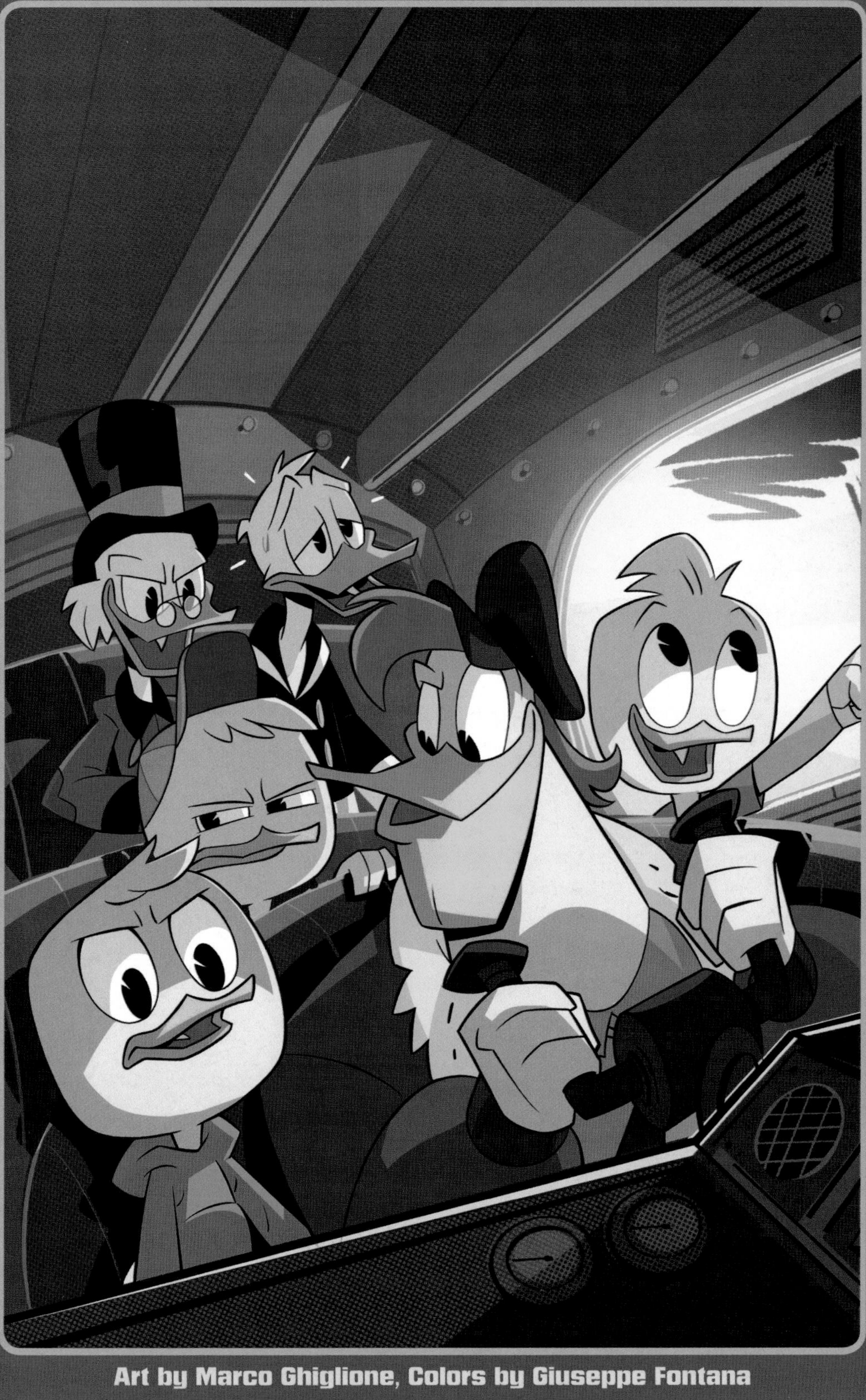

Art by Marco Ghiglione, Colors by Giuseppe Fontana

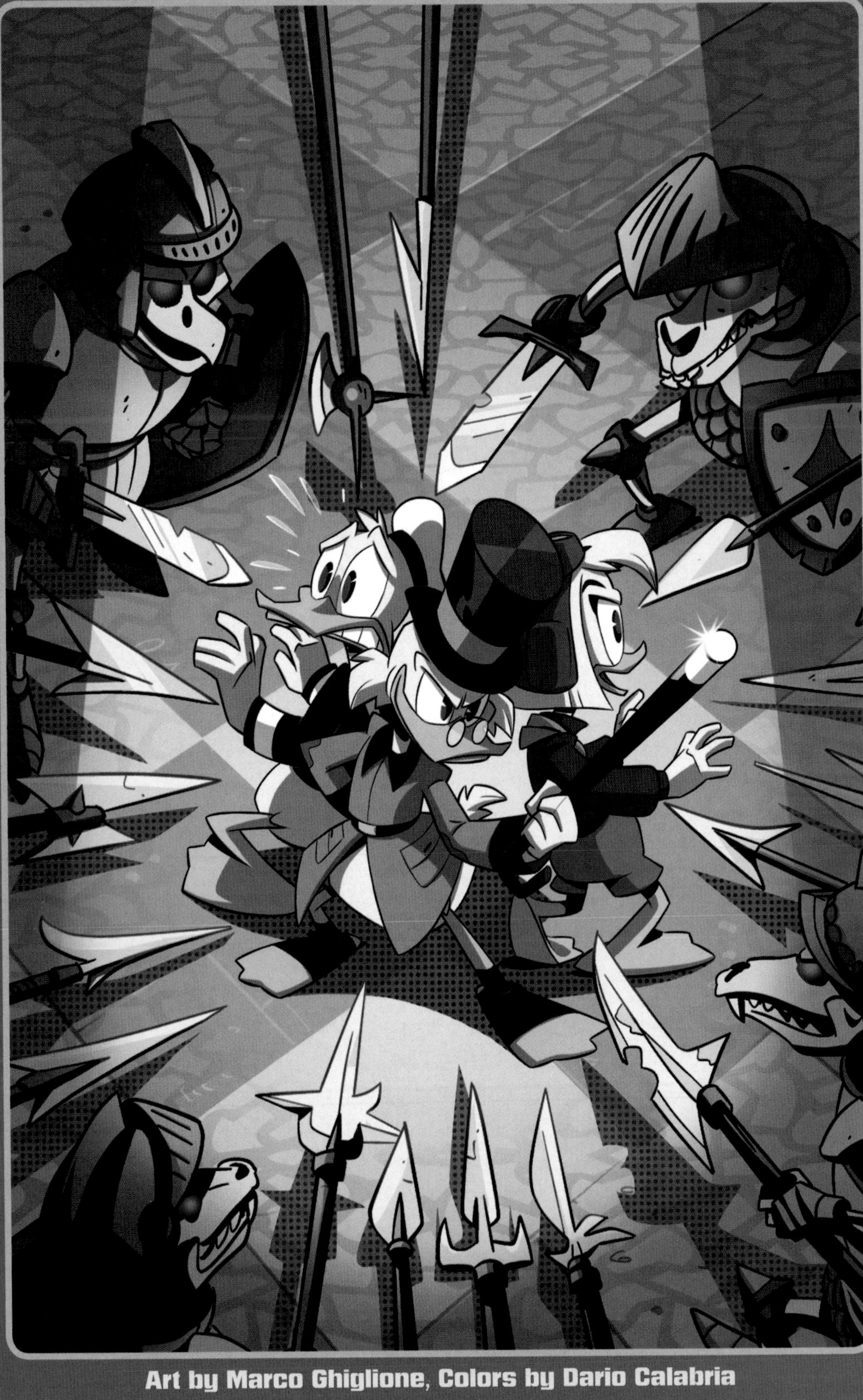

Art by Marco Ghiglione, Colors by Dario Calabria

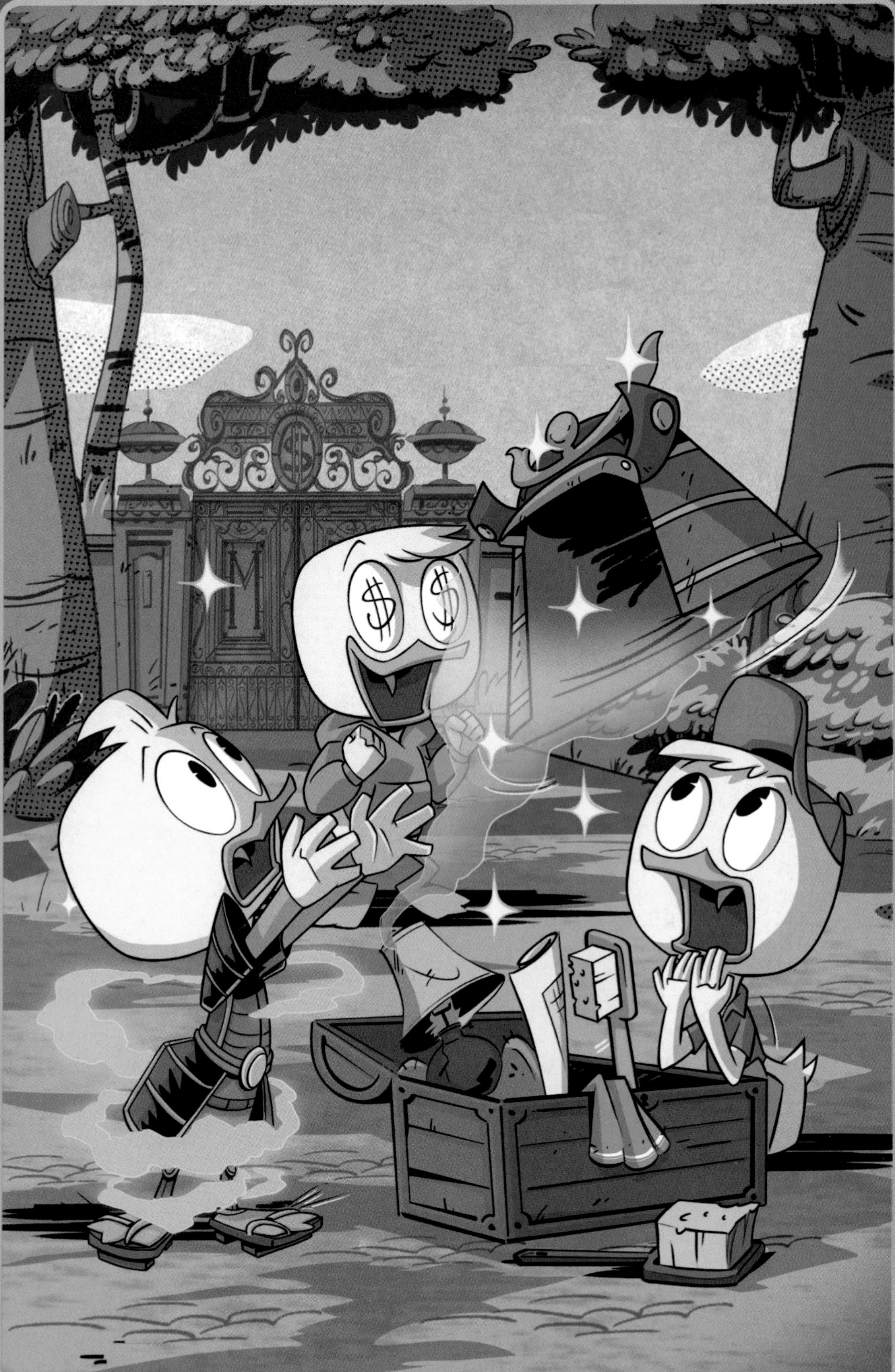

Art by Marco Ghiglione, Colors by Dario Calabria

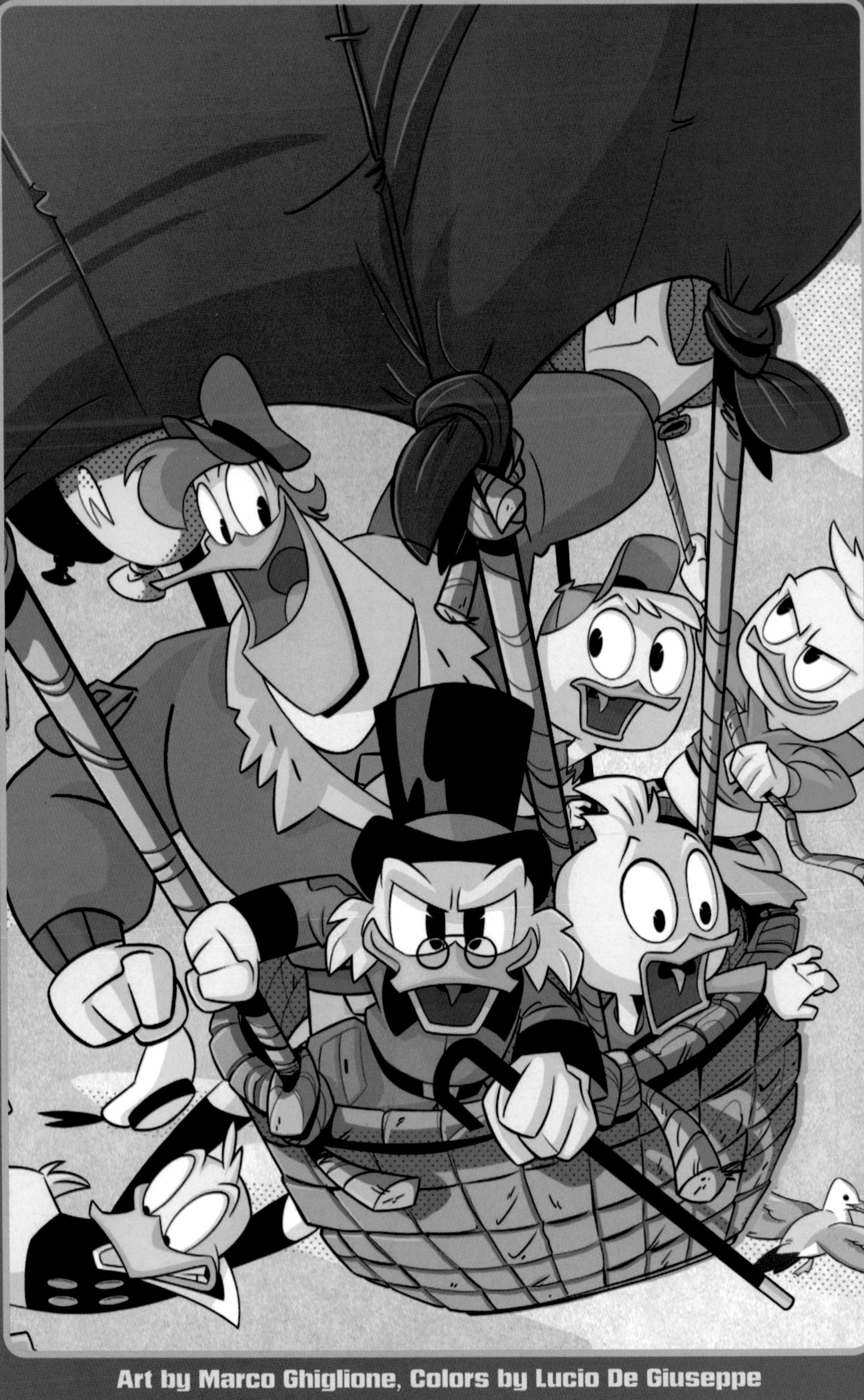

Art by Marco Ghiglione, Colors by Lucio De Giuseppe

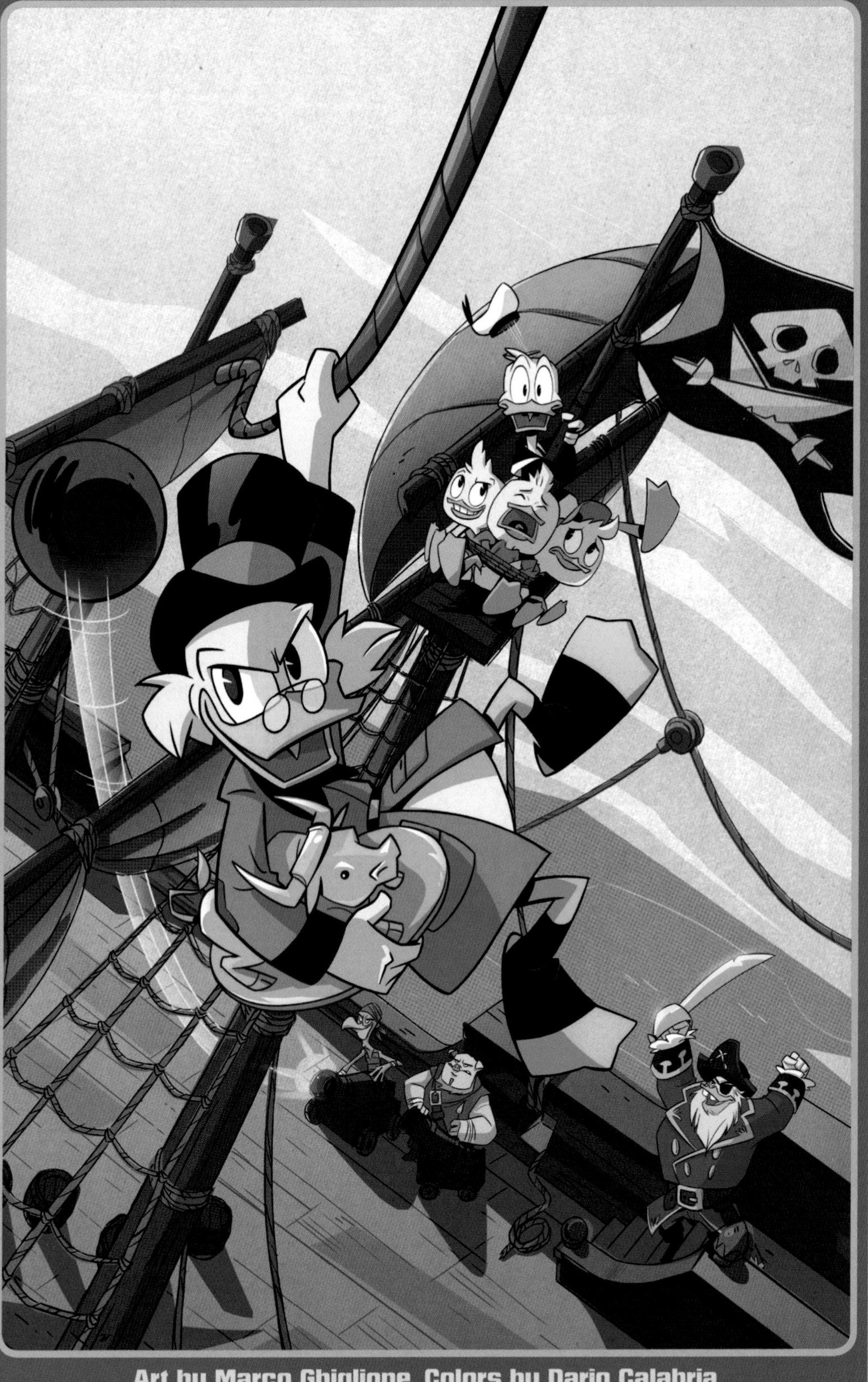

Art by Marco Ghiglione, Colors by Dario Calabria

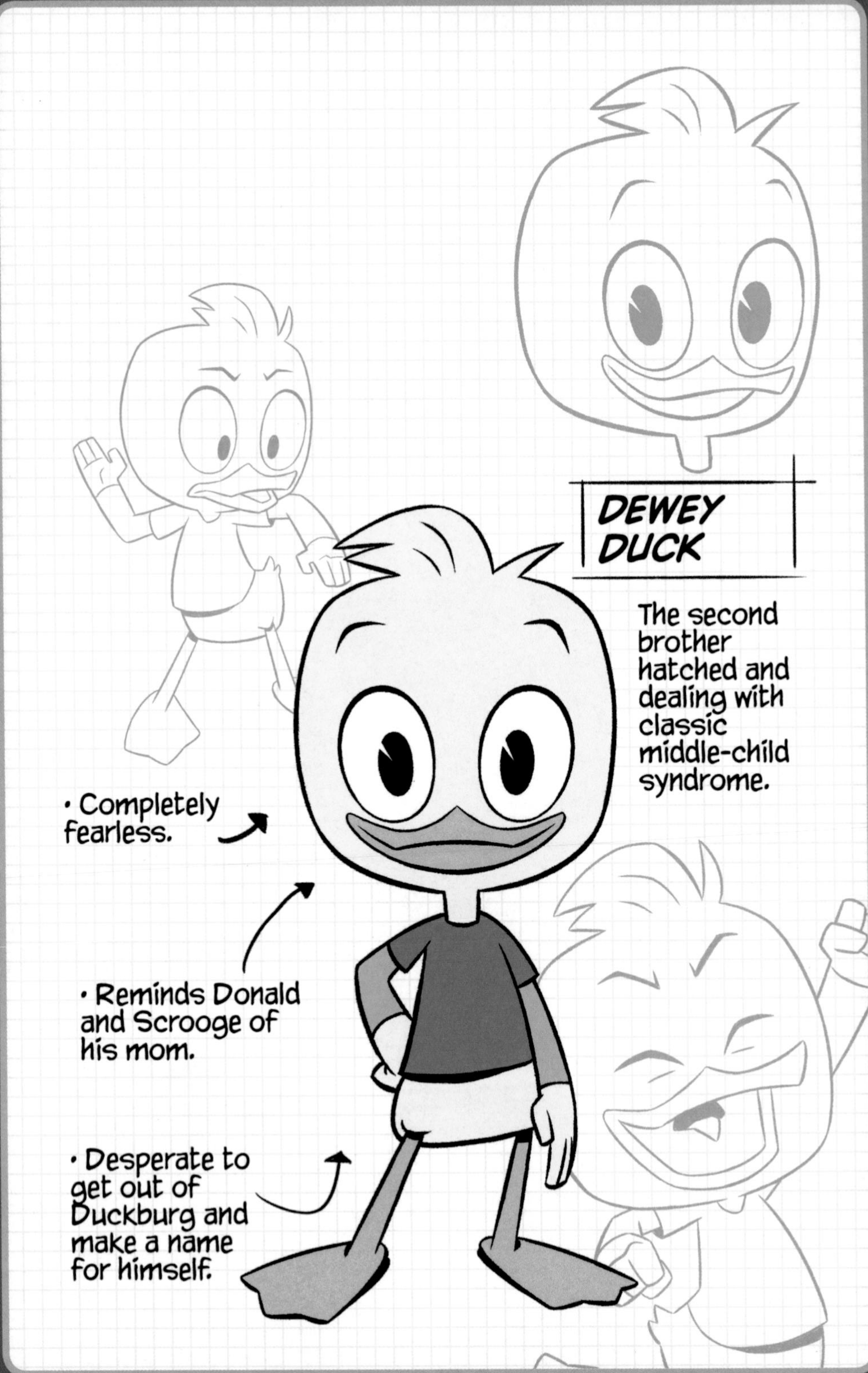
DEWEY DUCK
The second brother hatched and dealing with classic middle-child syndrome.
• Completely fearless.
• Reminds Donald and Scrooge of his mom.
• Desperate to get out of Duckburg and make a name for himself.

Art by DuckTales Creative Team

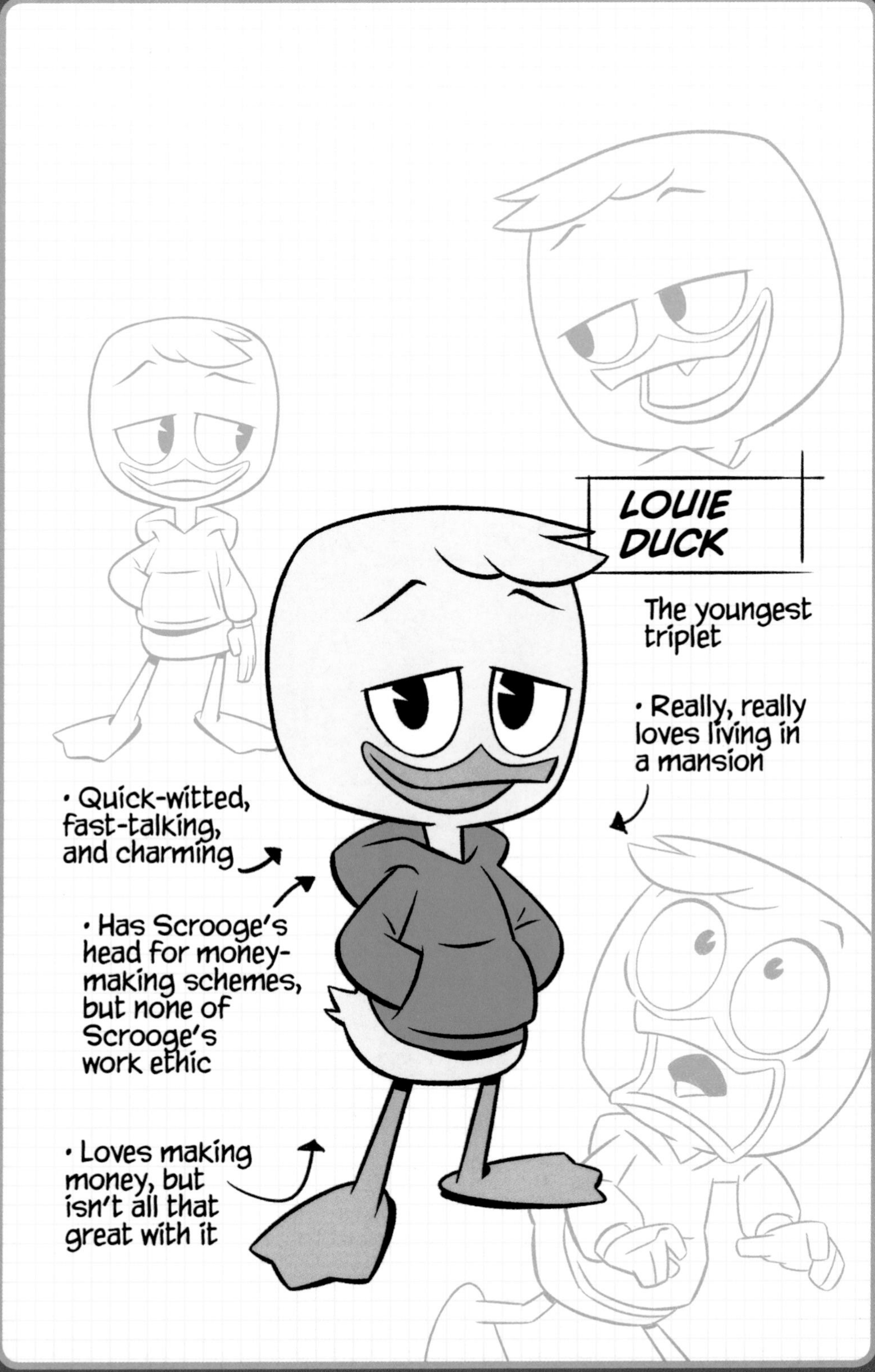
LOUIE DUCK
The youngest triplet
• Really, really loves living in a mansion
• Quick-witted, fast-talking, and charming
• Has Scrooge's head for money-making schemes, but none of Scrooge's work ethic
• Loves making money, but isn't all that great with it

Art by DuckTales Creative Team

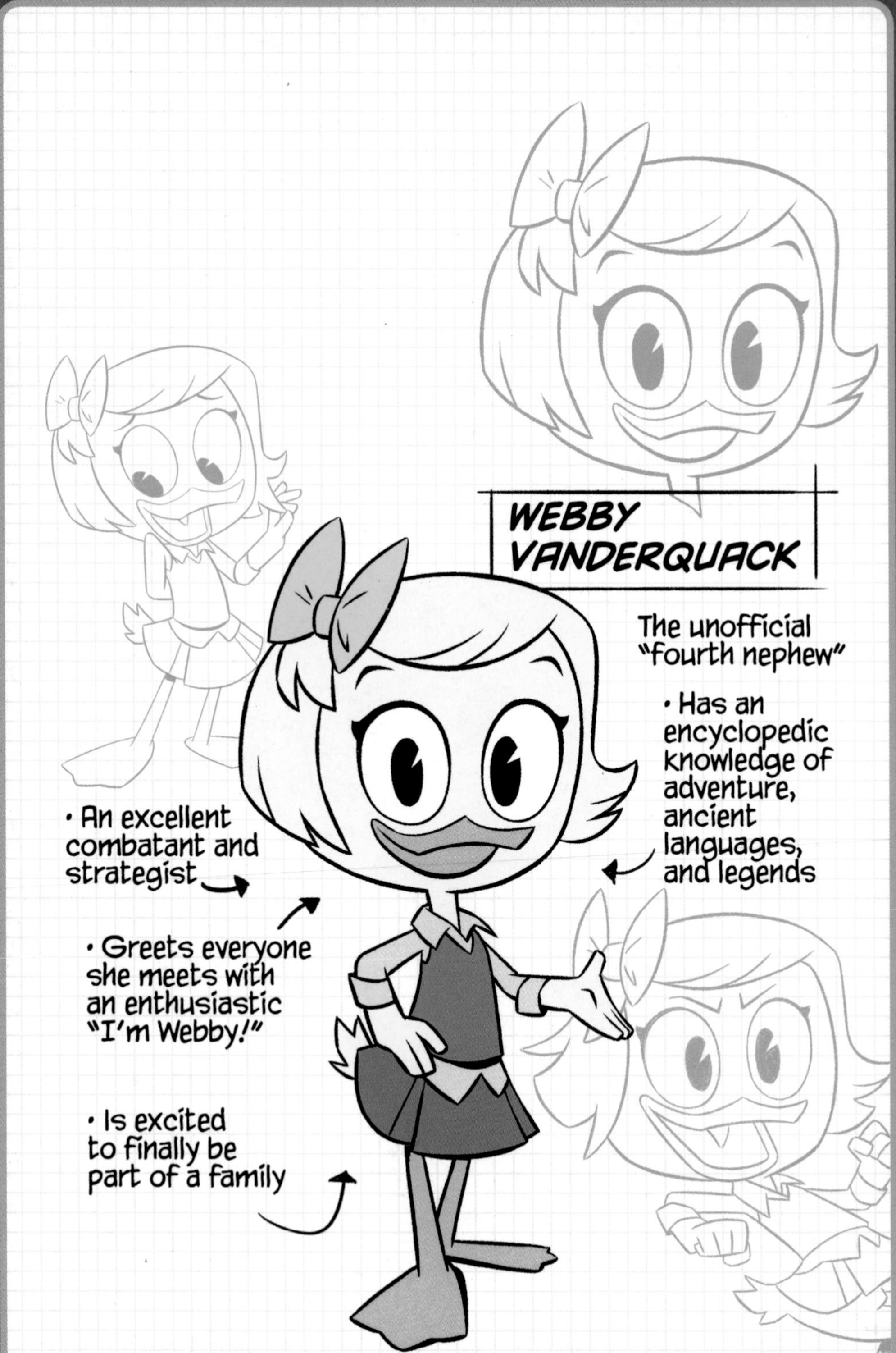
WEBBY VANDERQUACK
The unofficial "fourth nephew"
• Has an encyclopedic knowledge of adventure, ancient languages, and legends
• An excellent combatant and strategist
• Greets everyone she meets with an enthusiastic "I'm Webby!"
• Is excited to finally be part of a family

Art by DuckTales Creative Team